Bayou Roux

A Cajun Murder Mystery Series

Season 1

L. SCOTT SILVERII

This is a work of fiction. Names, characters, businesses, places, events and incidents are either the products of the author's imagination or used in a fictitious manner. Any resemblance to actual persons, living or dead, or actual events is purely coincidental.

Laissez les bons temps rouler – Until somebody gets killed of course.

Chief of Police, Scott Silverii
(2014)

Table of Contents

Dedication

Season 1 of A Cajun Murder Mystery Series is literally "in the books." Owing so many thanks to an amazing writing community, I dedicate this work to you who've mentored me daily.

Finding one's voice is a lifelong journey. This work is but one step in an evolution of creative efforts I trust will span my lifetime. Your time, talents and truths have inspired my journey.

This book is also a portrait of real life work experiences I've had and actions I wish I could have taken. Living my law enforcement career vicariously through each character has been a blessing and a serious reminder of the range of humanity each cop experiences and carries eternally. This work is also dedicated to my family in blood and in Blue.

About the Author

Chief of Police Scott Silverii blends over 24 years of heart-stopping police experiences with an action packed writing style seasoned by the Mardi Gras, hurricanes, humidity and crawfish étouffée.

This gumbo of experience serves up a unique perspective in his writing—but don't let the Creole smile fool you. Chief Silverii spent 16 of those years working in policing's special operations groups with thousands of undercover narcotics and SWAT missions. He's bought dope, banged down doors, and busted bad guys.

A Cajun Murder Mystery Series is an episodic adventure that takes readers behind the badge and along the bayous of south Louisiana to experience the raw rush of cop life. As Chief Silverii likes to say – *Laissez les bons temps rouler* – *Until somebody gets killed of course.*

Follow him on:
facebook.com/CopsWritingCrime
twitter.com/ThibodauxChief
and
www.scottsilverii.com

Lock & Load – You with Me?

Chapter 1

— District Attorney Gaudet —

"HOW MUCH BLOOD CAN ONE body hold?" I peered around the detective's shoulder and saw there was more than one body. Many more.

The ancient cypress camp buried deep in the heart of Cajun country buzzed with flies as the humidity and creole sun baked the dismembered corpses. The taste of rotten fish heads and human blood sat thick on my tongue.

"It'll take days, maybe weeks for the coroner to piece parts together." Detective James Walker's hand sandpapered his nail-hard jaw. "Headcount. Get it?" Walker tried that joke on me. I ducked my head as my lip twitched. The last thing I needed, as the District Attorney in an election year was my ass on the front page chortling over decapitated bodies. I pretended not to hear him, though he knew I did.

The bayou boys did good work in a pinch, but I wasn't getting guts on a brand new seersucker suit. I needed it for the big Labor Day announcement. And hell yea – people do actually still wear them. At least the alums and I from Tulane Law School. True Southern lawyers and gentlemen.

"Y'all got any leads, Walker?" I knew better, but there was no need debating the obvious. I figured best to play the back seat gawker and let the deputy dogs have a go at it.

"We just got here. Ain't like they left a note." Walker replied, gnawing on the tip of his ink pen.

I guess that question bugged him more than the house full of dead.

"Settle down, old fella." I'd worked with cops for twenty years and appreciated the challenges of their job, but they can be temperamental. I guess after all the crap they'd seen, the last thing they need is some smart-ass blue blood second-guessing them.

This one wasn't in the mood for my usual hazing. Walker curled his lip to release a low guttural sound as he flung his grizzled, bone-thin fingers open to release three blowflies into my face. Stupid hick thought I'd flinch.

Though I'd never admit it, I hated the smell of murdered flesh, and I damn sure hated tasting it on the legs of those nasty blowflies when they landed on my lips. Hell, they look like metallic helicopters carrying death.

"Them bugs scare you, mister lawyer-man?"

"Not at all, detective." This gumbo of brackish bog water and sticky heat had me in no mood to tolerate him, and I wasn't about to back down to this local yokel. "Ain't my first time with the dead. Saw eleven sawed apart in Bossier few years back."

The big bastard stamped my shoulder with a soiled rubber-gloved hand, smashing a fly on my coat.

"You son of a bitch. You gonna pay for cleaning." My voice cracked, but I didn't care—I was pissed.

"Maybe so, but you stepped in that blood pool on your own. They used to be nice Saddle Oxfords." Walker's eyes sparked with silent sarcasm.

I ducked out from under his hand and snaked into the camp's living quarters. Not much alive in there. Detectives were placing number tents near each of the displaced heads.

"What'cha think?" Walker crowded me in the doorway.

"I think the person's a badass killing machine. I mean, seriously—twelve butchered and not a clue?" Grinning at my assessment.

"How'd you know it was twelve?" Walker asked.

"It doesn't take a G.E.D. to count a dozen in headless math." I jerked my jacket off on purpose and shoved it against his meatless chest. "Dry clean only."

I heard the Sheriff's entourage arrive. Media whore. Camera crews tagged along, tripping over their equipment for a shot of "the law" stomping his way across the lawn. *Why not beat him at his own game?*

Snaking my forefinger inside the knot, I loosened the plaid bow tie. I rumpled the front of my light blue button-down, and tugged it just a tad over my belt. Since the detective was paying to have my favorite summer suit cleaned anyway, I brushed the bloodstained leather shoe tips across the creased shins of my trousers.

No one expected me to be on scene, so I flung open the old cabin's tattered screen door. Sheriff Benjamin Martin pitched onto the heels of his box-chain bought cowboy boots, standing stiff in the yard at the civilian side of the stretched plastic crime scene tape. The media crews nearly ran up his ass. In control, I coolly eased off the crooked porch toward them.

"Benji, grizzly sight in there. Not sure what's with the crime in this parish, but you need to get a handle on it." I stuck out my rubber-gloved right hand. Typical white-hat, he froze. I let my hand linger in the emptiness across the yellow 'Do Not Cross' tape. The cameras devoured Martin's indecision.

"Gill, why you here?"

I played to the same television stations that just abandoned their escort. "I'm helping these dedicated officers determine who's responsible for the vicious murder of twelve innocent people." Angling my best side for the cameras, I forced a look of concern across my brow.

"But why you Gill?" he'd just opened another door of opportunity and I hesitated while tucking in my shirttail. Even the mosquitoes stopped buzzing to hear my answer.

"Because somebody gotta do it, Benji." Rolling my neck around, I eased my chest out and planted my hands onto my hips. The way my elbows pointed in opposite directions musta made me look like a giant grinning scarecrow. That was the purpose, and that little birdie stood there—fat and silent.

The media panned over to Sheriff Martin in time to see his bulbous cheeks flush like cherry tomatoes. He tried to fan himself with that ridiculous Stetson. Thinning patience led the reporters into a barrage of questions that bit into his soft, chubby hide like anguished piranhas. Meanwhile, I basked in the stench of rotting flesh that wafted from indoors.

The million-dollar question about crime details surfaced, and I thought—*Don't do it, Benji.*

He stuttered, "I, uhmm, don't know how many are dead. They didn't tell me."

Yep, and there it was—the career killing comment.

Chapter 2

— Detective James Walker —

IT WAS JUST A MATTER of time till the earth shook. In this case, the earth was Sheriff Martin. The shaking was his career tumbling apart with an election year looming and a potential challenger with fearless intentions set on the office.

"I want this case solved ASAP. You hear me Detective?" The jowls flopped blood red against his spaghetti-stained white shirt. The neatly stitched Sheriff's star and his name overextended across a gut enlarged since he was first elected to his initial term four years ago.

Never much of a cop, the entitled public official really pissed me off when he tried throwing his weight around.

"Yeah Sheriff, I'm on it. Matter of fact – we're all on it. You think it sets okay with us that twelve of our citizens in this parish were butchered?" For his safety, it was best to not make eye contact. One more word and I was about to explode. I was retirement eligible – didn't need his shit.

"Just stop dicking around and get 'er done." He pointed to the "Re-elect Martin" button pinned onto his shirt. "If I'm out, you're out Walker. I'll make damn sure of that."

"Excuse me, Sheriff Martin," my frame shook like it was full of rocket fuel and fury as I stretched over him. The whites of his eyes were a dulled yellow and the red in his fat neck had drained colorless.

"Maybe you should think about the dozen families grieving this tragedy instead of your next campaign plate lunch." I lowered my voice back to its usual whisper.

"I have Walker, but maybe you should also think of me." I think even he was shocked at how stupid that sounded bumbling from his coffee-crusted lips.

"I'll check with the District Attorney tomorrow to give him an update and see if he or the Coroner had gathered any more information." It was best I change the topic. I could be diplomatic on occasion. Rare, but I could.

"Boy, you stay away from Gill Gaudet you hear me? He's the enemy. Don't tell him shit until we're ready to break this case." Martin had stepped back to give his wagging finger room to fling in front of my face. Being diplomatic and remaining diplomatic were two very different things.

— D.A. Gill Gaudet —

"LUCY, ANYTHING FROM THE SHERIFF'S Office on them killings?"

It'd been almost a week. The Sheriff was still pissed at me, but I didn't care.

"I tried a few times but they keep telling me he ain't in." My administrative assistant, Lucy Bates, knew the game of political cat and mouse. She'd attached herself to me shortly after graduating from UL-Lafayette and worked for me in one capacity or another over the last twenty years.

"I know them lying bastards are covering for him so I'll keep trying." She's one persistent bitch. That's why I keep her around.

"Any luck on them shoes?"

"Are you freaking serious? Why didn't you make that deadwood detective clean them along with your suit?" I'd ignite her fuse. That's exactly the tenacity I needed for my next request.

"How about you drop these oxfords off to your favorite detective later tonight?"

"What do you think I am – a badge bunny?" Though she might not have admitted it, she was kind of a cop groupie. At least where her attraction to Walker was concerned.

"Tell Walker I said hello." I eyed the female powder keg. "Second thought, tell him to kiss my ass."

Match placed to fuse.

— *Lucy Bates* —

CAN'T BELIEVE I'M CARRYING GILL'S *bloodied shoes in this grocery bag.*

I usually did as told, but if that damn James Walker left me standing under his porch light after one more knock, I'd leave the bag on his step.

Finally, the door edged open. "Hello, baby. Didn't hear you. Shower." He shadowed himself behind the door as he hurried me inside. He wore only a towel this time, and my eyes flicked over the length of his long form. He knew exactly what he was doing.

"Not bad for a 55-year old man, Walker." He looked half that. I held the bag out to him. "Gill wants you to have his shoes cleaned too."

"Take care of me first, then we'll discuss the shoes." His primal growl excited me. He was rugged—unlike the sophisticated-acting Gill Gaudet.

As I said, I do as I'm told.

"What's that jerk up to now?" he asked, helping me up from my knees. I swiped bare knuckles across my raw lips as he pulled me in for another kiss. Kissing for him was lagniappe.

I told him my boss was worried how he' solve the case. I think Gill was more afraid of Walker than jealous. Walker was silent, but eyed the clear plastic bag that I'd brought. "Leave 'em on the tile."

He'd do what I wanted. I knew he was falling for me. Just had to let him have his way first. I set the bag just off the old shag wall-to-wall carpet, below the paneled walls.

"What size shoe does Gill wear?" he quizzed as he ran his fingers across the knot I'd retied in the towel around his waist.

"Eleven and a half. I should know – I shop for his lazy butt."

The towel parted along his muscular thigh as he leaned to inspect the shoes. "Why's the number thirteen written in red on the soles?"

"His unlucky number. He's obsessed with it." I stepped toward the front door, having delivered both goods and services.

His hand journeyed from the base of my neck and into my hair. I relaxed, expecting his mouth against mine.

If he kept it up, I might actually consider staying the night.

"How obsessed?" Walker's kind, light grey eyes narrowed to slits.

A warning bell blasted in the back of my mind. "I don't know. He's always talking about it. Doodles it. It's in his personal e-mail address. Tattooed on his dick." I jerked my head out of his tightening grip.

"Him too?" Disappointment mixed with disgust flashed in his normally oaken expression.

"What can I say—I do as I'm told." I spun away, and left him limp in the threshold.

— Detective James Walker —

"SHERIFF MARTIN. I'M DROPPING BY the dry cleaners before heading up to Bossier City."

"Uhh, okay Walker." He was more concerned about re-election anyway. His cop skills were minimal – like his election chances.

I dialed the DA's office once I hit the interstate. "District Attorney Gaudet's office. May I help you?" asked the new receptionist. It didn't pay to know their names.

"Detective James Walker calling for Gill." He hated being called by his first name to the staff. That's why I did it.

"Gaudet speaking." His words more snarl than greeting.

"I dropped your items off at the dry cleaners. Said three days at least." I wanted to test his patience.

"Three days?" He spouted, but I throttled back my contempt.

"Laundry claim ticket number is thirteen."

Chapter 3

— Detective James Walker —

AFTER FIVE IGNORED CALLS FROM Lucy and six hours into north Louisiana, I checked in with the Bossier Parish Sheriff's Office. Their idea of a decent place to perch for the night was slightly better than the fileted-flesh fishing camp I'd collected skulls from two weeks earlier. I was there to investigate, not vacation.

Detective Albert Robinson was an old timer like me who understood the value of arriving early. There's clarity in those earliest morning hours that the length of day disrupts. After three decades of public service, we both knew how important it was to stay focused.

We walked out back to whisper while the sun crept up over the low-sloped hills. We eased onto the damp, welded pipes fitted as parking barriers. I liked him. He was a lot like me except he wore his years of service more visibly. His dark grey skin sagged from his jaw and elbows. The faded polo shirt embroidered with his name and Sheriff's Office star was threadbare over his chest. His experience as a black man in the Deep South's law enforcement had to be a hell of a lot different from mine. It showed, but not in an angry way.

"Gill Gaudet? Prosecutor?" I threw it out there.

Neither of us faced each other. Just in case the answers became dangerous.

"Yep." He drew from the cup of muddy coffee.

"Eleven dead bodies. Missing heads?" I dropped the veiled intention—we spoke the same language.

"Yep." I saw him nod, then try to shake the memory. Didn't seem to work. He placed the coffee cup in his trembling left hand as he ground his right palm into the corner of his eye. The skin might thicken, the mind might steel in its suspicions of others – but the hardened hearts of men who've witnessed the violent things people do to each other, always save tenderness for hope.

"I know, Brother. Never gets easier. Just stay afloat." I patted his shoulder and walked away.

No telling how many mornings Robinson re-lived that gruesome scene in the name of justice. Where's the justice in destroying an honest man's life for the sake of investigating an evil man's crimes? It'd not been long enough for my mind to toil over my twelve-headed mystery, but it was just a matter of time until my devils called in the chips.

"Walker. Go to Natchitoches." He stood and gazed over the field before moving to the back door. "Ask about the ten." Then he fought with the electronic key code to get back inside the office building.

He was right—my digging had already turned up information that the Sheriff's Office down there had handled a multiple murder the year before Robinson's case.

— D.A. Gill Gaudet —

"Lucy. Come in please." I still hadn't heard back from Walker, and his crack about my laundry ticket being number thirteen was driving me mad. Worst of all, with Labor Day this weekend, that smart-ass wouldn't tell me which dry cleaner had my suit.

"Yes, what may I do for you?" Her flirtatious singsong question rolled from ruby lips.

Her way of asking aroused me.

"A favor. Please." I always threw in the niceness when it involved unofficial duties.

"Sure thing." The distance disappeared between us as her head vanished below my desk.

"No. Thank you, but that's not what I was asking." I yanked her back up by a fistful of blonde hair to look into her pointed, flushed face.

"You sure? I'm already here."

"Seriously. Not now."

She struggled against my grip, but I had more important things for her to do.

"Please call every dry cleaner until you find my suit. If you don't find it, call the store and buy me a new one but charge it to that a-hole, Walker. You understand?"

"And what if I don't?" She twirled her index finger in the air as she spun away on her heel.

"You will. You always do what you're told."

— Detective James Walker —

SINCE I WAS ABOUT AN hour away, and in no real rush to return to the hotbed of re-election season with a fledgling incumbent, I took I-49 South back down to Natchitoches Parish.

A friend of a friend said I'd be safe connecting with Captain John Torres. An old Narc, he could be trusted with sensitive information.

My friend also said Torres once had a run in with Gill and Lucy at a bar outside of Goldonna. The town was so small that word lightened its way throughout the parish. It was the undercover agent who took the heat from the Sheriff of course.

"Torres, thanks for meeting me out here." The guy was what I expected—overweight, under bathed, reeking of last night's alcohol and today's cigarettes.

"You wired?" He never blinked.

"Are you fucking kidding me?" That bastard almost caught me off guard—first time in thirty years I'd been asked that question.

"Sorry, gotta ask. Come round here mentioning Gill Gaudet and people get concerned." His hands slid over the back of my flannel button up, "Old habits, sorry."

"You caught ten a couple years back?" This wasn't old-timer Detective Albert Robinson, no need to tread lightly.

"Not me, but detectives did. I went out for the hell of it. How often you gonna see ten heads cut from the body? Shit was amazing." He sucked the fresh cigarette near all the way through the filter. Reliving that memory seemed to excite him.

"How so? If it's not too painful." I didn't like him to start with but liked him even less now. First time for that in thirty years too.

"Gill pranced in the house dressed like he was heading to church. That place was bloodier than the old slaughterhouse on Boone Road. Started asking stupid questions – small talk you know? Got upset when he stepped in blood with a fancy pair of leather shoes." He smashed the butt into the ground with an exaggerated heel. His leathered face flatten to avoid expression.

"Saddle Oxfords?" I just had to ask him.

"What the hell is that? I saw him step into the blood with my own eyes. Don't know why he'd act like it was an accident. That's what we argued about months later. Saw him and his whore at a bar. Got up in my face—started yelling I owed him new shoes."

"And then?" I knew my body language showed way too much enthusiasm, but my mind ached with questions that needed asking. I knew he wasn't the one to answer.

"Then nothing. Not long after the case went cold, he transferred over to Bossier Parish to work for the District Attorney's office." I thanked him, but couldn't shake his hand again—I still had hours to drive and the thought of his filth on me turned my already hollow stomach.

Chapter 4

— Detective James Walker —

I MISSED GAUDET'S SURPRISE ANNOUNCEMENT at the Labor Day celebration, but wasn't shocked the arrogant bastard was running for Sheriff. Of course, I'd been busy crisscrossing the state interviewing cops about eleven similar cases.

I knew the DA wanted an update, but I wasn't sure if he actually wanted it solved until after November 4th. My suspicions were quickly confirmed as Gill ramped up the campaign intensity with just weeks until Election Day.

I'd watched corrupt Louisiana politicians sodomize citizens my whole life, but he made a bold promise. Gill Gaudet was so close to being elected Sheriff of this parish, but I knew the secret behind that promise. My investigation would soon reveal it.

— D.A. Gill Gaudet —

"FOLKS, I WANT TO BE your next Sheriff."

The audience erupted. I was trying as hard as I could to contain my shit-eating grin, but these swamp people love me.

I stared straight into my opponent's dull, wandering eyes. "Benji, can you or can't you bring the killers to justice?" Not waiting for his stupid reply, I teased him with the tip, and then jerked the microphone away. He nibbled after it like an infant for the nipple.

"I promise that upon my election as Sheriff, I'll solve this case within one week." Illiterate bunch of hicks went wild whooping and hollering. Sounded like a Saturday night in LSU's Tiger Stadium.

— Sheriff-Elect Gill Gaudet —

"...SO HELP ME GOD." I lipped that last part of the Sheriff's oath of office. I'd repeated those words before, and just like every day of catholic school and catechism, I despised being a religious hypocrite.

I swiped my hand off that Bible, cleared my throat, and turned to the small crowd of strangers in my office. "Thank you for doing the honors, Judge Chiasson. Now back to business. I've got a murder case to solve. Thank you for coming. Lucy will see you out."

"District Attorney—I mean Sheriff Gaudet. You rang?" She bounced back into my now empty office.

"You better get the title straight." I snapped.

"I'm sorry. It's just that this is your thirteenth different public office over the last twenty years." She spun her right wrist around, dismissing my affliction with the number thirteen.

I didn't intend to hit her that hard. Probably should've helped wake her up, but she knew better than to throw that damn number in my face. Besides, I put up with her obsession for all these years. She should respect mine.

I left her body crumpled on the floor. No time to play doctor. I had a killer to catch.

— Detective James Walker —

MY STOMACH TWISTED FROM THE latest information dump. "Sheriff Jones thanks for giving me access to those records. Had no idea Gill Gaudet started his career in Lafayette Parish that long ago."

I had Gaudet by the balls but nothing to squeeze. No evidence, no witnesses, no DNA—nothing but twenty years and twelve locations matching his employment to sites of increasing numbers of dead.

Not to mention—he was now my boss.

Regardless, I'd make my move as soon as I got back home.

Her name flashed across the cell's screen marquise again. "Honey, where you been? I need to see you." I liked when Lucy called me that. Too bad it was insincere.

"I don't have time for a quick visit. Coming back from Lafayette." It was my twelfth follow-up on this overdrawn murder investigation.

"Walker, it's important. I'm taking a risk, but you need to hear this." Her tone was serious. Desperate.

"Lucy, are you okay? Is it Gill? Tell me, what's going on." My heart had begun to actually race at her words. Wasn't sure if I'd fallen for her, or was just getting old. Either way, I knew the feelings were one-sided.

"Baby – can't talk over the phone. You're in jeopardy, James."

That got my attention. Not the jeopardy part, but the fact that she used my first name.

"I'll be back in town around nine o'clock tonight." I mashed the accelerator.

"Okay, come by the Sheriff's Office." She hung up.

The next incoming call was an unknown number. "Hello? Yes, this is Detective James Walker. Hello, Judge Boudreaux."

Would this be the nail in Gill's coffin? Waiting on the elder judge's deliberate conversation was like anticipating the slow, lumbering horse-drawn Mardi Gras floats as a kid.

"I first hired Gill as a prosecutor. Damn fine man." The lead telescoped to a dead end as the Appellate Court Judge droned on about Gaudet's accolades. He even mentioned that Gill prosecuted a suspect for a decapitation case nineteen years earlier but lost on verdict. "The man was devastated, I tell you."

Bile boiled up, "Sheriff Gaudet seems like the perfect man, Judge, thanks for your time."

"Well, he ain't perfect, Detective Walker. He's got an unhealthy obsession with the number thirteen and women. One kept him under fear and the other kept him under thumb."

"I've heard about the numerophobia, but women?" *No way was Gill afraid of women.*

"Let me say, woman. As in one. Some girl from college out here." I didn't want to consider it, but I knew he meant Lucy.

I SKIDDED ALONG THE VINYL seat against the back wall of the café. Hated to admit it, but I was flat exhausted. Between the driving, the phone calls and reality of what waited just across the parish line—I had to muster my strength.

It was easy to charge into battle as a young buck, but I'd learned to pace myself. Even if that meant grabbing something to eat at the grimiest joint in bayou land. Damn cell phone just wouldn't stop.

"Hey Lucy, still okay?" I was concerned about her, but the non-stop questions were wearing me thin.

"Yes baby, I'm still out of town but will meet you around 9:00. Yes, at the Sheriff's Office."

"Sir, you looking like you got the world on them shoulders. You married? Need a good woman?" The young waitress tried to make small talk. Hell, I hoped she wasn't flirting.

"You offering dah'ling?" Through my cold coffee, I grinned over the cup.

"Oh gosh no mister. You could be my grandfather or something." So much for the tip. Probably creeped her out the way Torres did to me out in that crawfish pond near Natchitoches.

I stretched my spine, but I couldn't get the sensation of his fat paw running against my shirt and belt. I knew he was checking for a recording device, but thought for sure he would've picked up on the second weapon I kept tucked in my back.

I decided to tip the waitress anyway. She did a decent job and after all, I was the one who asked. Thought it was funny though—a grandpa. I dug into the back pocket for my wallet but didn't feel the usual bulge of that snub-nose revolver.

"No wonder that fat Narc didn't catch it, I left it in the glove box for the ride." I mumbled walking out the door. She must've really thought I was old and talking to myself. Personally, I was a little disappointed in myself for having forgotten the gun in the first place. Wasn't like me – maybe age was catching up. I replaced that trusty tool the second I hopped in the truck.

MY HEADLIGHTS SCRAPED ACROSS THE Sheriff's Office parking lot. Gill's car was still there. It was an easy mark—newest ride in the fleet. My tires crunched the gravel-covered concrete as I skidded to a stop.

I didn't bother going through the Detective Bureau's entrance, and there was no secretary on duty this late, so I stormed headfirst into the Sheriff's lavish office.

"Walker, you better try knocking." His spine arched.

His arrogance enraged me.

"Knocking is the least of your worries. Where's Lucy?" He never flinched, much less bothered to sit upright in his executive leather chair.

"Lucy? Off doing what she does best." He smiled.

That comment threw me off track, but I had to stay focused. I was gambling on a hunch. No evidence.

"How could you?" I knew that came off as childish, but my mind washed over who was more evil between the two.

A slow grin spread across his features. "How could I? Easy. She loves to kill, and I love her."

"What?" The coldness of his words sucked the warmth from my soul. He was the devil's own son.

"She's the killer. Hell, she killed them all. That's what she does – besides working for me."

I could have put my fist through his face. "Why didn't you stop her?"

"I tried once. She threatened to leave me. Promised to stop at thirteen. She knows how much I hate that number." A quick shake of his head distorted his face.

"Tried? You're the Sheriff." Was I really having this conversation?

A small cone of light escaped beneath the shaded lamp and lit his frame bowed across the desk, "You're a good detective, Walker. Got this all figured out."

"I asked you where is she?" My thumb separated the snaps on the leather holster.

"I promised my constituents." His soulless eyes darted the dimness.

"Has she gone to kill thirteen people?" My spine twisted cold. I unleashed my weapon and spun to look behind me. Nothing.

"Found twelve." Gill's forked tongue hissed without regret.

His eyes dipped more than once, so I nudged around the edge of his desk. Lucy's motionless body lay jammed beneath desk drawers.

"What in the name of Sam Hill?" I stammered.

"Impossible to find thirteen people in this small town." He glanced away with admiration and angst. "She knew I hated that number." He flinched his face again.

I locked eyes onto him as I crouched into the deep darkness beneath his desk to check for signs of life. I'd fallen for this woman after all.

"Did she come back here to make you number thirteen?"

"Not me." Gill's chair flew back.

Lucy's legs twitched to life. Shadows broke streaks of hallway light, and the lamp toppled across the glass desktop. Stunned, I fell into the credenza. Gill towered over me and stomped his shoe across my weapon.

She let loose an inhumane wail. Lucy lunged with a jagged bloody knife.

"You're number thirteen, Walker."

Chapter 5

— *Sheriff James Walker* —

HOWARD JONES WAS DEAD ALL right. His brand new road bike was destroyed in the process. Jones lived on that bicycle and the irony was that it's what killed him, or at least on what he died. People didn't much care for him or his habit of trotting through their stores, clip clopping like a showboat thoroughbred in carbon-soled cycling shoes.

Why is the death of a disliked man who cavorted in spandex pants important? Well, to start with—it's illegal to kill anyone for no good reason. Second, he was a federal agent and my friend. Third, and most important, is that I'm the law along this bayou parish and murder ain't allowed. Especially not one of my cycling buds.

Coupled with his murder, my gut was set to explode with that third helping of thin-cut fried catfish. I asked the waitress to hold off, but being the new Sheriff meant everyone wanted something done or fixed. I saw the speeding ticket stuffed in her apron.

The young reporter and I squeezed out of the booth and tried to escape around back of the restaurant to watch alligators belly up along the bank looking for treats. Restaurant staff had hand fed them marshmallows for years—it was a tourist favorite.

"Sheriff, sorry 'bout yo friend. Sure he was a good man." A hard and weathered old man in faded coveralls bounced his fist on the scared wooden counter next to the register.

I didn't bother acknowledging the farmer. Dropped four dollars in the glass tip jar instead, and shoved the back door open. I waited until my lunch companion joined me on the porch before picking up where we left off.

"Son, pay attention to the way folks say things. It's as important as what they say." I feigned interest in mentoring this cub reporter, but I did promise his editor, my cousin, an interview with the new Sheriff.

"Yes sir, but why?" That response was naïve even for a LSU graduate.

We eased down the steps from the shaded porch. I paused at an old wood bench. Its green paint had faded and blistered under the cloudless sky. Lumber was the only material that wouldn't burn a customer's butt too bad. My rawhide had grown used to it—young Jackson Andrews was about to find out.

"Oh shit," Jax yelped.

I smirked. Yep, always pays to touch it before planting your ass on it.

"Jax, you rather stand?" Rubbing my palm across curled lips hid a grin, but the laughter in my question was obvious. I drew another gulp of sweet tea and swirled ice around the extra-large Styrofoam cup.

"Can we get on with this? My boss is bitching at me to talk to you, and it's hot as heck."

The kid's Polo was already dappled with sweat. Where'd he grow up anyway, indoors?

"Jackson, you do realize I'm just the appointed Sheriff until the parish holds a special election." Those words deflated an ego I didn't realize I'd gained.

The kid's upper body looked like it'd lost its spine as he slumped his shoulders with a twist of his mouth up to the left.

"Okay, you want to know how I got this Sheriff's gig. Easy enough."

I dug my boot heel into a small anthill and watched the tiny specks pour from a pinhole. My stomach wrenched, not from fried catfish, but at the possibility of losing the elected seat I thought I didn't want.

"Yes sir, Sheriff. How did you go from being a detective to the

Sheriff—acting Sheriff?" Avoiding eye contact, his enthusiasm waned.

I rehearsed the way I'd answer this question if ever asked outside of a courtroom. Actually, there would be no trial, and the Louisiana Attorney General's office cleared me in the shootings as justifiable homicide. Smashing ants with my boot wasn't going to make answering any easier.

"There was this evil ass District Attorney named Gill Gaudet and his whore, Lucy Bates who loved murdering people. They murdered plenty of people—like Bonny and Clyde, except they robbed lives instead of money. Gill beat my former boss in the last Sheriff's election, and then they tried to kill me. Got it?"

Honestly, that wasn't exactly how I planned on it coming out. He was the first to ask since it happened a few months back.

"No way." The kid's shorts had stained wet, but I was hoping it was from sweat. Either way, I'd give him benefit of the doubt.

"If they tried to kill you, what happened?" His blotchy beard failed to hide the tension in his unwrinkled face.

"I killed them instead." There, I said it. No therapist, shrink, or medications needed to get back on my feet.

The muscles clinching in my chest wouldn't let me forget how close I was to becoming their thirteenth victim. How I let Gaudet trap my Glock under his boot, I'll never know. It eased my stress each time the top of my hand patted the metal bulge shoved into the back of my waistband. I was thankful for my back up revolver—it wasn't the first time it saved my butt.

Loose leaves of notepaper fluttered in slow motion onto the uncut yard. His pen bounced against the stone pathway toward the gators. Those spoiled bastards never flinched, just laid there sunning themselves with snouts full of creamy snacks. Kid never moved either. Jaw on chest, eyes unblinking and both arms fixed from the thirty-five degree angles he held for note taking. He had this odd *uhmmm* sound coming through the rubber bands intertwined with his braces.

"Jax, you okay?" My jaw twisted in the pain of regret—*best to keep my mouth shut about that.* Citizens can't understand the adrenaline of taking another's life. They surely can't imagine the pain afterward.

The casualness of the boy's question unleashed the problems that ate at me constantly and had threatened my sense of normalcy since the incident. Jax wasn't the cause of my problems, but I sure just dumped them all on him.

"How bout I get you home and we'll do this another day?"

The dusty oyster shell parking lot off Highway 90 was silent, except for the scraping of our shoes crunching across it. I'd wounded his young spirit by answering one simple question. Jackson Andrews existed in a world different from mine. I used to resent people like him—called them sheep. Maybe because I'm five years past the half-century mark, I'd finally started developing a sense of compassion or pity for the flock.

After a moment, Jax rallied back, "Sheriff, tell me about that farmer in the overalls back there. You said I should listen to how people say things as much as what they say." Jackson's thoughtful inquiry sounded like he was trying to mend the breach I created. I appreciated the question, but more than that I admired his resolve.

"Son that man couldn't care less about Howard Jones and even less about me. He flies under the radar for a reason. That act was to gauge where he falls on my shit list."

"Help me understand. What radar and why does he care whether you like him?" His notepad back in his lap for note taking. I liked this young reporter.

"That old farmer, who looks like he ain't got a pot to piss in, got more cash than we'll ever see. It's all illegal—the Cajun Mafia."

I saw him Googling it on his cellphone and then like the predictable countdown, "No way. That old man looks poor as dirt." His skeptical chuckle showed discomfort, but not disbelief. He jotted notes in fancy shorthand I'd never seen.

"His name?" Jax asked without turning his stare away from mine.

His bright eyes shone bluer thanks to sunbaked cheeks, and reminded me of my own boy—God rest his soul.

"Saul Dugas. But leave it be. Some old dogs are best left lying on the porch." My temples pulsed—I'd just lit a fire under this neophyte reporter hotter than that park bench.

Chapter 6

— *Coroner Susan Lambert* —

BUCK WALKER'S LANKY BODY FILLED the doorway to my examination room, and I squashed a giddy flush before inappropriate ideas popped up. This wasn't a social call.

"Hi Sheriff, thank you for coming over so quickly."

"No problem, Doc. He was my friend and I'm gonna bust somebody's ass for this." Buck Walker was a tough man to rattle. I'd never known him to talk like this. I didn't blame him though—Howard had suffered horribly. Besides the deceased and his killers, I was the only one who knew exactly how horrible it was. Buck was about to find out.

"Buck, I'm sorry to be the one to go through this with you. I'd only met Howard once. His wife tried to set me up on a blind date with a friend of theirs. I didn't go of course." What just fell out of my mouth? I took another deep breath to focus my thoughts.

His chin dug into his shoulder as he tried to hide a grin that made me think of a sunrise over the bayou. I couldn't swing my gaze from his gray eyes as they barely squeezed through slits in his rugged bronzed face.

"Do they still call it a blind date?" He tried easing my embarrassment. I wasn't sure now that I hadn't said it on purpose. Either way, I'm sure he was just being polite.

I busied myself around the lab looking for a rock to crawl under. I found the coffee pot instead.

"Thanks Doc."

"Ok, onto the reason you're here. I'll speak to you as the Sheriff and not Howard's friend. Is that understood?"

He looked like I'd stabbed him in the stomach by the way he suddenly hunched over in his chair. He'd broken out into slight sweat. Maybe the flirtation mixed too harshly with his best friend just feet away—Howard's chilled body in pieces under a thin white blanket.

*Da*mmit – *too harsh. Get it together Susan,* I reminded myself. "I'm so sorry Buck, I mean Sheriff." Maybe I'd confused his reaction with grief. His broad back vibrated as the tips of my fingers rested on his shoulder. My hand popped back with what felt like electricity invading my senses. *Focus Susan.*

"Doc, we go way back. Not many people still call me Buck, but I prefer that to Sheriff. I'm only the temporary boss anyway." Buck leaned to stand up from the swivel chair—his faded denims pulled tight across the flexing quadriceps. I needed to focus, but I'd admired him over the years.

"Sorry, I know this is hard for you. I'll just get to the facts." Heat soaked through my lab coat as I struggled to center less on steamy Buck and more on the cold corpse. I reminded myself I wasn't a desperate teenager anymore.

He propped himself up with his elbows on his thighs, a frown settling down his forehead like a shield against the worst kind of report I give in my line of work. I noticed he began to ease up on the deep exhales, and once he finished wiping moisture from his lips, I gave it a shot.

"Obviously this was no farming accident. Official cause of death was suffocation." My eyes locked onto the metal clipboard but I didn't need to see the words. I just couldn't bear to cause this man any more pain.

"Suffocation? I thought the John Deere Harvester crushed him?" He sprung up looking to take action, but what I saw in his face was only confusion and fury warring in his eyes.

I chewed on the tip of my pen as a way to ignore how my tummy felt—it burned as if it was full of spicy Tobacco sauce. Cause of death was the easy part.

"Sheriff, the tox screen showed he also had anhydrous ammonia in his system. Looks like someone tried to poison him or slow him down on that bicycle." I watched as he struggled to process what I had told him. I slowed the feed of clinical information to give him time to do so.

The empty coffee cup trembled in his left hand. Steel eyes glinted while a weathered hand twisted the wrinkled skin covering his cleft chin. The rock jaw looked to have endured that habit for years during the thought processes of solving mysteries, but it was still hard and handsome.

The same way I change personas before cutting open autopsies, I witnessed his transformation back into the tough-souled lawman. I fanned the clipboard slightly to cool my reddening face. Shame covered me for the way I allowed my thoughts to wander over this man while Howard Jones laid waiting for closure.

"Doc, where'd the fertilizer come from? Was it poured in him after he was killed?"

"Definitely not. It was premortem. It had a chance to get into his bloodstream and began to metabolize at the time of death."

"How in the world does a man cycling through a sugarcane field near Nottoway Plantation get anhydrous ammonia into his system? Hell, for that matter, how does he get run over by a sugarcane harvester and end up buried under bagasse?"

His eyes opened a bit wider as I watched the expression of grief morph over his face. He lifted his chest and slapped his hand across his knee. The #2 pencil snapped in half, "I'm sorry Susan." His words apologized for the pencil, but his thousand-yard stare showed his mind was far removed.

"He must have been one tough son of a gun, Sheriff. He fought to survive. The amount of chemical wouldn't have killed him, but the crushing of his body by that tractor should have. The weight of the equipment was so great that it severed his limbs. I also found carbon fiber infused into his tissue and embedded into bone."

"Doc, I guess that bike is now more a part of him than he'd ever have imagined." Buck's comment shocked me. It was without emotion, and the callousness concerned me.

My shoulders fell as I tried to loosen the wrenching in my back from hunching over the body all morning. Moreover, this next part was going to really be painful to tell—and for him to hear. But, maybe not. Possibly I'd overestimated his depth of compassion.

He sidestepped my instruments table and poured himself another cup of caffeine.

"Sorry, there's more, Buck. Howard Jones was still conscious after the tractor rolled over him. There was dirt under his broken nails and the tips of his fingers are cut and scratched. All typical with grabbing or crawling—being alive."

"Tough as an oyster. I'm not surprised." The right corner of his mouth curled as he looked to gain hope in his friend's noble effort to survive.

"There are ligature marks across his neck and brush burns under his jaw consistent with rope, but not with hanging. More like he was dragged by the neck." I swallowed hard.

"Like, with a noose?" Buck stopped his pacing to study my expression. His chest pumped with shallow breaths. The man, usually so controlled, looked to have finally allowed his feelings to be pierced by loss. He was seconds away from a full-blown anxiety attack.

"I guess he must 'a been struck off highway 405 around Nottoway Plantation. Your detective's report said his car was parked in White Castle, so I guess he rode his bicycle from there. Must have consumed the anhydrous ammonia along the way. Then..."

"Percle's Country Store." Buck gripped the autopsy table until his knuckles blanched white. "Oh God, I'm sorry, Howard." His face creased and he fell back into the chair.

"What about Percle's?"

"We always stop there to refill our water bottles. Someone had to slip him the chemical there. But why?"

"How would they know he'd stop in?"

"Clockwork. There's only so many decent roads to bike down here, so we travel the same routes religiously. We're both cops—should have been better about avoiding a routine. But biking?"

His thoughts reflected through glassed eyes as his hands pounded together. Buck was mentally stitching this thing together, but it wasn't going to get sewn in this lab. He thanked me on his way to the door. I knew he knew, but I didn't want to know.

"Buck." I had to finish the briefing.

"Yeah, Doc." He spun back to me with his chest pushed forward like a sprinter in the starting block.

"Someone buried him alive in Sinclair's bagasse. That's where he finally died. His lungs were filled with that fiber." I felt an unusual sadness in sharing the death details. Almost twenty years processing the dead and consoling families and it never got easy. Especially when it's someone you care about.

Chapter 7

— *Reporter Jackson Andrews* —

I'D MADE SUCH A JERK of myself the last time I spoke with Sheriff Walker. Hope he'd give me a second chance. I got good information this time. He did say to call him anytime. He answered after the third ring.

"Hey Sheriff, this is Jax. Got a second?"

"A little busy but I'm on the road, so go ahead." Howling winds through his open window made it tough to make out his voice.

"I'm following up on the Hispanic girl's body they found this morning. I know it's out of your parish but its close."

"First I hear of it, son. Sorry, got nothing for ya."

I rushed ahead before he could kill the call.

"Cane farmer found her not far from Nottoway Plantation." The background noise lessened.

"Jax, you sure? Anything else?"

"Heard that a Wildlife and Fisheries Agent is taking major heat over this. Seems he stopped a boat last night with three guys and this same girl. Frogging they said. Let 'em go."

"Did the Agent identify the people?" He either rolled up his window or come to a complete stop. My Spidey senses said something was up. This might be my big break.

"No sir, but I'm heading over to Percle's Country Store. Heard the boat's moored there."

"Son, stay away from there. They might be involved in Howard's murder. Stick to reporting the facts, not becoming one of them."

"But, Sheriff—" Now I was sure I was on to something big. No way was I going to miss this scoop.

— *Sheriff James Walker* —

I WAS OUT OF MY jurisdiction, but someone was gonna tell me the damn truth. I'd planned to slip into that old general store like any other customer. Buy a bottle of water. Shoot the shit about the weather. Play it cool was my plan. That was, until I got there and the realization slammed into me like a piling driver. That store was the last place Howard Jones had stopped before being tortured and left to die.

Curious about a commotion around back, I eased a peek around the corner of the building. A boat was docked down by the launch. Two jackasses guzzling beer were scrubbing it with deck brushes. The bleach they used to clean the boat wafted through the stench from the bayou's brackish water.

I walked back to the front of the store and propped myself against the porch railing. Speckled light dotted my vision and I blinked my eyes. Walking was impossible until I managed to control the fury whipping through my chest. My fingers rode the beats ripping through my arteries—gotta control this blood pressure. So much for playing it cool—I drew in a few deep breathes.

I tugged my t-shirt down over the holster and slipped the badge into my pocket before returning to the rear of the store. "You boys doing any good out there?" I knew they were up to no good, but had to ask.

"Naw, sir. Just cleaning it up fer later on." The skinny one's snickers made him look dumb, and I pictured cracking that brush handle across his skull. The second one just sat there—sweat sliding between rolls of neck fat shadowed with beard stubble.

"Nice boat you got there. No trawl motor?" *Frogging my ass.*

Three decades of evolved intuition shivered my body, so I pressed a thumb against my t-shirt to ease the snap on my holster open.

"Why we need dat, mista?" Skinny asked.

"Seems like you'd need that and a q-beam. Maybe even a gig pole, unless you're fond of grabbing them by hand."

"Grab what, you jackass?" Fatso spoke.

"Frogs. How'd the frogging go last night?"

"Whose you? Da game warden?" Now I knew they were at least two of the three. I checked to make sure my back up revolver was tucked tight behind my belt. Ensured my stance in the slippery mud and loose gravel—this was going to get bad—and quick.

The fat one crumpled his beer can against his thigh. Beer spurted through the cracks in the aluminum and onto his torso. He'd be easy to take out. The other one was gangly. I'd punch him in the throat to start. I'd have preferred to talk to these two, but I sensed they'd killed the Mexican girl. Faces void of expressions showed they were aware I knew also.

"What ya trying to do mista, get your ass whooped out here asking crazy questions?" He tried to slam his beer can down onto the ground, but stupidly struck the hull instead. They looked at each other and he shrugged his shoulders.

Rolling my neck and rotating my shoulders a few times, I limbered up like a boxer in his corner. I rocked onto the toes of my worn leather boots. The air stunk of stagnant marsh, but I shot quick breaths to steady my heartbeat. The two men were slightly down the levee from me, so I had the advantage of momentum right off the bat.

"Hey Sheriff, thought that was your truck out front."

My head twirled backwards like an owl, and my knees buckled at being caught off guard.

"Jax, I told you to stay away from here. Now get in your car and go." I had to nearly drag that kid back to the gravel parking lot. I hated to take my eyes off those two killers but the kid's safety came first.

It was too late. I heard the roar of twin Mercury engines. I dashed down the levee's boat launch—there was nothing but a rooster tail of water and middle fingers. I whipped out my weapon to pop off a few rounds, but noticed a wrinkled face peeking through the store window's cloth curtain.

"Guess we were both right, huh Sheriff?"

I couldn't punish Jax. He wasn't my son. I kind of admired his gumption. We were both after the same thing—the truth.

"Jax, you were right, but you just let two killers escape. I'll call you with anything that I find out, but you have to watch it out here. This ain't the LSU campus, son." I felt the abrasion of cloth under my palm as his shoulder jerked away. I'd insulted him again. When will I learn to just be quiet?

Jackson sped out of the parking lot as fast as that hybrid would allow. I ducked into the country store and stomped to the counter. The ancient shopkeeper's face resembled an alligator's, minus a couple dozen teeth. His dusty eyes lit up and he sucked in before muttering something.

I leaned in, angry, "Huh?"

He lifted a bony finger and pointed over my shoulder. "Behind you."

— Creola Parish Sheriff Tyler Robinson —

"BUCK, WHAT THE FUCK YOU doing sneaking around my parish?" I should've left Buck's ass in Percle's Country Store, except it was hard for customers to step over him while buying bait.

"Tyler, what happened? Why am I in the hospital? All I saw was a giant fist when I turned around."

"What happened? You stuck your nose in official law enforcement business and got knocked out. What more you want to know?" I wasn't sure if I was pissed at him for coming into my parish without notifying me or that someone in my parish attacked a cop. Either way, this kinda crap don't look good in my jurisdiction.

"Tyler, we go back to the undercover days. Don't treat me like I'm some state police rookie on a ticket-writing binge. Howard Jones is dead, and now you got a Mexican female murdered."

Buck was right. If there was anyone I trusted: it was guys from the old days of busting down crack dealers' doors together.

"Who hit you like that?" Buck was tough as steel, and I shuttered to think what man could best him with one punch.

"The Rougarou." His face flattened with hollow expression.

"The what?"

"You know, the Cajun Big Foot. Guy was humongous."

I figured the meds had kicked in, but he didn't look sedated.

"Buck, get yourself some rest and soon as you check out of this hospital, I'll give you the run down on all I know."

"Thanks, old friend. This is personal." His eyes were practically shut by flaps of overlapping purple and black skin stretched to the limits across his face. I still saw the wrath in them, though—somebody was going to get hurt. Just hope it ain't in my parish.

"You got people on the way. Need me to call your family?" Damn it. Wish I hadn't said that. "I'm sorry Buck."

He laid his hand on my arm. It lacked the usual strength and patted my wrist more like a grieving victim than the hard-as-nails cop I'd known for over twenty-five years.

"Chief Deputy St. Pierre's on her way." He rolled his battered face away from me and sighed something about the bright hospital light, even as one tear slid to the pillow below.

Chapter 8

— *Sheriff James Walker* —

I WAS COCKY AND GOT my ass knocked out. What's been with me lately? I let that kid walk up behind me at the boat launch—I wanted to annihilate those two jerk offs instead of interviewing them—and then I let the alligator man freak me out so that I missed Rougarou hiding behind the Twinkie aisle.

Maybe I wasn't over the shooting.

Even the detectives seemed glad to have me back at work. I patted my feet while waiting for whomever it was in the men's room to give it a break. Of course, no one missed the opportunity to kid me about the two black eyes I couldn't conceal under bifocals. Finally, I heard the flush.

"Detective Stone. What'cha got for me?" The young detective who replaced me once I moved up to Sheriff reached for my hand and I recoiled. "You wash that thing?"

"Sorry, Sheriff. Sir, look like you could use a few days off. You okay?"

My frowning face had to have hollered, *Oh, hell no*, but the reality was, I'd already wasted enough time. I poured two cups of coffee, offered one to the greenhorn detective, and repeated my question.

"I got the numbers for the boat out back of Percle's. The registration comes back to a company out of Iberville Parish—the Jean Laffite Bayou Estuary Conservatory."

"I'm not sure what you're talking about, Todd." I needed to hit the head something fierce, but now I was hooked by the boat information.

"The one Jackson Andrews called in the numbers to. Said you wanted to know about the boat because it was for sale." Detective Stone lifted his shoulders with his hands palms up. "I thought you told the kid to call."

"Todd, that's the boat the two killers escaped in from behind Percle's Country Store. Jackson is trying to scoop the story and tricked you into giving out official police information." Todd Stone might be a rookie detective, but was a seasoned road cop. He should have known better. Forget going to the pisser, we had to save Jackson Andrews.

"Stone, you drive. I'd already put the prescription eye drops in and it was blurring my vision." I ran my hand along the wall for stability until I reached the Communications Office.

"Call Sheriff Robinson in the next parish and tell him to meet us at the Jean Laffite Bayou Estuary Conservatory immediately. It's a matter of life or death."

THE CONSERVATORY LOOKED LIKE AN old cattle auction and slaughterhouse. Red brick and rusty piping created a dangerous obstacle course across the overgrown property. I could barely make it out at dusk. Injuries from the Rougarou's punch and the stinging medicated drops left my eyes swollen and vision strained.

Detective Stone tried to be helpful as he picked our path to Sheriff Robinson's Tahoe, but he flinched each time I grabbed a fist of his shirt to avoid adding a sprained ankle to my list of injuries.

Robinson held his silence until we stepped beyond the arc of his headlights.

"Buck, one of my deputies found a light blue car around the other side. A little hybrid or something like that." He started to return to the abandoned vehicle but I reached out to stop him. "That's Jackson's car. He's already here."

I turned to my detective, "Stone, call Jenny at the paper. Ask if Jax said why he was coming here or what he knew."

Stone stood stiff, anxiety engraved into his face. Just a rookie, his defeated posture showed he also knew it might be too late to save Jax.

"Son, I need you to go, now." I patted him on the shoulder.

"Robinson, my eyes haven't adjusted yet. Wait for me, will ya? Robinson?" I found myself without escort and still blurred vision.

A minute after he disappeared into the night, the deputies' cruiser headlights exploded across the field like brilliant starbursts branding my dilated pupils. Heading into that direction would only make finding Robinson more impossible.

No way was I going to stand here helpless. Measuring each step, I slid my boots across the broken plain of asphalt and cracked cement-parking stops. A rusted rebar spike from a concrete pillar jammed into my shin. Hell, I was a mess. The kid was in a bigger mess though. Jackson had discovered who the killers were and came to investigate. No time for pain. Job to do.

I stopped fifty yards from the shadowed opening. No way I'd go in alone. There were too many other cops in the area to play John Wayne.

What the hell was keeping Stone? Crouching next to a dirt pile, I shaded my cell phone's screen light to check for messages. Nothing. I stamped out a text message to him.

[where r u?]

Blood sucking mosquitoes buzzed around the light. I jerked away and fell against the mounded earth, and immediately felt the tickle of ants attacking my palm and wrist. Fire exploded up my arm.

The phone screen flashed with an incoming text, highlighting the red devils crawling everywhere.

[on phone w/your cousin jenny]

Vision was less twitchy so I crept closer to the threshold and further from the ants. Pressing against what bricks remained, I willed my senses to compensate for the shitty sight. Why the hell hadn't I worn a vest?

A hot wind picked up and whistled past the empty windows of the warehouse and through the vacant halls. The aroma of rotting flesh built up over decades of butchering beasts greeted me. Metal, boards, and pulleys across broken ropes twisted making eerie sounds from another world. Despite the screaming wind, I could still hear my own drumming heart.

The wait had me inside out—I knew Jax needed help. He needed me. I pushed off from the brick frame and peeked into the abyss. Robinson's cruisers cast streams of light into the tumbledown building. Helpful, except for the false shadows.

I drew my Glock and pointed it at the opening before flipping on the flashlight attached beneath the barrel for a quick swipe of light to shock anyone hiding inside. Sometimes crooks get antsy waiting to do bad things. I'd fooled a few crooks with that trick.

No such luck this time.

My pants pocket buzzed. I figured it was Detective Stone texting me again. I'd already begun my breach into the opening. My weapon swept left to right as I sped across the opening and moved toward the left corner of the building. I killed the light switch and dropped to one knee. Quiet – looking and listening for motion.

[stone – call coroner asap]

Chapter 9

— Coroner Susan Lambert —

THANK GOODNESS SHERIFF WALKER HAD sent a deputy to pick me up from my house. This warehouse was God forsaken. I'd never have found it on my own. The collection of cop cars, ambulances, detectives and K-9 gave it an almost carnival atmosphere. If it wasn't for the white male strung upside down from a meat hook that is.

I knew Sheriff Tyler Robinson from before coming on as the Coroner in the quad-parish area. After a quick greeting, I allowed my eyes to wander back to Buck Walker. A chill buzzed up my neck at the hollow, tortured look in his eyes. Classic case of PTSD. The man was carrying a cross heavier than anyone, but he was doing everything he could to hide it. I motioned for him to sit against the police cruiser.

"I'll be fine, Doc," he said, refusing to lean against a cruiser that was lighting the scene. "I know what we got, but tell us what really went on."

"I can't give you a definite cause of death until I perform the autopsy, but the ligature marks around his wrist and ankles indicate they bound his hands and feet. The bruising on his torso indicates physical blows before they hung him upside down. Glass shards embedded around his eyes are from his eyeglasses that were shattered as they struck him. Whatever they used to beat him wasn't heavy enough to break bones. Just enough to cause plenty of pain. Internal injuries."

I watched Buck. His dedication wouldn't allow him to walk away, but the mind has a way of shutting itself down for self-preservation.

"So, interrogated, then murdered," Robinson said.

I agreed with Robinson's assessment. "Seems about right, given the bloody pool of urine on the cement below the body.

I realized this kid worked for Buck's cousin Jennifer Adams at the newspaper as I saw the LSU student ID card and a few prom pictures that fell from his wallet.

"Why you used the word *they* Doctor Lambert?" Robinson asked. He'd been laser focused despite managing his staff and the media's phone inquiries.

"Just assumed it would be hard to manage a twenty-one year old by yourself."

Buck's fingers scrubbed his eyes before crawling across his scalp. "Twenty-three. He was twenty-three."

"The puncture and ripping wounds are what eventually opened his organs and probably killed him. They don't appear deep enough to have pierced vital organs quick, so he bled out. It was probably the same weapon that was used to cut him open from groin to throat."

Buck's torso finally caved over the hood of the Ford Crown Victoria. "Son, I'm so sorry. I failed again. It's my fault."

I tried to comfort Buck—just a pat in the back. The contact was a wholly different sensation than the last time we touched. My soul wanted to take his hurt, to help him heal.

"He followed me to the boat launch that day. They saw him."

"Who, Buck?"

A uniformed officer coughed behind our huddle. "Sheriff. Look what I found in that corner." He held something wrapped up with a handkerchief. Anxious to show off what he'd discovered during his grid search, the heavy-set deputy gasped for air after sprinting across the smooth cement-killing floor.

A gig pole for frogging.

— *Sheriff James Walker* —

HOWARD JONES WAS DEAD. HE was a federal agent and knew the risks in life. Jackson Andrews was dead. He was a brave boy and had no clue about the evils in life. The Hispanic girl was dead. I had no idea how the three connected. What I did know was there were at least two people I was going to kill. Maybe even the Rougarou if he was still hiding behind the candy aisle.

It was time to get to the bottom of Jackson's discoveries. My cousin, Jennifer was his boss at the newspaper and had to have known he was heading to check out the business.

"Jennifer, I'm sure you've heard about Jax by now. I need to know everything he discovered in this case. See you soon."

Detective Stone remained at the crime scene. I was okay to drive and had to meet my cousin at the Creole Café in thirty minutes. Honestly, the food there was horrible, but I needed fuel and I must've forgotten to replace the last of the protein bars I normally stash in the glove box.

Headlights dulled by the grime of sugarcane and love bugs swept over the empty parking lot. I backed my truck into the shadows furthest from the front door. I sat in the dark cab and waited for Jenny to arrive. I also had a gut wrench that I was followed. With no one else lurking about, I slipped from the truck to greet Jenny at the front door of the café. We grabbed the booth in the deepest corner. There wasn't anyone following me—maybe fatigue was making me jumpy. Maybe my age was showing.

"Jenny I'm pissed and pressed for time. Just point me in the right direction." Our hands lay atop one another for the moment. It jolted my mind to replay our childhood together. We were both so happy. How'd my life change streams?

"Buck, I'm so sorry about all of this. Had I known Jax would have gotten himself into this, I would've never put you two in contact. After losing your son, I thought it might be helpful to—" her words blended into a dark static.

The porcelain coffee cup exploded in my hand. That depth of darkness had never entered my soul, but watching the black sludge run from the tabletop told me my time was also running out.

"Details, Jennifer." I shot a glare at the approaching waitress. She stopped short and returned without interrupting us.

"Buck, you're terrifying me. I don't know who you are right now." She reached across to touch me but I jerked back into my seat. She busied herself with sopping up the coffee instead.

"No time for that, Jenny. Tell me where to start."

"Buck, please remember these are the files of a novice reporter. I'm almost afraid to tell you what he thought." Her own coffee leaped onto the table from rattling hands.

"Instinct said I could trust that kid. Go with the facts." I growled with impatience.

"A bogus investors group uses the Jean Lafitte company as a front for buying properties and other investments. They bought the old Belle Cove Plantation in White Castle over a year ago."

"Belle Cove Plantation—the Queen?" My mind washed back to childish days of camping along the bayou. Neglect, Civil War, and ignorance had destroyed the majesty of that antebellum mansion. We didn't help much by sling shooting rocks through what windows were left or riding four-wheelers through the seventy-something rooms. I was too stupid back then to realize what a treasure it was.

"I know what you're thinking cuz. You little bad asses tore that place up and your poppa busted butts with a switch branch." Her taunt brought me back to focus.

"I thought that place had been demolished?"

"Almost. Investors said they were reclaiming the historic beauty of the Queen as a luxury B&B."

"In White Castle?" How could no one see the farce behind that claim?

"Buck, promise me you'll stay calm and hear me out. This is only a boy's theory."

"Promise." I would've agreed to chew the crushed coffee cup if it got me out of this diner and into the mode of retribution.

"Cross my heart."

"Jax thought the investors were involved in human trafficking. Prostitution. The Queen had become a makeshift brothel and dungeon for the girls kidnapped from—"

"Mexico."

"How'd you know?" Her eyes widened with surprise.

"Was Howard Jones investigating this?" My eagerness for disclosure drew my body across the table.

"Seems your friend Howard Jones was involved."

"Hell, I knew he'd be on their case." I pumped my fist in celebration of my friend's pursuit of justice—even if it did cost him his life.

My confidence in Howard Jones was halted by a raise of her hand.

"No. Jones was a silent partner in Southern Consulting, LLC." Both hands invaded my scalp as I dug fingers through my hair. I exhaled it all before I faced her again. In my heart of hearts, I wasn't surprised—just disappointed. I'd seen enough good men go bad behind the shield.

I'd learned not to judge their action until I knew their intentions. However, a dirty cop still pissed me off every time. Knowing Jones was a reason that honest arrow was tortured to death really flipped a switch in me.

"Who's the not so silent partner in Southern Consulting, LLC?" I had to get answers and go—or that café would never be the same.

"Dugas. Saul Dugas."

Chapter 10

— *Sheriff James Walker* —

I PULLED INTO THE SAME parking lot I had pulled into for over thirty years. Only difference was I slid in-between two yellow stripes with a metal sign that read SHERIFF WALKER. That didn't make me special, just responsible for my staff and the flock in my parish. It made me the shepherd.

I let the engine idle while I listened to the end of an old hymn on the radio. It soothed my perspective. I knew the next time I pulled into the parking slot I'd be a different man. I would've done something I'd hunted people down for doing. Some things have to be done no matter the consequences—as long as they're for the right reason.

When I noticed the deputy standing on the sidewalk in front of my vehicle, I damn near came out of my seat.

"Sir, sorry to startle you, but Sheriff Robinson told me to get this to you no matter what."

"What you got, son?" I was in no mood for games or get-well gifts.

"Said it belonged to you and that you'd know what to do with it when finished." The black nylon rifle pouch was zipped from end to end. There was a bread tie woven between the two zipper handles. The thought of Robinson's idea of security brought me a slight smile.

"I'm sorry, Deputy, but he doesn't owe me a rifle."

"Sir, he said you'd say that. He told me to make sure you accepted his gift."

I nodded and the deputy quickly exited the complex for his own jurisdiction.

After I Googled the Belle Cove Plantation in White Castle, I hit the road for about an hour's drive. It was already late. I was seeing things in my peripheral vision as I ripped up rocky roads and pitted highways. The bread tie was unscrewed and I tried working the sticky zipper with one hand.

Google assured me I was getting close, so a slow rolled into a wooded patch that left me about a mile out. I tugged up on my socks and touched the backup revolver just to make sure.

ONE LAST, LONG GULP OF coffee and I checked the map again. I grabbed the black pouch more out of frustration than curiosity and finally tore the zipper apart. It was the gig pole used to kill Jax. I hesitated to touch the evidence. Did Robinson send this as a mistake? I recalled the deputy's words—"... *that you'd know what to do with it when finished.*"

There'd be no one left to arrest for my son's murder. "It's Jackson, not my boy," I whispered. "Keep it straight."

This gig pole wouldn't be needed as evidence in a trial that would never occur. I was six-foot-four inches tall, and in damn tough shape. I'd lived my life so hard that callouses blistered my heart. I didn't care that I didn't care—until I held that bloody pole. Images flashed in my mind of what that innocent boy went through. I was ready to make someone hurt for that.

I set off into the night, wiping the waterworks. Not a great way to start a killing spree, but it was the best way to justify what I was about to do. It took me fourteen minutes to get there. Not bad considering how many times I had to duck into the weeds when cars flew by. This highway led nowhere, so I figured the cars were customers at the Queen.

The Belle Cove Plantation sat a couple hundred yards from the road. The dark covering approach would make getting close easy. The sheer size of the structure would make finding my targets impossible. Failing to recall the mansion's interior proved my childhood memories weren't as detailed as I'd hoped. I just knew the place was enormous and I'd have to clear it quickly.

Even in the darkest of night, the Greek columns that survived the latest fire stood out as a symbol of the old south. About twenty years ago, an arsonist with deep sentiments over the Civil War's outcome decided to set it ablaze to do what the Union army couldn't complete.

I thought of the hundreds, maybe thousands of slaves forced to give their bodies to laboring in these fields. Hundreds of years later and there were still slaves forced to give their bodies to the highest bidders like bales of cotton at market.

My wrist ached as I squeezed the pole in rage.

Halfway between the road and the giant front porch, the roar of twin Mercury engines split the silence. I dropped into the wet Bermuda grass next to an abandoned bush hog. My body's heat could've created steam.

I knew it was *go time*–time to protect the sheep from these wolves. The switch in my soul had become easier to flip at times like these. It wasn't easy to take another's life, but in this case, it was the right thing to do. I'd deal with my consequences later.

Fatso and stupid dragged a young girl by her hair toward the front door. I sprang to my knees and lifted the gig pole as they approached. My muscles were warm from the run, and my vision had finally settled to see more than just shadows and surface breaks.

Twenty feet. Fifteen feet. Ten feet. They were almost on top of me, and I coiled in the anticipation of ambush. Was it the right time?

She begged in a string of Spanish curses and almost pulled free after a handful of hair ripped from her head. The gangly one just stood there holding her tresses as she dashed back to the road. Fatso also stood there. Why didn't they chase her? I steadied myself with a predator's tension. If they let her escape, I would kill them both right now.

She sprinted ten yards, and then her feet flew forward and her neck jerked back. The leash around her throat wasn't going to budge the fat, hairy one. They dragged her back the way they probably dragged Howard Jones. The tall one started kicking and giving her demands that I knew she didn't understand.

Butterball pushed him away. "Stupid fucker. You know Boss Saul likes 'em pretty and unpunished."

Saul's inside?

Now, where was Rougarou lurking?

I looked up and the trio had made their way onto the massive set of stairs leading into the house. Tough call—stay and wait for dumb and dumber to return, or rush inside and find who I could. My heart told me to rescue the girl, but reality is she's better off waiting until I could clear them all out.

Shit. My heart dropped out of my ass. What was that thing?

Chapter 11

— Sheriff James Walker —

THE SHADOWS PARTED AS A figure slogged into the haze that had settled from the marshlands. Wasn't an alligator. This thing was walking upright. Crap, it was him—the son of a bitch who sucker punched me—the Rougarou.

I tapped the revolver in my back, but this wouldn't be the time for popping off shots. The wooden gig pole would just tickle his big ass. The uncoated wire came untangled from my pocket.

I skulked up behind and jumped onto his back. Both fists wrapped around each end, and the cord sunk into his throat as I let my weight fall back onto the ground. I had to land on my feet to keep him upright and off balance. If he fell to the ground and I lost the tension I'd be shit out of luck.

That beast swung me like a child's doll but I wasn't letting go. He growled, but the razor wire slicing into his esophagus quieted him. My biceps seared as I pulled to separate his melon head from his useless body.

His fists were hammers to my skull and I tucked my face between the muscles of his neck and traps. I kept whispering into his ear, "Go night night. It'll be over soon. I'm here to kill you." It seemed to unnerve him. My body began to struggle, but my resolve was solid. I had flipped the decency switch to off and focused on the killing.

He arched forward, rocketing my feet off the ground. One boot stayed where it was. His head flung backwards and my nose crunched.

I don't know how he did it with his head sawed half off, but he laughed.

I squared my feet back on the ground and arched to keep him off balance. He gave way and I relaxed for a second. Then his ass thrust into my gut as he threw his shoulders forward again to lift me from the earth. I couldn't stop the momentum. My feet flailed over my head and I landed on a pile of dirt and concrete. The wire was fileting my palms. I never let go.

He fell to his knees sitting upright. I thought he'd busted my gut with a cinder block. It was his head. It had cut clean through with his last effort to free himself. He was free all right. From life.

I was beat, but the adrenaline coursed through me like high octane. Blood was everywhere, his and mine. I couldn't get enough air in me. My nose babbled blood and seared to the touch. I wasn't sure I had the physical strength in me to fight the other two. I decided to make it easy and shoot them. I knew Saul Dugas was still inside. He was way too old, so no chance of him fighting or running away at the sound of gunfire. He'd be easy picking, like them frogs in the bayou.

I found my boot and the gig pole, and then stumbled parallel to the dirt road leading back to their boat. I'd take advantage of the wait to catch my breath and disable the boat. I didn't have to wait long. I made out two distinct figures in the pre-dawn fog.

Waiting in silence to kill people is one hell of a feeling. I'd struggled with it earlier in my career, but tried to numb it from my soul. It was just a job—it needed doing.

They came closer without regard for stealth. My mind raced through scenarios a thousand times. The way I did before SWAT and undercover missions. I always expected the unexpected.

They lumped a girl's mutilated body into the hull.

I didn't expect that.

My mind blanked with rage and I launched out from the other side of the boat. My boot caught the edge of the hull and propelled me across the open cabin. I think I yelled out as I flew through the air before plunging that gig into fatso's bloated belly. He slurped in air and fell to his knees.

The stupid one, stunned, almost had a smile. His clothes and mouth covered in the girls' blood, he still savored his kill.

"Huh?" was all I heard from him. My legs felt youthful as I rocketed off the ground. I formed a C-shape with my thumb and fingers to catch him square across his windpipe. His head jerked forward then flung back as he gasped for breath before slamming to the ground.

Both disabled but alive, my plan was to torment them the way they tortured Jax. The thought of either alive for any longer than they had to be sickened me. I didn't bother looking behind me, fatso was gurgling as life was escaping him. He tried pulling the gig pole from his fat girth but didn't have the strength.

I knew the skinny one was going to be the challenge. He curved up onto his ass, so I swung behind him and clamped what law enforcement officially calls a vascular neck restraint. In my Nekodo training, we called it choking the shit of out somebody. My left forearm settled across his carotid artery. I locked in with a quick right hand behind his greasy head. He went out. The trick would be to end his life. I stood to let his unconscious frame flop to the gravel and mud.

I blacked out for just a second. Dazed, I felt my own blood running over the back of my neck and into my ears. I tried to shake the affect, but my ears still rung. I spun around to thrust my right arm up in a forty-five degree angle and block fatso's next strike of the gig pole. I deflected the blow, and then wrapped my left arm behind my back. My reliable snub nose revolver was still tucked behind the small of my back.

Two bullets to the body, one to the head. He dropped the pole. Dead.

I felt the blood running off my skull and anger replaced the fatigue. Skinny rustled himself to kneeling, so I grabbed the same gig pole he killed Jax with and brooded over him.

"Hey, that's mine."

"Really? Here, have it." I ran that spear clean through him until I heard the metal tip scrape against the rocks behind him.

I collapsed onto the boat trying to regroup. I'd give anything for a drink of water or coffee, for that matter. This stuff ain't like you see on TV. I was physically drained, and now the emotional battle would begin. The man I used to be fought through—I'd just killed three men. The man I'd become returned—I'm the flock's shepherd—and one wolf remained.

The dawn was going to race me to the finish. I had to be gone by then. I must've looked like Quasimodo dragging myself back toward the old Queen. My body had been through it, but my mind stayed razor sharp. The light of day wouldn't save Saul Dugas.

Covered in blood, I pulled myself up the massive marble staircase leading toward the sound of screams and objects striking flesh. I almost couldn't look. My eyes had witnessed the most horrible sights a human's soul shouldn't see. As I tried to avoid making noise, the sounds from a giant open parlor grew louder. I flinched with the sound of each smack against skin. Honestly, I doubted that I had the heart to turn the corner. But I had a job I swore to do.

I leaned against the threshold of an ornately carved frame—my bloody palm print mashed into the design.

"Oh Lord give me strength to face this." My stomach tightened as the crack of a whip rent the air. I knew those poor girls were on the other side of the wall, but I was frozen with fear for the unknown. I'd already let one girl die tonight because I hesitated.

My Glock in hand, I wiped the sweat from my brow. The blood draining from the open wounds in my palms made holding the weapon difficult. One-step back, a giant gulp of air, and I pivoted to launch myself into the parlor. My eyes were keen and scanned the entire room within one second. I was tensed and ready to shoot anyone who harmed another—especially Saul Dugas.

The man in the middle of the parlor was tied with ropes and rags. Covered in blood, a towel shoved in his mouth muffled his screams.

His face was mangled but I saw the wide-open eyes begging me to save him. He writhed like an inchworm on the marble floor. His dick, hacked off, lay in a pool of blood and feces.

My mind immobilized my body while it processed the startling sight. I lifted my weapon from its ready gun position and the three senoritas stopped striking him. We were all stunned. It was dead silent—except for the man's muffled screams and scuffing on the ground.

Honestly, I wasn't sure what to do. The women's bruised bodies, in tattered blood and semen soaked dresses had inhumanity in their empty black eyes.

"*Policia?*" Her eyes locked onto the barrel of my duty weapon, and she dropped the rusty machete covered in blood.

"*Señor* Dugas?" I nodded toward the dickless maggot. My intestines wrestled over disgust and delight.

"*Si.*" All three nodded in confession.

"*Yo no Policia,*" I said and walked out.

Chapter 12

— Sheriff James Walker —

WISH I COULD'VE SAID THERE were menacing morning clouds under which we laid Jackson Andrews to rest, but Mother Nature had another plan in mind. I saluted my deputies as they balanced their slow-rolling iron hogs past the metal gates. Another funeral escort well done, and a showing of proper respect to the dearly departed.

"Buck, the family asked me to thank you for helping with the funeral procession, but they'd rather not see you at the church reception." My cousin Jennifer Adams' watering eyes were glued to the perfectly manicured lawn at Memorial Estates Cemetery. Without waiting for a reply, she withdrew from my touch. I didn't ask why and in the quiet, she repeatedly crossed and uncrossed her slender arms.

It stung, but I understood.

I ran the calendar through my mind. When was the funeral for Homeland Security Special Agent Howard Jones? He deserved what happened to him, but it was his crooked dealings that got Jackson murdered. Pretending to honor him as a fallen law enforcement officer will be the worst thing I've had to do.

Jenny spun away without making eye contact. I disappeared between the white washed mausoleums and turned my face to the sun. The grass crunched under my boots. It was just before noon, and the South's summer was in full swing. The endless rows of above-ground gravesites and family mausoleums created an orchestrated maze. I soon found myself uncertain of which plot to avoid.

Nipping the tip of my nose to swish mosquitoes sent a shockwave through my skull. The bone-crushing blow from the back of Rougarou's head only four nights ago had provided an alibi for visiting with Doc Lambert. She'd also been kind enough to not ask questions about that or my sliced open right palm.

My personal pain gave way to the sound of someone else's tormented weeping. Instinctively, I ducked down a row to my left looking to make sure they were safe. I know it's a graveyard and people come to cry, but this wailing was hauntingly familiar. I jogged, looking through the breaks in eternal cement housings. I still wasn't sure where or why I was now running to the sound of grief.

Another piercing shrill like nails down my back – I spun right. The forward momentum in my arms caused them to flail out to the sides while both knees twisted into the spongy turf.

She was hunched into a fetal bead so I didn't immediately recognize her. Time had passed without friendship or reconciliation. Spasms twisted my head to side-to-side and I crumpled with the sense of dread. Then I dropped, clutching my stomach. I vomited off to the side and drew my bandaged hand to wipe the residue.

It was my only son's tombstone. He would've been thirteen today.

"I'm sorry," and patted his mother across her shoulders.

— Deputy Chief Genevieve St. Pierre —

I'VE DEALT WITH BIG WIGS and political hotshots for years. I love when the big boys come a-calling and expect the lil' ol' deputy to pant over their presence. Well, the state police commander is a damn fine looking man, but his arrival this afternoon was unexpected. While I appreciated their advanced security team scoping the area in preparation for the governor's visit this evening, Sheriff Walker was dealing with the grief of the Andrews boy's funeral and his son's birthday. I wouldn't be surprised if Buck didn't show up at all tonight.

Punching the electronic keypad, I entered the Detectives Bureau. It was quiet—each investigator was tucked away in their cubicle. Except for the music coming from the back corner.

"Detective Stone, get your feet off the desk." His shiny dress loafers hit the floor's tile before my next words formed. "Sorry mam." Pausing to allow the nervousness to set upon him, goofing off wasn't going help him succeed as a rookie detective.

"Now prove you deserved the transfer into Detectives, and find Sheriff Walker." I liked jerking his chain – there were probably ten or fifteen better candidates, but Walker said he saw something in the boy.

While he skittered off, I turned to the Chief's assistant. "Miss Martha, would you mind calling Sheriff Walker to make sure he's okay?"

"Is there something wrong, Genevieve? Deputy Chief, I mean." Her kind, easy ways were calming in the adrenaline junkie environment, but we needed to light a fire for finding Walker.

Approaching the coffee pot, I saw eyes darting between each other and me. Four deputies halted their conversation. It was obvious from their worried expressions that I was the topic of discussion.

"If you're waiting to get into the toilet, then okay. Otherwise the citizens of this parish don't pay you to stand around gossiping." They scattered like piss hitting concrete.

"Why's she being such a bitch?" I heard Deputy Jacque Hebert's snide gripe, so I leaned against the corner to eavesdrop.

"Heard she's mad cuz Walker's gonna be officially appointed Interim Sheriff. As if."

After twenty-five years and five different bosses, you'd think I'd know the value of a level head. Hearing Deputy Debi Benoit run the screws through me was disappointing. And a female at that. Trembling with adrenaline, I pushed off the painted cinder block wall. I tried to exhale that calming breath crap, but it didn't work. Instead, straightening my uniform shirt before confronting these two know-nothings gave me a second to cool off.

"But you know, she's one of the best cops we got. I'd hate to see her stuck in the politics. I'd rather see her working with the real cops." The shift in my day went full circle – Debi Benoit had just redeemed herself.

"Smart kid" I whispered.

"You talking about me?" Detective Stone asked at my back, scaring the shit out of me.

"Watch where you're going, Todd."

He blinked at the tone in my voice. "Found Sheriff Walker. Behind the tank battery off Highway 307. Empty whiskey bottles." Stone's look teetered between empathy and disgust.

"Todd, don't judge so quick. He saw something special in you despite the obvious. Don't you know what today is?" Buck's business wasn't anyone else's, but before Buck lost the confidence of a potential protégé, the kid needed to understand.

— Deputy Jacque Hebert —

I AIN'T NEVER SEEN NO shit like this. I just had to call the Chief of Police—it's in his city after all. Besides, ain't nobody seen the Sheriff all day.

"Hey old boy, what ya doing?" The Chief was gonna get a kick outta this crap.

"What, Jacque? I'm getting ready for the governor's visit this evening."

Poor guy was my bud and all, but ain't no way he's gonna get appointed temporary Sheriff. Walker got that shit all locked tight. Too bad though.

"Come on over to the Geaux Roar Truck Stop. You never seen shit like dis. I guarantee."

I hung up on him as Stone came storming my way like he was better than me now that he wore a suit.

"What's up Hebert, what we got?" Young punk had this smug look like I was supposed to kiss his ass or something.

"Not sure, Todd. I called the Chief to see how to handle it."

"You called Deputy Chief St. Pierre?"

"No, Chief of Police Roberts." I wasn't about to call that bitch St. Pierre. She's too worried about being in charge.

"Your funeral, Jacque. Where's the crime scene?"

"The cage is around the other side." He could go, but I was waiting for Tom Roberts to take charge. Maybe solving something like this could get him elected Sheriff, and me a job in Detectives.

Chapter 13

— Detective Todd Stone —

THE RING-A-DINGING OF SLOT MACHINES paying out customers in quarters filled the building. The aisles were jammed with elderly people staring blankly into the screens of brightly lit, fluorescent, one-arm bandits. A rare triple seven on the wheel prompted an adjustment to one old man's portable oxygen tank's breathing hose. Purposefully windowless, the time vacuum concealed that the morning had slipped past high noon.

Hurrying through the vapor of musty cigarette smoke and collected ash, I felt a constant vibration shaking through my feet and hips. An army of eighteen-wheelers rumbled at attention in the massive cement parking lot. Stepping outside, the steam wafted from the blacktop mixed with diesel and humidity as the truck driver's cab windows glossed over with air-conditioned comfort.

Moving to the tiger's cage, I was amazed by the lush garden of plants and flowers that spotted the animal's living quarters. Iridescent lighting and simulated jungle noises bathed the massive cat. He purred, standing over a blood-soaked mound. A tattered flannel shirtsleeve and scraps of denim were strewn across the floor.

How would someone have gotten inside the cage? Or for that matter, why? More importantly, why would someone keep a full-grown tiger as a truck stop casino mascot?

Collecting my thoughts before making notification to Sergeant Brooks, I watched the gathering crowd. Most only peeked through finger slits while gasping in horror, while others vicariously enjoyed the feast and snapped pictures.

The manager Linda was easy to spot – late fifties, overweight with soft fat from fast food and casino buffets, chain-smoker, and a seventy-two ounce soda in her trembling hands. I wanted the owner, the jerk responsible for trapping this tiger in a truck stop.

Boys from the state police gaming division were just arriving. Those dapper Dans were harassing the manager over permits and gaming documentation. Couldn't imagine them getting down and dirty with a homicide investigation. Sure wish Sheriff Walker were here, it was going to be one hell of a jurisdictional battle royale.

"SO-212 to SO-147." If Hebert didn't answer his radio and get his butt over here to start taping off the crime scene, I was going to bust it.

"SO-147 to Todd—I'm busy briefing the Chief." I hated to be a rat, but my next call was to Deputy Chief St. Pierre. Hebert was up to something, and it had nothing to do with solving this crime.

The two men rounded the corner a few moments later. Trouble. Hebert was a second career deputy who thought he'd grace the Sheriff's Office after retiring from a chemical plant along the Mississippi River. Two years on the job and he'd only grown increasingly bitter. A know-it-all who pushed everyone around, he'd do better to push himself in the gym. At least it would keep his navel from hanging over the duty rig.

His escort, Police Chief Tom Roberts was a different story. He was a lifetime lawman. Had the resume of a presidential candidate, but something didn't stick. He gave me the willies—just a little too polished past sincerity. I respected but avoided him.

A thunderous roar ripped the silence and everyone jumped except me—I nearly crapped my pants. In grand appearance, the casino's owner arrived and entered a section inside the giant brick and titanium cage, cracking a whip. The tiger responded like... Well, like a tiger.

The beautiful beast looked to be over ten feet long and at least five hundred pounds. Well cared for and fed, it swatted at the whip that was more for show. Johnny Jones wasn't going to harm a hair on his prized possession. He hadn't felt the same way about his last few wives though.

In the open parking lot between the gas pumps and casino entrance, the crime scene had become a circus and I was responsible for securing the three-rings.

"Jones. I need you to get out of there right now."

His look of contempt told me that he knew exactly who I was. He hid a sinister grin with a ringed hand that smoothed over his dyed black hair. Elvis crossed with Satan.

"If you make me come in there and get you, I'll shoot that animal first." Under my breath, but purposefully aloud, "and you next."

"Detective Stone, a moment please?"

I'd heard that voice on television and radio, but never up close. A wicked chill ripped up my spine.

I spun toward the sun to face the two other men. "Yes, Chief Roberts, how may I help you?"

Hebert basked in the police chief's shadow, licking his fat chops. This felt like a planned tactic. I kicked at loose debris along and studied the scuffed soles of my shoes while I scraped gum off a parking bump. I really wanted to avoid a confrontation.

Roberts swung between the tiger and me, and presented the greater threat.

"Yes, sir?" Suddenly feeling tired, I straightened my necktie.

"Stone, I need you to stand down until my detectives arrive. They'll handle this matter appropriately. I understand you've never actually investigated a death, so we don't need you interfering in this one now that the media is all over the place." I fought to keep him from seeing my concern, as I looked up into his face.

Hebert smirked and bobbed his shovelhead. He'd clearly run his mouth to the Chief. Now, I really wished Sheriff Walker would get here.

— Sheriff James Walker —

SLUMPING AGAINST THE RUSTED TANK battery, my eyes were cast across sprouting sugar cane fields. The thick green stalks were a peaceful contrast to the night my son was murdered. I always sit in the exact spot his body was discovered. For the last five years, I try to imagine what he went through. For the last five years, I've tortured myself for failing to protect him.

I saw Genevieve St. Pierre's cruiser dragging a dust trail long before she skidded to a halt. I tried throwing the glass bottle into the wetlands but it caught the lip of a tank and rained down shards.

"I forgot his birthday. I've so much shit going on that I forgot. Genevieve, what kind of dad am I?" I stuttered in uneven breaths. My attention blurred while starring at his little league-playing card while she patiently waited.

"Buck, we go back a long way, but I don't feel like I know you that well. I do, however, know what you're going through. When Tommy died in that crash years ago I surrendered the dream. No kids. No husband. I buried myself in this job. Let me tell you, Sheriff, it's no way to live your life. It smothers your soul." Her jaw clenching, the emotion was still raw and just under the surface.

"I'm so sorry, Genevieve. I know you suffered..."

"Suffer Buck, I still suffer." Fists beat hot air until she pressed a finger into the corner of her tearing eyes.

Cop life's a bitch – here we sit in the middle of nowhere, both shredded apart on the inside and neither can show weakness or support. So much for the thin blue line.

"I need closure. The motherf'er who killed my son is still loose. How many more families is this bastard going to destroy before he's caught?" No need to palm press my eyes. Screw it. I'm pissed and it hurts. I'd never tell her that each day begins with searching for reasons not to end it all. Revenge now fuels the life that love once fed.

"I can only sympathize with you. I've no idea the pain of losing a child. I swear to you that I'll do anything, and I mean anything, Buck, to help catch this guy." Wrangling the duty rig up on her hips, her shoulders pushed back and she held out her hand. "But we gotta go. Now."

"I really don't give a shit about the governor or her appointment." Dizziness swept through my already battered skull as I lurched to my feet. I tried brushing the grass stains off and straightening my clothes. Dark spots from wiped tears dotted my shirtsleeves.

"Buck, we need you. This parish can't afford a prick like Chief Tom Roberts to get this job."

"Think he's any worse than Gill Gaudet, or Benji Martin?" I dragged my bandaged knuckles across dried lips and thought about the long list of horrible Sheriffs this parish had survived.

She punched me lightly in the shoulder. "Hey, at least Martin didn't try killing you."

That was possibly the first time we'd actually joked with each other. Genevieve was all right.

Chapter 14

— *Coroner Susan Lambert* —

I WASN'T GETTING INTO THE middle of this three-ring circus. My blood boiled watching that giant cat prance over his prey, devouring crucial evidence. Between the pampered state boys bartering for documents, the rookie Sheriff's detective fighting for respect, and the overbearing Chief of Police clamoring for media attention, I didn't really have any other options. I only wanted that cat sedated.

No one even noticed that I'd walked across the parking lot with a tranquilizer rifle. A single 20-centimeter dart was serum loaded. I stood at the observer's barrier, called out "Hey cat," and then pumped him full of Ketamine. Beast barely flinched when it hit above the shoulder so I began to load another dart.

Screaming civilians hit the floor or hid behind cement planters while cops ran toward me. Except for the troopers, the other cops knew me.

"Drop the weapon, lady." A trooper who looked like he was holding his weapon for the first time outside the shooting range trained his weapon at my head. His hands shook like his voice.

"Please settle down. I'm the Coroner. How about you place that pistol back in your pocket before you hurt someone."

He looked to his partner, whose eyes were as wide as the tiger's eyes were getting droopy. With his partner's nod, he holstered it.

"Susan, what the hell are you doing?" The sheen from Chief Roberts' slick persona slimed everywhere and everyone he crossed. Of course, he asked with a smile for the media's sake.

"I'm doing what you failed to do. Securing the evidence." I snapped while my eye zeroed through the iron sights on the stumbling tiger.

The snarky look across Chief Roberts' face seemed out of place considering the situation. A flash shot across my peripheral vision and I screamed while tucking my head for the high-speed impact.

An exploding crash jammed against the reinforced metal cage. Violent bodies flailed. Realizing I escaped the impact, I peeked under my left arm to see Detective Stone on top of Johnny Jones. The older man writhed angrily in pain. Metal cuffs bit into his wrists once the detective snapped them tight.

"Detective, have you lost your mind? Do you know who that is?" Roberts's head swiveled toward the news cameras.

Chief Roberts looked like he'd seen a ghost, but instead what he saw was an honest officer doing the right thing. That idiot Jones tried to run right over me.

"Thank you, Detective Stone. Someone had to step up." I was most appreciative. The scene was chaotic and full of machismo, but I wasn't exiting the fray this time. I was a finger twitch away from launching the second tranquilizer dart into Chief Roberts, but I didn't think it would help matters.

"Chief Roberts, I'm going to respectfully ask that you take your hands off me. I'm making a lawful arrest. Please, either assist or stand by, but don't interfere." It looked like the police chief was trying to pull the detective off of Jones, instead of helping to arrest him.

Either heat or insanity had just forged this young officer into a man of steel. I tried biting the inside of my cheek to cover my laugh.

"You've just ruined your career. Detective Todd Stone, is it?" Chief Roberts had an anger in his face uncharacteristic of the façade he tried to portray in public.

"Yeah, dumb ass, you're screwed." The man who'd tried to body slam me looked around at the arresting officer with bloodshot eyes, somehow ignoring the fact that he was the one in cuffs.

"Tom, take your hands off my deputy or I'll arrest you. Hebert— you're fired." Buck Walker's deep voice discreetly cut through the sounds of the scuffle in front of me. The shadow cast by his six-foot-four inch frame was powerfully dramatic, and sent my heart into heavy thuds.

— Sheriff James Walker —

I ALLOWED JONES TO REMAIN on site, but in cuffs because he knew more about that tiger than anyone. Convincing the others to gather in a private room was a chore, but this scene had spiraled beyond the possibility of solving the mystery. I wasn't surprised that Chief Roberts elected to leave, but instead assign a rookie officer to take notes. His time in front of the cameras would serve no purpose in solving this case.

Meanwhile, my deputies were playing tug-of-war with a mostly sleepy Bengal tiger. Dragging over five hundred pounds of muscle, teeth, and fur into his night cage was no easy task.

Deputy Chief St. Pierre stood watch over the cage. Everyone from PETA to the governor's advanced protection team had arrived, including a parish veterinarian and a lady from Wal-Mart who'd offered giant tarps to cover the cage to give investigators privacy and offer dignity to the deceased.

I gotta admit, this was a first. It definitely helped take my mind off the last few months, but not my son's birthday.

Everyone seemed agreeable to the delegation of duties, mostly because that carcass wasn't going to smell any less rancid and Chief Roberts wasn't there. Detective Stone was the lead detective. Tackling Johnny Jones had earned him high marks in my book. The events of this investigation would test Stone's mettle.

"Deputy Chief St. Pierre, has Jacques Hebert left yet?" Too bad that snake hadn't been in the cage instead.

"Yes sir, I made sure Deputy Benoit drove him to the station. The Patrol sergeant will meet them to collect his equipment, vehicle, and commission. If he's behaves, I said it's okay to drive him home." St. Pierre is a square dealer and would make a good Sheriff.

She stepped closer and lowered her voice. "Buck, nothing leaves us I swear. Is there anything you need to tell me? You okay?" I appreciated her concern, but I'm not the guy who cries in his beer.

"Just make sure Stone gets the right resources to close this fiasco. Get the District Attorney up to speed and let Judge Boudreaux know we'll be needing warrants." The switch I'd flipped a few nights ago was proving hard to turn back. Since leaving Saul Dugas to get what he deserved, I'd had nothing but flashbacks and sleepless nights. This pile of meat needed to be identified and the case solved, but I didn't have the focus to supervise it.

"Will do, but you know everyone who thinks they're anyone will be at that reception? Including Chief Roberts."

I snorted despite the crushed bone in my nose. The Republican governor hates Tom. Not because Tom's a Democrat, but because he's a jackass.

"Genevieve, I'm going back to the station and then home to change. Please stick around to make sure Stone gets it right. Also, make Doc Lambert put that tranquilizer rifle away."

Chapter 15

— Detective Todd Stone —

"YOU HAVE THE RIGHT TO remain silent. Anything you say can and will be used against you in a court of law. You have the right to an attorney. If you cannot afford an attorney, one will be provided for you. Do you, Johnny Jones, understand the rights I read to you?"

"Boy, you are making a life-changing mistake." The black clad casino owner hissed.

I ignored his threat. "You are not under arrest. You are being questioned as to the events leading to the death of an unidentified person. Do you understand your rights?" I paced while he sat. Standing wasn't an option for him. His cuffed wrists were locked to a chain running between two eyebolts screwed into the table's top. He initially tugged on it before realizing he wasn't going anywhere.

I didn't have to keep him cuffed, since he wasn't under arrest. It just seemed like a good time to pinch him. In silence, we both examined the eggshell colored ten-by-ten dry walled room. It had the usual one-way mirror, a table, three chairs, and a smoke detector. No one ever guesses that the hidden camera is in the smoke detector.

"I bet you think it's your chance for payback. I want another deputy in here, and I'm calling the FBI about the way you slammed me into that wall." I pretended to ignore him.

I guess he was right about me wanting payback, but I'd taken an oath and would never abuse my position of authority. Regardless, he would sit there in shackles. "Are you willing to answer questions that may assist us in identifying the person and determine what events led up to the death?" I rubbed my forehead until it started to ache, and realized he'd gotten to me. After all. Maybe I did need to get Detective Graza in here. A change of pace with the old good cop/bad cop routine?

Johnny "JJ" Jones was fidgeting for a cigarette, so I made a mental note for later. He peered to the door as if planning an escape attempt. Using everything I learned about interview and interrogation, I slid a chair between him and the door. His eyes dropped and he became agitated, looking around the room again.

"JJ, you ready to talk?" His Adam's apple bobbed as strange noises emitted from his throat. "You thirsty?"

His eyes brightened at the offer. "Yeah, just a sip of water, please."

"You ready to talk?" It was just a matter of time until I discovered his triggers.

"Ok, but can I have something to drink please?" I'd let him perform before the reward. He launched into a charade of theories and conspiracies. Forty-five minutes had blown by. I needed a chance to think through the insanity of what he'd just said.

"Now can I have a cigarette?"

"I'll get you something to drink." He wagged his tongue like a puppy, but I made him wait a little longer. My cell had gone nuts with messages, so it was a good time for both of us to break. Difference was, I walked out of the interview room and met with Detective Graza.

"Thanks for the water, Jose. What we got so far?" Detective Jose Graza and I swore in with the Sheriff's Office on the same day. He came through the military, and was straight-up rules and regs. Nothing went undone when he was on the case.

"We yanked video surveillance from the lobby and the cage. Interviewed the night crew, some of the truck drivers staying in the barracks, and housekeeping." This dude was thorough and exactly who I needed helping with my first real case.

"That all?" I joked, trying to lighten the tension.

"No, we had to shovel what was left of that body into a bag for the Coroner. I'll never eat meatloaf again." Disgust glazed Graza's gaze.

"Body that bad, huh?" I winched at the image.

"Not really. I ordered the meatloaf before we left. It was horrible."

Deputy Chief St. Pierre curled her index finger, so we hurried into her office. The heavy wooden door eased shut.

"Good work so far. Catch me up to speed, will ya?" We both knew the drill. This case had to be closed today. Graza and I switched glances, avoiding direct eye contact with her.

"JJ's claiming innocence. Still sweating him though." I bumped Graza's knee to cue his turn to unload what he'd learned.

He glanced sideways at me, his expression telling me he was unimpressed with my opening contribution. "Video shows the victim is none other than Lonny Tucker. Get this—folks call him Lonny 'The Trucker Fucker' Tucker. The manager said they let him come into the trucker's lounge on occasion to sleep off a bender. Personally, I also think he's a lot lizard."

If my face looked anything like St. Pierre's, Graza had a lot of explaining to do.

"A prostitute." Graza chuckled.

"At least my heart isn't heavy over it anymore." St. Pierre broke the uneasy vibe in the small cluttered office. "Go on."

"Tucker stumbled in to the night desk. Surveillance behind the counter shows the clerk giving him a key. Next video picks up at side door. You see an arm pointing, and Tucker fumbling to open the side of the tiger's cage."

I had to get into the fray, and asked the first question that popped into my mind. "No hall cameras to ID the person pointing?"

"Yep, but it just so happened to be out of commish."

"Bullshit," St. Pierre murmured.

"We tried cleaning up the imaging and can tell it's a white guy, but that's it."

"Johnny Jones, maybe?"

"No, this dude looked like he'd be fat. Thick arm and potbelly poked out of doorway, but he knew to stay out of the camera." Graza was sharp, and I felt like the student instead of the lead detective.

"So now Tucker's in the cage. What happened? I saw earlier that there were sections to the whole enclosure. This cat can't just walk up to the side door, can he?" Her impatience obvious.

"There are four sections separated by locked doors," I jumped in, happy to have something to contribute. "The room accessing the side door has two of those locks before getting to the night cage. Someone must've left those two doors open on purpose."

"Good call, Stone. I have a blueprint layout of the cage from the Audubon Zoo. They arrived to take custody of the tiger. They're examining him with an x-ray and fecal monitor over the next seventy-two hours." Graza's attention to detail was on display.

"Fecal monitor?" I repeated, looking from one face to the other.

"Watching his shit. No telling what that tiger ate." St. Pierre didn't even try to cover up her laugh, before asking, "Was the cage key found?"

We both sucked wind on that one, and I shrugged. There was still a lot of work to be done.

Chapter 16

— *Sheriff James Walker* —

CHECKING MY CELL WOULDN'T MAKE it ring. I was getting bits of information, but I wanted that case closed so I could shove it in Chief Roberts' snarky face. The guy was just too cool, too wrapped tight. No need bothering myself over him.

I flipped on the small desk lamp in my bedroom and dug the tattered cardboard box out from beneath the antique dresser. It was only worn, never dusty. Hour and a half until the governor's reception was plenty of time. I spread the files over my comforter. The pictures were saved for my office. It was too painful to look at them at home.

Five years, and nothing new. Not a clue or a suspect, just more children. His last swim meet picture sat unframed on my nightstand. It had begun to curl but I didn't dare fix it. He put it there and his little prints last touched it.

I wasn't going to my grave without solving his murder. I still couldn't sit alone for long looking through these reports. My heart went cold, black and it seeped into my conscious once again. Just in case, I dropped the snub nose to the nightstand drawer. I hated watching TV, but I needed noise.

I kicked off my boots and rested on the mattress for a bit. It felt odd but nice sitting at home under the twirl of a ceiling fan during the workday. Sheriff Tyler Robinson graced every news channel I flipped through. Seems he'd detained three Hispanic women for the murder of four men just outside of White Castle at the Belle Cove Plantation home.

The media applauded him for releasing them after he rescued fifteen other human trafficking survivors held as sex slaves by the four men. I eased further back against the pile of pillows and listened to the uneven beating of the fan blades against the air conditioning vent's breeze.

I must've dozed off. My cell was ringing and I pounded my temples forcing the nightmare from my skull. All that did was cause me to shrink in the pain screaming through my stitched palm and aching head. It was taking longer for my body to recoup. I had no expectation of my soul getting there though. It was broken.

I bounced, well rolled, off the side of the bed. There were twenty-five minutes left until the seven o'clock event. I threw the nicest jacket I had over my shirt, but hesitated before stuffing my back-up revolver in the rear of my pants. Ballistics would match the holes I left in fatso.

How could I've been so careless? My revolver. I was in a zone that night and trying to beat the sunrise. I had time to think while I sprinted the mile back to my truck. I'm better than that. Maybe my age was making me fuzzy after all.

I removed the revolver and locked it in a concealed cabinet.

The drive to the Acadian Cultural Complex took only about fifteen minutes. I usually liked to have a few of my staff accompany me to events. Someone inevitably tries to occupy my time, so they get passed along to solve their problems on my behalf.

"Oh shit." Shoved my size 13 boot through the floorboard, and the full-sized pick-up truck skidded to a sliding halt. "Now I know I'm losing my mind. I forgot the gig pole at Belle Cove. That damn thing has my prints and DNA all over it."

No way would I call Sheriff Robinson. He'd never trust me again and if he got within a thousand miles of that thing it could ruin his career. I'd head back to the plantation as soon as this farce ended. Probably best that I'm going alone.

— *Detective Todd Stone* —

I HAD UNCUFFED THE JERK after the first few hours. Rambling makes for no good confession. He lay back in the scarcely padded metal chair and used the insides of his hands to brush his hair down. The way his forefinger and thumb split under his nose to trail down each side of his mustache curled my gut.

There's a flow to the interrogation process, a give and take. I'd noticed his personality patterns early on. The markers that give away thoughts, feelings, and unintended responses are an investigators advantage. How a person says it is as important as what it is they say. Sheriff Walker taught me that lips lie, the involuntary body doesn't. I knew this flow had run flat. Either Jones was innocent or I wasn't experienced enough to crack him. I wasn't giving up. He was going to snap. Time for Graza.

The door slammed behind us this time. The air turned thick and hot in that ten-by-ten. The handcuffed man straightened his rail-thin frame and uncrossed his legs. He snapped to an uneasy attention in the chair. His face turned grey, looking much older than when he arrived. His eyes never left Detective Graza, but sunk low the way dogs concede to the alpha by shunning direct glances.

Jones' withdrew his gaze and seemed to suppress a panic attack. Graza remained silent. He stalked the limited open spaces as I imagined the tiger would. Except JJ had no performer's whip. He bounced his right knee and his frail hand took an unsteady ride upon it. He began to gnaw on the yellowed cigarette tar colored fingernails of his other heavily-ringed hand.

Graza lurched into the open chair. Jones nearly toppled backwards out of his. My body was sweating, and covered with goose bumps watching this brilliant display. Heck, I wanted to confess.

"Who led Tucker into the tiger's cage?" Graza swooped his hand above his head and demanded an answer. Jones cowered by burying his paper-thin jaw into a pointed shoulder. Overwhelmed by the rush of adrenaline, I slid in front of the door to block anyone from disrupting Graza's momentum. Jones' eyes darted to survey my actions. His pale cheeks rapidly puffed air as his hand white-knuckled the silk shirt over his chest.

Graza spun a quick peek back to me. I could only roll my shoulders toward my ears. I wasn't a medic. Graza slapped the narrow table with a hand thickened from a life of hard labor. Jones babbled with pleadings to spare him.

"Before you leave this stinking earth come clean, JJ. What did you do?"

"Help. I need a doctor." He groveled.

"Tell me what you did." Graza stared a dying man in the face. His nose, mere inches from the last breathe expelled by this devil, he never flinched. "Tell me."

— Sheriff James Walker —

A RECEPTION LINE? SERIOUSLY, THIS is the parish civic center—not a presidential ball.

"Hello, Governor Jewel. It's great to see you again."

"James, what in the dickens happened to your face?" Soft people are easily appalled at injuries. Cops rarely notice. It's a badge of honor. Politicians are not honorable.

"Ma'am, I ran into chicken wire." She smiled with slight relief that I lied to spare her from having to care.

"Put something on it son. Now where is your lovely wife? Don't you have a boy too? Sheriff Walker, where's the family to celebrate this moment with you?" Thank goodness my throat clamped around its spine, otherwise the lump of bile would've ruined her pantsuit and pearls.

"My son is...." I wouldn't dishonor his memory through insulting her. It was only a question after all. "Ma'am, it's good to see you again."

I joined Deputy Chief St. Pierre along a rickety buffet table. Pans of food and such were set on park benches covered by bed sheets. Looked damn edible.

"I'm glad you're here but what's the latest on the mysterious feast?" She knew how to buffer the politicians and assholes from bugging me. I was glad she was here. Knowing how badly she wanted to become a Sheriff, I admired her dignity by supporting me.

"Doc Lambert got the carcass and Audubon Zoo got the cat. The boys are sweating JJ something fierce. Stone texted not long ago asking what's the worst case scenario if Jones died of a heart attack." I finally laughed, and then the wool blanket of worry over the snub nose revolver quickly covered me.

"Damn James, ya'll still terrorizing Johnny Jones?" The slickster had slid in behind our conversation. There goes my chance to smear an arrest in his pie hole.

"Chief Roberts, it's a pleasure to see you sir. Thank you for the high-level assistance your agency provided at the crime scene today." I had to either mock him or knock his greased comb-over out—the jerk deserved it.

"Sheriff did you say there was a crime today? Anything serious?" The parish councilman was genuinely concerned, though I was growing weary of the eavesdropping.

"Yes sir, and Chief Roberts was kind enough to leave my rookie detective on scene by himself. Of course the Chief threw a tantrum over not being in charge. That's real teamwork – right Tommy?"

The paste cracked on his polished smile. Vibrating muscles through his neck and jaw tensed as he struggled to control a seething inferno for responding in kind. He drew slow, measured breaths and pried his razor thin lips apart over chalky clinched teeth.

"Fuck off Walker."

Chapter 17

— *Coroner Susan Lambert* —

"MIND IF I JOIN YA'LL?" There was no way I'd miss this event.

"Hi, Susan. Didn't think you'd make it. Isn't someone waiting for you back on a metal slab?" I knew Genevieve wasn't interested in Buck, but for the life of me I couldn't figure out why she was being such a bitch.

Buck came to my rescue. "I'm sure you've already pieced him back together. Come, join us."

Genevieve nibbled on her bottom lip as her look trailed off, then went up and down at my outfit. I leaned over my right shoulder to gaze down and back up her length. "Nice uniform."

Governor Jewel was kind, but got elected for her connections not her competence. I hated to bash another female, especially a successful one like Eleanor, but she'd done nothing to move this state forward. The old south had served her family well and she saw no reason to upset that crawfish pot. Although biased, I'd agree that tonight's decision was her best one yet.

"Buck, Detective Stone just sent a message that a trucker at the Geaux Roar Truck Stop remembered seeing someone hanging around the night clerk's desk. A heavy set white male, though he wasn't an employee." Genevieve's hand cupped against her lips and Buck's ear to shield her conversation, but was said loud enough to signal the case was moving along.

"Has Detective Brooks confirmed anything else on his canvass?"

Buck sat back to allow me into the investigative loop.

I leaned across his right shoulder, eyes cresting my eyeglass frame. Chief Roberts, just across the table had craned his ear our way. Bumping my left ear onto Buck's chest not only quieted Genevieve, but also alerted them that Roberts was present.

"Well, Brooks did confirm that Tucker was a trucker fucker."

What the hell did she say? I recoiled and nearly grazed Buck's chin with the back of my head. He nervously chortled as he rapped the table with his knuckles. I saw the faint sheen of moisture breach his forehead and upper lip.

"Deputy Chief St. Pierre, please." He looked unhappy with St. Pierre's comment.

Her shoulders slumped. "We're all tense Genevieve– forgive me." Buck said.

I shuffled in my chair for comfort. I'd heard the mayor ramble on before and I was confident this would be no different. My shoulder tingled at Buck's touch. When I smiled to meet his eyes, he pointed out that the cell inside my purse was buzzing like mad.

[call Audubon zoo vet asap] the text message read.

Hopefully it was good news, but it was show time and the reason I was here, to support this fine man in his official appointment as interim Sheriff. I squeezed his arm in excitement as Governor Jewel graced the lectern. The high school's seal still hung from it following the graduation ceremony in the spacious hall. No one else seemed to notice. The thirty or so parishioners gave a good attempt at applause, but patience was wearing thin.

Governor Jewel glanced our way and smiled at Buck. Grabbing his arm, I sensed his nervousness. I was so happy for him. Jewel's eyes seemed to light up as I hugged him.

"I see that Sheriff Walker's lovely wife has joined him. I'd like to wish them the best in supporting our newly appointed Sheriff, James Walker."

Silence.

Awful, dead silence.

Buck's body collapsed within my grip. There was no place to hide for either of us.

"Buck, she didn't know." Genevieve wrapped her arm around the back of his shoulders. "Your boy would be proud," she whispered.

A dense quiet filled the room but for a slight snort like a bull from Chief Roberts.

Buck inhaled and sat back upright. Genevieve and I leaned back, watching carefully, as he twisted around to lock eyes on a smirking Roberts. Buck silently mouthed, "You're next."

The coldest, dead chill surrounded my spirit because I knew he meant it and could darn well do it.

— Sheriff James Walker —

IT FELT LIKE WALKING THROUGH a wall of sand—boots nailed to the floor with every lift and thump of each leg. The thirty-yard plow to the governor's lectern was slightly less soul-searing than trudging through the church for my son's wake.

My hearing waffled and dizziness pushed me off-balance. The thin scrapping of my boot soles pounded the waxed floor to echo in my skull. The chipped wooden high-school seal hanging off the podium looked like a tunnel with streaking flashes of confusing lights.

Governor Jewel's bewilderment by the dead quiet showed her honest error, but Roberts' actions only served to flip my switch against him. The walk was taking longer than I anticipated and the closer I got to accepting her outstretched hand, the farther away she seemed.

"Congratulations, Sheriff Walker, and best of success serving this parish." The fancy certificate embossed in gold foil and blue ribbons made it clear that this was only an interim position. No need to be too excited.

"Thank you, Governor." It was official, at least until the parish council decided whether to hold a special election or allow me to serve out the rest of what would've been Gill Gaudet's three and a half year term.

Jewel patted me on the back as I turned to walk away. I expected her to follow the half-hug with an apology, though nothing should surprise me.

"James, you go easy on old JJ now. You hear me?" Not sure if she felt the stiffening of my spine or the quivering heat of rage, but her hand sprung off of me like bread popping up in the toaster.

I nodded to Genevieve and Susan as I made the arc around the bleachers toward the exit. My switch was about halfway flipped and between Chief Tom Robert and Governor Eleanor Jewel, I'd had enough of politics and playing nice.

— Deputy Chief Genevieve St. Pierre —

TUGGING DOCTOR LAMBERT'S SILK SLEEVE left a slight residue of mac and cheese, but she got the point. It was time to jet out of this reception. We had work to do and a case to solve.

"I got a call from Audubon Zoo. I'll meet you in the parking lot." She snapped the cell to her ear and began speaking in hushed tones on her way out of the double wooden doors.

I'd been reading a novel's worth of messages one text at a time from Detective Stone. This younger generation of cops smashes out messages faster than we ever could. Although I was pretty fast on the electric typewriters when I started.

Buck had tossed the framed document onto his front seat and looked agitated trying to call someone.

"If that damn Stone doesn't answer his cell, I'm taking it away from him. That's why this department pays for it—to answer when I need him." For once I felt uneasy approaching Buck. I wasn't afraid of him hurting me, but I'd not seen the emptiness in his eyes—ever.

"Sheriff, he's probably still in the cube. You know how intense interrogations are. He's doing his best to break this case, and it's important for him to please you." A little soothing psychology sometimes helped defuse situations. I knew that whatever had broken this man ran much deeper than kind words and reassurances.

"I want to know exactly where we are on this case. Someone's ass is going to pay for this. I don't give a damn if it was only Lonny Tucker. He deserves our best." With that realization, I stopped while shame washed over for the earlier comment. Tucker did deserve our best effort, not my childish name-calling.

"Zoo vet said the tiger finally crapped. The tranquilizer slowed his intestines down along with everything else. Sedation had worn off, and he said that big cat looks like he had a massive meat hangover." Susan actually seemed to crack a joke with that announcement, much less formal than I'd known her to be.

"Good news I guess. Did he shit a confession?" Even Buck lightened up. Obviously there was something brewing between these two. Maybe neither was aware.

"Found a metal LSU keychain. Passed right through."

"Not sideways I hope." I just had to throw that in there. The mood lighten up.

The buzzing cell distracted him. His pinched lips and skin drawn tight around his rockish jaw signaled something was going down.

"Buck, you okay?" Although I'd not briefed him on Detective Stone's latest, the intensity had just ratcheted back up.

"That jackass Jacque Hebert is back at HQ to turn in his equipment and uniforms. Dispatcher says he stirring up all kinda hell about Johnny Jones still being interrogated and won't leave the building." Buck had that focused edge. Tonight wasn't going to be a good night for former deputy Hebert.

"I guess we'll all meet at HQ then. Buck, I'll check in on the interview while you'll want to escort Mr. Hebert somewhere."

Susan looked a little lost but not intimidated, "I'll meet y'all there."

"Helped that guy get hired as a favor for a friend. This is what I get." Disappointment colored his scowl, probably from the letdown that not everyone who asks to do this job has the heart to do it right.

"I'll take my car and meet y'all, if it's okay. The Vet said one of your deputies, Debi Benoit has already been into the city to pick up the key chain." The excitement in Susan's information was encouraging, but it would take more than that to break this case.

"Genevieve, make sure to have Detective Sergeant Brooks run the key chain for prints under live scan. Maybe that cat passed it so quickly, prints survived. Unlike Tucker the Fucker that is." Nudging, his sly smile was his apology and without words, I fully accepted it.

Chapter 18
— *Sheriff James Walker* —

THE DRIVE TO HQ WAS short, but even shorter as I was blowing past cars on the highway. Jacque Hebert had the nerve to disrespect my office—my house—that I sacrificed thirty years serving. That pompous asshole was going to regret ever wearing my badge.

I answered the cell on the first ring. "This is Walker, what ya got?"

"This is Todd Stone, sir. Jones is still refusing to talk but he hasn't asked for a lawyer, or died from a heart attack. He did piss his pants when Graza whispered in his ear. Said he was suing us."

"Let him get in line behind the other idiots."

"Detective Brooks got a partial on the guy who pointed Tucker into the tiger's cage. The witness was already in his rig moving cross-country, so communications have been between cell phone and CB radio. Said he'd pick him out in a line up. Thought Tucker was security, but figured he was trying to pick up on the desk clerk the way he was hawking her."

"Know who she is?"

"Once Detective Brooks finishes printing the keychain, he's heading back to the truck stop. Of course the owner's being an a-hole and won't tell us."

Hanging up that call I realized how much Stone still had to learn. The night clerk should've been a crucial and first witness to identify. Thinking back, I guess the whole agency hadn't had much in the way of leadership or training to make them better. Sheriffs Benji Martin and Gill Gaudet, no way would I follow in their footsteps.

Security lights bounced a soft glow around the parking lot. Piloting into my parking space, I sat in my truck and let the engine quietly idle. My mind began to drift as I gazed through the office blinds that I kept open all the time. Running my fingers around the corners of the cherry wood certificate frame, it began to overwhelm me. I've seen and done plenty in these last thirty years. I've bitched about bosses, criminals and co-workers—some of whom were one and the same. I'd lost my only boy, and then his mother.

While I was always highly focused, at times I'd lost sight of who I wanted to be. Scars graced me inside and out to prove I'm a survivor. No, not a survivor—a warrior. I'm the shepherd in this parish and the flock looks to me for protection. This wasn't me being self-righteous. I swore to an oath over and above every personal desire I ever had. It was time to rid my house of someone who blemished that same oath.

Maybe it was best that Stone caught me in the squad room. My march into the lobby to intercept Hebert was beginning to make General Sherman's look like a picnic hike.

"Sheriff, good news. We grabbed a print from the LSU keychain. Both partials but got a front and back hit. Probably thumb and forefinger is what Graza thinks."

"Live scan hit?" This would be too damn good to see. Talk about getting revenge. Busting the killer by the key he gave to the victim that ultimately was passed through the tiger who ate him.

"Waiting on it, sir. Should be any minute." I bridled my enthusiasm because we still needed a positive identification from that cross-country trucker.

"Brooks is also getting the identity of the fat guy and the night clerk." Stone was in a zone.

"Good job, Todd. Don't let up on Jones till he confesses."

Now to take the trash out.

I heard Hebert's loud mouth before I shoved open the metal door separating us from the rest of society. I knew the lobby was under video surveillance, so I kept it low key.

Hebert didn't have such qualms. "You chicken shit mutha-fuka. Ain't got the balls to tell me I'm fired. Gotta send a skirt to do your dirty work."

Stay calm. Be cool.

"Mr. Hebert, I'm going to ask you to leave this building now." I looked behind me at the people waiting in the lobby. Most were dirt bags like him, but a few of the homeless actually looked like they needed our help. Empty, expressionless eyes darted back and forth, bouncing off me and landing on each other.

"I gotta turn in my shit? Here it is, bitch."

The uniform shirts and trousers didn't soften the blow from his leather duty rig and radio that caught my chin and swollen nose. It all fell to the ground with a muffled thud, except for a shirt that hooked on my collar brass. I dropped it on the pile at my feet.

"Thank you Hebert. You may go now."

Curling my toes kept me from launching myself through his face. Deep breathing. Flexing my fingers open. I felt unable to control that switch from flipping.

You know what? Screw the lawsuit. I arched my spine while the loud mouth kept taunting me. He never noticed me slide my right foot back so I could use balance and force to knock him out.

Canting my shoulders slowly, I knew the radio dispatchers in the office behind me were watching. I looked out through the exit doors behind Hebert and there she was, Doctor Lambert, shaking her head and begging me with her eyes.

— *Deputy Chief Genevieve St. Pierre* —

DOMINO EFFECT. I COULDN'T BELIEVE how quickly everything tied together. Stone had done a great job relying on the more experienced detectives. That's what a good criminal investigations division does—

work together.

I knew Buck was either kicking Hebert's ass, or his own for not kicking Hebert's ass earlier. He was about to get the good news and the bad news. Detective Brooks had learned that the regular desk clerk was given last night off. A temporary worker, Donna Hebert, had filled in. So many of them in the parish, it didn't ring a bell, but the LiveScan came back with a positive confirmation on the LSU keychain prints.

Driver's license database made the match. Buck was gonna love that.

Stubborn ass Johnny Jones hadn't stroked out yet. Buck was gonna hate that.

Truck driver finally e-mailed back on a photo-line up, and he picked the guy. Buck was gonna be shocked at that.

Now to find Buck and lay it all out before any arrests were made or media called. Dispatchers monitored the building's surveillance systems and always knew where everyone was.

"Hi ladies. Know where Sheriff Walker is?"

Crowned with high-definition headphones, one of the dispatchers pointed her finger up for me to wait and to hush. The other dispatcher pointed to monitor number eight. There he was.

"Thanks."

"Deputy Chief St. Pierre." I caught the doorframe and looked back in.

"Sergeant Hottie with the state police called to advise that the governor's motorcade was leaving the civic center." She grinned at the mention of the handsome motorcycle officer who liked to visit during night shifts. "Said Chief Tom Roberts would be leading the procession and wants us to stop all traffic through town."

"Uhhh, no." Seriously? We had more important things to do.

Rushing around the corner toward the lobby, I fell face first. No time to worry about the excruciating pain running through my ankle.

By the time I made it to the pile of uniforms and police gear in the lobby, Buck was gone.

One old woman pointed toward the double glass doors. Buck gestured angrily on the other side.

When I saw he was arguing with Hebert, I launched myself at the heavy doors. "Buck, wait. Stop him!"

Buck spun around at the sound of his name.

Already forty yards ahead of Buck, Hebert took off, barreling out into the employee parking lot. I tried running, but my slip outside the radio room left me hobbling.

"Buck, don't let Hebert get away."

Chapter 19

— *Sheriff James Walker* —

UNDERSTANDING WHAT ST. PIERRE WAS yelling through the lobby doors, I regretted not dropping Hebert on his ass inside. He heard her too and took off into an awkward sprint. Albeit, a slow one.

Breaths snapped uneven as my body's sudden bolt left me feeling stiff. I was gaining ground on him though.

"Stop, you're under arrest." I commanded.

"Fuck you, James Walker. Roberts is right – you ain't worth a shit." Hebert called out in more of a desperate plea than a statement.

"I said stop! You're under arrest." The roar bellowed like a lion. Everything got quiet and stopped.

Everything that is, except Jacque Herbert and the line of black limousines escorted by state police motorcycles. That murdering bastard never noticed them as he puttered out of the parking lot and into the highway.

Cars bearing State of Louisiana flags tangled with skidding blue-lighted motorcycles and their radio antennas. The motorcade eventually crunched to a heap about fifty yards away.

I found Hebert's maligned body another twenty yards away in the opposite direction. His moans led me straight to his mangled frame. There was just enough life in him to glare up one last time before twitching to eternal stillness.

Heels clipped over the asphalt behind me. I glanced up, and signaled Doctor Lambert to stop.

"Jacque—you forgot your LSU keychain."

Chapter 20
— *Sergeant RJ Ruiz* —

SWARMING THROUGH THE THRESHOLD, MY tactical team fanned out within seconds to cover every section of the location. Submachine guns swept each corner, alerted only by the quick step of trained SWAT Operators and their laser red lights leading them through the darkness.

A putrid cat piss and rotten egg cocktail invaded my facemask and permeated the air tank's respirator. Gasping for air, I focused on the quiet whispers over their headset's bone mic. I couldn't hold it. I gagged at smells resembling pickled foods and shitty diapers as I moved closer to what would be the meth-cooking lab.

If I hadn't gone to school with her older sister, the corpse's identity would've remained a mystery. Maybe fifteen years old, but definitely still in high school. She'd scratched her skin off from head to toe. I leaned closer. Even the islands of intact flesh were destroyed in her fight against the imaginary crank bugs crawling over her body. Crystal meth is a bitch to kick, and this child had lost.

As I labored to breathe, fog formed inside my facemask. Aching shoulders and fatigued quadriceps screamed when I bounced the tactical air pack harness back in place. Entombed inside this thick plastic coverall, I was drenched in sweat with my hands and feet taped off in rubber gloves and booties. Glancing into the chemical mist covering the cracked bathroom mirror, I looked like an extra-terrestrial.

Claustrophobia set in and passed. There was no time to panic with a mission to accomplish. The self-contained breathing apparatus only gave me sixty minutes of air. Less time after panting like a dog looking for drug dealers inside this shit hole.

Communications with my team was limited to hand signals and expressive facial gestures through the protective facemasks. The SWAT officer covering my back took one look at the girl's body and gasped inside his hazardous chemical protective suit. He spun into the threshold, rammed his head into the rotted wooden doorframe, and crumpled to one knee.

I don't think he intended to land on the teenager's body, but the body armor, tactical gear's weight, and the air pack drove him onto the roach-infested floor. His *yulp* was muffled but distinctive. I'd heard the sound of sickness enough in the military's teargas training chamber. I yanked him to his knees and saw the vomit slosh inside his facemask.

"Get outside. Call the Homicide Detectives." I yelled through the hard plastic shield while waving my bright green rubber-gloved thumb out the door. The officer crawled past me until he cleared the threshold, and then stumbled to his feet out of the mobile home.

Sweat poured down my brow and burned into my eyes—*focus, this is where bad shit happens in places like this.* Still on red alert for the suspect, I held the sub-machine gun steady at the closed corner door until backup arrived.

"All clear," whispered an officer over the tactical radio channel.

"Negative," I hissed back. "One unclear in southwest corner. Got eyes on. Send backup."

Shaking, my right arm struggled to hold the fully loaded weapon on target. My left forefinger and thumb clumsily fumbled for the activator button to communicate instructions to my team. The plastic hood and heavy ballistic helmet muffled the tactical headset and microphone. My eyes strained to cut through the fog building inside my mask when a shrill whistle rang through the earpiece. The rifle's butt slipped away from my sore shoulder as I was startled by the two-minute alarm. Fighting to regain control of the firearm, I tried slowing my breathing. The air tank would be drained in less than one hundred and twenty seconds.

A sense of comfort returned with the squeeze over my left shoulder. It signaled go time. Moving to breach the closed door, my new partner and I avoided standing directly in front of the threshold's fatal funnel. We made eye contact just as he tried the doorknob—locked. Taking one of my last breaths from the respirator, I stepped back and slammed my boot into wood.

The hollow core door splintered with the force, exposing piles of shit heaped inside the small room.

Thirty seconds of air remained.

Leaving my partner without first clearing this space was out of the question. Sweat exploded over my face, nearly blinding me. I swung the weapon's muzzle toward the floor as he crossed my path entering the room. Letting out a last breath of relief as the SWAT officer gave a thumb up to signal *all clear*, I stepped back as he crouched backward.

Fifteen seconds of air remained.

The junk on the floor parted as a pistol was thrust through the crap pile. Gulping the last of my air, I shoved my partner onto the ground with my left hand. The young girl's feet kicked from beneath the pile of clothes, plastic chemical buckets, and busted ephedrine blister packs.

I never actually heard the shot fired.

My partner jerked the girl to him by the ankle and fell on top to shield her. I could see all of her teeth as the small mouth stretched wide open, but couldn't hear the screams escaping it.

The bullet's impact left my chest caving against both lungs. Desperate for air, I shook my head in fury. It replaced the need for oxygen in the tank. My gloved forefinger slid into the trigger guard. Bouncing around this shooter's chin, I steadied the red dot. The selector switch was set to a three-round burst. I rattled off a lightening eruption of 9mm ammunition—dickhead's dead right there.

Chapter 21
— Sheriff James Walker —

THESE PART-TIME PARISH COUNCILMEN HAD yanked my chain once more than I thought I'd tolerate. I got along with most, but a few figured they had me by the balls. They'd hold the decision to have a special election over my head as a carrot, or maybe, the stick. I tried to put the worry aside as I prepped for another busy day at the office.

The hot coffee cup felt good against the stitching scars left across my right palm. Still cringing, I relived the sensation of the Rougarou's head plopping into my lap. The slashes caused by the cutting wire would serve as a constant reminder. I was finally settling back into a grove to focus on the daily duties of being the top cop in the parish.

My tires crunched gravel across the cement as I muscled the truck into my parking spot.

"Who the hell's in my parking spot?"

Just in time I noticed unmarked civilian vehicle in my space, and I stood on the brake, sending coffee sloshing over the rim. My chin grazed the top of the steering wheel.

I shoved the agitation aside, only to be replaced by emptiness as I entered the building. Officer involved shootings bring out the best from some in tough times and the fear from others.

A handful of deputies huddled in the hall, their eyes hollow and afraid. They shifted weight from one foot to another, silently muttering. All eyes turned to me.

"Good morning, deputies. Sarge gonna be released once the tubes are yanked. Collapsed lungs will be good as new." I assured them.

One twenty-something year old deputy spoke up. "Sheriff, how can this stuff go on in our parish? First the tiger murder case, and now this poor girl gets killed and Ruiz shot." He oozed fear. This was probably his first officer shooting.

I clawed my cheek wondering whether his question was inexperience or doubt over my ability as Sheriff. "Son, bad stuff happens all the time. We don't create it, just investigate it."

Now to see who was in my parking spot.

Deputy Chief St. Pierre hustled the group back onto duty as I approached Ms. Martha. Her usually calm, dull eyes looked strained. An experienced administrative assistant, she seemed rattled as she tried speaking from the corner of her tightly pressed lips. Her gaze darted back and forth between the closed office door and me.

I slipped into my office and saw a man, his back to the door, studying a picture from my bookshelf. I glanced back to reassure Ms. Martha it would be okay as I eased my office door shut. "Councilman Chiasson, you find a place to park?"

He fumbled the glass-framed picture back to the uncluttered bookshelf. "That's your boy? Ever figure out what happened to him?" His squat ass didn't have the decency to look at me while feigning concern over my child.

"Can I help you, Tony? I've got the State Police coming in about eight-thirty to begin their shoot team investigation." I bit my lower lip and wished I'd not said that. Anthony Chiasson had made it clear in each of his four terms on the council that he cared nothing for law enforcement. Possibly because we put his stealing ass son away in Angola State Prison.

"James, now that you mention it, what the hell is going on in this parish? Seems there has been nothing but bloodshed since you took over as Sheriff." He smacked his thick, chapped lips while delivering his threat. He'd never kept it secret that I wasn't his choice for this position.

"You telling me there was no crime in this parish until I came along?"

He plopped the saran-wrapped pants stretched across his bloated butt into my desk chair. I shouldn't have, but I'd had it up to here with him. I nudged onto the corner of my desk and perched right over him.

"It does seem that way. How else do you explain things lately?" His eyes darted between us. I wasn't budging and he couldn't escape. He'd planted himself into this pigeonhole, now he'd shit on the paper.

"You telling me that the last candidate you supported for Sheriff was the right choice?" I scratched my palm's itching scars across my unshaven chin. Doc Lambert warned me that once the nerves begin reattaching, I'd feel twitching sensations.

"Who, me?" His voice raised an octave.

"Yeah you, Tony. You still got the 'Elect Gill Gaudet' bumper sticker on your car." There weren't many dumb enough to leave those stickers on, but I'm sure he couldn't care less.

He waved my comment aside. "Let me get to the point. The Governor's still pissed at the way you treated Johnny Jones. Then you ran Jacque Hebert into the road and got him killed. Chief Roberts is still shaken up by the whole damn thing. You're a train wreck, James Walker. I just don't think you're the man for this job." His eyes blinked and he rubbed his bulb nose.

I swallowed my retort. The silence allowed him to chew on what he just said. His neck fat jiggled under the golf shirt as he fidgeted in my overstuffed leather chair. The old-school politician first folded, and then uncrossed his arms repeatedly.

"I've got work to do," I said after a few long moments. "You'll see yourself out." Speckling lights burst behind my eyelids and goose bumps exploded up my neck. *Stay calm*, I breathed. *Just get him out the door.*

"You know, it's smart to leave those bookshelves empty," he managed while squeezing between the credenza, desk, and me. I wasn't budging. Once past, he tucked the wrinkled shirttail over his soft potbelly.

"No need for clutter. My work is out in the parish," I replied.

He twisted his mouth unimpressed. "You should really take that picture down. It's kinda creepy seeing that he's dead and all." The councilman flipped his fingers up to dismiss my son's memory.

Regardless of his feelings toward me, only the evilest could dishonor the memory of a child.

As soon as I was alone, I collapsed into my chair. It never failed to amaze me that such vitriol could spew from another human. A single tear escaped as I glanced at my son's framed photograph from five years earlier.

Chapter 22
— Deputy Chief Genevieve St. Pierre —

FIFTEEN, RAPED, POISONED WITH CRYSTAL meth, and dead. That's one hell of an obituary. I kept the high school yearbook page open to her sophomore photo. Doctor Lambert's autopsy pictures shattered my heart. I needed balance.

I surveyed the officers sitting across my desk who waited impatiently for their assignments. "Lieutenant thanks for coming. I'll have Ms. Martha call Detective Stone so we can begin." It was going to be a struggle to keep my emotions from influencing the Drug Task Force supervisor, Remi Leblanc. Someone had to pay for yesterday.

The newest detective knocked on the doorframe and walked in to join us.

"Hey Todd, congrats on the CID promotion. Never thought you'd make detective." Remi Leblanc's cocky-ass swagger made you resent him while jutting your hand up to volunteer following him through hell and back.

"Thanks, Remi. Couldn't see being a Narc—I'm not about earrings and goatees," Stone said with a half-sure smirk.

I drifted to watching the news channel behind the two officers. I hushed them and turned up the volume as Sheriff Walker explained to a skeptical television crew how heroic his SWAT sergeant was in saving the eight-year-old's life.

"That's why we're here, boys. What the heck's going on?" I muted the screen and set about trying to refocus them—and me. I have to admit I was a bit distracted by both of these officers. They were the kind that I had found myself in bed with on more than a few occasions as a rookie officer.

Focus Gen.

Stone leaned back in his chair with a glint of admiration for Remi and possibly intimidation, also. I couldn't finger Remi's draw, but damn, the man commanded attention without saying a word.

"The turd we shot yesterday is Bobby Hale. A nobody kick-about who just happened to know enough chemistry to become one hell of a meth cook." His lines were delivered in a low whisper, like he'd spent a lifetime keeping secrets to protect others.

"Is he the main guy?" I asked.

"No ma'am. Just a low-level cook. He pissed off the bikers, and after they broke most of his rotten teeth out with a cordless drill, he landed on his feet working for someone else."

"Cordless?" Stone's face crinkled with his question. He was in a new arena—Undercover Narcotics.

"You don't think Hale sat still, do ya? Probably had to chase him down with that drill." Remi eased back into his chair. A grin crept across his bearded face and the shaggy hair nearly hid his look of savoring the idea. He looked me straight in the eyes as the scuffed sole of his worn leather boot tapped at the edge of my desk. He was measuring me.

"Remi, is there anything else?"

"Not now." Later, it would be.

"Well, we finally located the girls' parents. Social Service is holding on to the child. Looks like parents of the year material." Stone shuffled in his seat before leaning forward to wring his fingers between both hands and continuing.

"Both meth heads. Busted before. First time I've known them to lend the girls out for crank though." Remi clarified.

"You mean the parents left those girls there in a trade for drugs?" Stone's good heart showed his innocence. I let it ride since I trusted

Remi would use this to teach the rookie instead of ridicule him.

Remi was a hard man, maybe as hard as Buck Walker. His shoulders curled forward in revulsion of what those girls went through. Scratching his beard, a vulnerable look hid under Remi Leblanc's frown. And there was the power of his draw—his humanity.

"What's the game plan? I want this put to rest immediately. Definitely before the Sarge gets released from the hospital." I planted both forearms across the glass-covered desktop and leaned in. This was serious business. I also knew Buck was still beating himself up over forgetting his son's birthday, and battling the politics of being Sheriff. This was my chance to come through for him. He'd always been there for others.

"Stone, you pull those parents in and I'll squeeze 'em till they rat out their main supplier," Remi said. "Once we know who's really to blame for this crap, the Task Force will use them as informants to set up controlled buys before busting the big fish."

"Okay." Stone looked at me to interpret the language Remi lived. I brushed a loose strand of hair away from my mouth, and then tried to explain what he'd just said. Impatient, Remi unfolded from the chair. Exhaustion from working overtime and eternal nights showed in his posture. He straightened out his faded denim jeans over muscular thighs, and then shuffled across the room. Surveying with a suspicious eye through the small glass window facing the lobby, he laid a hand on Stone's shoulder.

"Just drag their asses in. I'll make 'em pay."

— Sheriff James Walker —

IDLING PAST THE OLD TANK battery off Highway 307, I eased the truck to a halt. No one was around, so I dropped my guard and unleashed my grief. Councilman Chiasson's comments ignited my buried emotions. They were becoming tougher to handle. It was getting harder to suppress the struggle, but nearly impossible to control the depression over my son's murder.

"Why, God? Why'd you let this happen to my boy?" I pounded my fist against the roof's interior. Praying, even bargaining for closure was insincere. I didn't want an arrest. Killing the bastard who filched my life was the only thing I lived for. God wasn't going to answer that prayer.

I clutched my sternum against the rage inside. I slammed the truck into park and leapt out seconds before I dry heaved into the sugar cane. The uncontrollable shivering and hand tremors concerned me. I'd avoided the doctors, but this was grief, not health.

I'd been here before and I'd be back again. I just couldn't promise myself I'd always be able to leave it. Once I emptied my stomach's contents, I readjusted the new snub nose revolver at the small of my back, and climbed back in behind the wheel.

Chapter 23

— Lieutenant Remi Leblanc —

THERE'S A REASON THE Drug Task Force office is separated from the others. The shit that walks in, and then crawls out would be impossible to explain to regular cops. Unhinging the clasps on my leather vest would make what was about to happen more comfortable. For me anyway.

I squinted into the setting sun as the black panel van skidded into the sally port. Agent Smith fed chain through the pulley as the metal bay door clanked until smacking the chipped cement. It was go time.

I jerked on the door's handle and shoved the sliding cargo van door open. Mister and Missus shit-bag parents crumpled their foreheads as they labored to figure out where they were. Agent Jones, their chauffeur, bailed out from behind the wheel. The stench in the van sent him stumbling off toward the bathroom.

The woman's body began tweaking from the days on end of smoking of crystal meth. Her wretched frame jerked uncontrollably with a nightmare case of the crank bugs like her daughter had—except her skin was calloused from the clawing at imaginary creepy-crawlies covering her body. No use talking to her at this point.

"Put the sack back over momma's head."

I stood ten feet away, but even so I felt the urge to bathe.

"Please help me. I ain't do nuttin to nobody," she cried.

I threw my hands up and walked away with a shudder. The thought of touching that mess made my own skin crawl. Instead,

Agent Smith stretched rubber gloves over his wide hands. He was one badass Cajun, but the sight of her apparently sickened him as well. In one swift motion, he draped a black cloth bag over her head. Strands of her unwashed hair slipped out from under the bag and fell across his exposed forearms. He flinched before glaring at me over his bowling ball-sized shoulders. "You owe me, Remi."

Fighting the urge to grin at the Agent's discomfort, I battled hatred in my heart for these scumbags. Agent Jones, who returned from the bathroom swiping grey lips, waited with us at the van's cargo door while Agent Smith handcuffed momma to a bench along the wall.

"Hey asshole, you can't treat us like this," Poppa spat, his eyes taped shut.

I drove my fist square onto his scraggly red-bearded chin. Agent Jones slapped him across the face a few times to revive him. "You say something, shit-bag?" I debated the degree of beating he'd be able to take. If I overdid it, he'd never cooperate with me. Clamping my teeth to contain any more threats, I extended my arm to help him out of the van.

Hands cuffed behind his back, he rolled onto his side, and then scratched across the non-skid, diamond metal floor of the van. "Screw you, pig." He tried spitting through a meth-mouth charred by cigarette lighters and dehydration, but it mostly hung from his chin. It was all I could do to put on a diplomatic front for his cooperation.

Regardless his situation, poppa continued to sniff the moldy air and lift his brows to peak beneath the duct tape. He licked parched lips with a black tongue, showing off brown and broken teeth, and tried once more to spit on me.

"Not this time." I pounded his ribcage so hard that his rail-thin body levitated before crumpling to the floor.

At the sound of his whimpers, Momma added her two cents. "Baby, what dey doing to ya? Call da police." They were too stupid to know we were the police. Or were we? We could've killed these two right here and now. I trusted Smith and Jones.

I sensed they felt it too.

Agent Smith hovered anxiously behind momma with eagerness in his eyes—just give him the nod. Agent Jones' latex gloves slipped from the chemical smelling sweat covering poppa's body.

"On your feet, douche bag," the older agent rasped. The child's death removed even the minimal restraints this Sheriff's Office expected us to exercise. No one knew they were here. They didn't know they were here. They were going to cooperate.

"You want something to drink?" I offered. It's all part of the game of getting information.

"I can't see." His voice shook. He'd break quick.

"No shit, stupid. It's called duct tape. Tell me what I want to know and I might remove it."

"I ain't saying nuttin. I'm calling da cops on yo ass." His face jerked up and pivoted as if trying to sense where I stood. If he spit again, I'd drown him in it.

"How you want to do this, hard or impossible?" I puffed out hard to calm my rage. My mind replayed that trailer scene, every agonizing detail of what those little girls suffered.

"Ain't scared of ya." Had to give him credit for defiance. It wouldn't last long though. I nodded to Agent Smith. He made momma hurt, which made momma scream. It wasn't important how he did it. What was important was that poppa started talking.

"We didn't mean for dem babies to get hurt. Da man said he'd babysit 'em while we got high." Somewhere in his hollow soul, he'd discovered a paternal gene. Still, his addiction to the crystal meth was stronger than the love for his daughters.

"Why did you leave the girls with Bobby Hale?" I demanded.

"Who?"

"Bobby Hale."

"My man is Diesel." His shoulders twitched while both restrained hands clawed at whatever skin the fingers could attack. I watched his physical reaction to what he said, and knew he told the truth.

"You got a name for Diesel?" Silent, I signaled to Agent Smith to ask if momma knew who Diesel was. It was best to play each against the other. No one keeps their story straight.

Raising both eyebrows, I tilted my head back to gaze at the emptied framework of metal beams and welded pipes that once supported suspended ceiling tiles. Whatever this warehouse used to be, it looked like hell now. I tried breathing through my nose to calm down, but had no luck tonight. My patience was razor thin.

Agent Smith shook his head side-to-side and mouthed no. I saw the ignition go off in Agent Jones' eyes while he looked over at the autopsy photos left on the workbench. I stretched out my right hand to distract him. Too late.

Agent Jones wasn't as tall as Agent Smith or me, but that swollen up—muscular bastard was wide, and strong—and pissed. In one smooth arc, he shoved the case file onto the bench as his arms swooped down to clutch poppa's throat in his vice grip. I moved too slowly to stop him as poppa's forehead raked upward and his mouth gaped open for air. His body was launched from the seat of the metal chair. The momentum of Agent Jones' anger smashed poppa onto the splintered wooden tabletop.

Momma called out in a voice scarred from a lifetime of cigarettes and drugs, "Baby, you okay?" There was no answer. Only silence, except for the echoing clank of the metal chair falling onto the cement floor, and a bag of crumpled bones striking the solid oak surface.

"Last chance. Who is Diesel?" The thud of poppa walloping against the wooden table was louder than the question. An unbridled wrath brewed within the room. It was time to contain it, or unleash it. Poppa had one chance to save them both.

"She got his numba in her pocket," he managed. "Honey, give dem dat numba. Dey gonna kill me."

Momma swung her shoulders wildly as Agent Smith tried to search her stained denims. Easily six foot-five, the younger agent resembled a professional wrestler as he snatched momma up with his paw clinched around her throat. With her hands zip-tied behind her back, her legs flailed until she ran out of steam. He picked through her pockets until he came up with a wrinkly swatch of paper, and then dropped her. She crumpled onto the cement motionless.

"You gonna make this call?" I suggested to poppa.

Chapter 24
— Sheriff James Walker —

PUNCHING THE INTERIOR OF MY truck wasn't the best idea, and I could practically hear Doc roll her eyes when I told her how these stitches burst loose. She agreed to meet me at her office after finishing up the autopsy on the fifteen-year-old girl.

A familiar pressure at the base of my neck told me someone was following me. Cold ran through my blood as I looked around and saw nothing. Didn't matter. After thirty years on the job, I knew better than to trust my eyes over my gut. Scanning all around, I clutched the steering wheel and chewed on who might be following me this time. Pointless, really. Between every dirt bag I put away, the Cajun Mafia for killing Saul Dugas, and Chief Tom Roberts for taking his governor's appointment—I was a wanted man – on both sides of the law.

I mashed the accelerator and barreled through the twisting bayou roads. With no shoulders on either side of the highway, it would be impossible for anyone waiting to leapfrog my truck. A tail would have to be right behind me. As soon as I careened around a blind curve, I slammed on the brakes, forcing the big truck into a skid across the middle of the slick hot asphalt.

Jumping out of the pick-up, I unholstered my Glock 9mm and waited for them to arrive. Enough of being the hunted. Who was following me? After five minutes, there was no traffic other than four cyclists working a rotating pace line that swung around my truck.

There wasn't anyone following me. Except for a few gators and nutrias, I was the only living creature.

I aligned my truck with the jagged edge of asphalt, scanned the highway for oncoming traffic, and then shoved my arm deep under the seat. The purple Crown Royal bag was heavy, but the pieces inside lay limp across my blood stained palm.

I'd had this Smith & Wesson snub nose revolver for over thirty years. It'd saved my ass on several occasions. Now it threatened to undo me. The past couple of nights I'd milled and bored it to pieces in my machine shop out back of the house. Piece by piece, I launched them into the swamps and bayou covering the tri-parish area. The only witnesses were crickets, and they weren't chirping to anyone who'd listen.

My cell jumped around the hard plastic center console. Had to be Doc. "Hey Susan, ready for me?"

"James Walker, this is Governor Eleanor Jewel." My shoulders squeezed in disgusted anticipation.

A little water snake slithered from the marsh grass at my feet and across the highway. My responses to this conversation would be similar.

"How can I help you?"

"Let's cut the crap, James. I picked you because Chief Tom Roberts is a hard-core southern Democrat." Her southern charm reeked like piles of sucked crawfish heads after Good Friday lunches.

"I don't belong to any party, ma'am."

"I know. Better no party than them bunch of jackasses. James, don't make me regret this appointment. If I gotta yank ya, we'll both look like idiots. Ya hear?"

Distracted and uninterested in her threats, I watched as the water snake edged down the other side without getting smashed. I pumped my fist for the reptile's victory. Back to the reality of the governor's call, I waited for my chance to escape without getting smashed along the way.

"I'm still not happy about the Johnny Jones thing. He's concerned that charges might be brought against him." She feigned a cooperative tone.

I leaned against the sunbaked hood. An orchestra of marshland sounds wafted quietly across the barren stretch of highway. Rubbing my eyes, I knew better but just couldn't resist. "Ma'am, you do realize a man was killed at his casino, and then your motorcade ran over Jacque Hebert?"

"James Walker, I couldn't give two shits about that Hebert fella. He ain't dropped one cent in the till." Her shrill voice, once unveiled, stretched the limits of decency. My head ached listening to the garbage this woman spewed.

"Okay, and?" If I were going to get an ax across my neck, then let's get on with it. I envied that water snake.

"I don't see any reason why a Sheriff busy with getting elected to a permanent position would worry about JJ. Do you?" She suggested.

The melody of baritone bullfrogs bellowing contrasted the conversation with Jewel. I allowed air, time, and the music of the swamp to fill her ear. It didn't matter, though. The vile woman would get what she wanted. I learned to pick my battles long ago, so I wasn't going to die on this hill today. There'd be other times to put Jones' butt in a bind.

"Sure, Eleanor."

— *Lieutenant Remi Leblanc* —

WORKING DOPE HAS BEEN ABOUT all I've ever done. Folks I knew along the bayou in my younger days are shocked when they find out what I do. I wasn't a criminal, just mischievous.

Pulling my feet off the desk to turn down Tab Benoit's *Best of the Blue Bayou* album, I tuned in to the voices in the hallway. Though muffled, tension resonated in Agent Smith and Agent Jones' words. A third voice I didn't recognize, but I knew these two men and it wasn't good. Should'a known better to poke my mug into others' affairs. This run-down warehouse may have been musty and rusted, but it was my office.

"You boys okay out here?" I eased around my office door, keeping my steel-toed boot pressed behind to limit how much further it'd open. Agent Smith's claw gripped a stranger's neck, whose unfamiliar yellow eyes pleaded with me for salvation.

"This is the girls' uncle, Roy Blanchard," Smith said. "Get it? Uncle." The hallway was already as small as a cattle shoot. Now crammed with conflicting bodies, it looked like a match box.

"How is Uncle Roy going to help us?" I asked.

Agent Jones answered. "He's feeling remorseful over the things he did to the girls as they grew up. He also knows Diesel personally and wants very badly to introduce us to him. Right, Uncle Roy?" Said the former Force Recon Marine who I could see had become frayed around the edges, but remained focused. Agent Jones refused to allow crap like fatigue, injury, or divorce to knock him off track. He was a soldier, on the battlefield or the bayou. The non-stop hours of ass-busting street-beating since SWAT Sergeant Ruiz took one to the chest was taking its toll.

Narcotics operations present small windows of opportunity. When the tide rolls in, you gotta ride the wave. This tide was high and Uncle Roy was about to get washed away.

I stared into the man's pleading eyes for a moment. "Call Detective Stone in on the loving uncle part. We'll help him ease his guilt by introducing us to Diesel."

Agent Smith rammed a heel palm strike to the base of Uncle Roy's neck, causing the gangly fifty-something-year-old's knees to buckle. The trio continued down the ill-lit hallway.

"Agent Jones," I called at their backs.

He spun to attention. "Yes sir."

I thought he'd salute. "Drop the rigid shit. Blend in, brother." He was scarlet and gold through and through.

"Yes, sir, okay."

"Put this case to bed soon. The girl's corpse haunts me. Make somebody pay."

The warrior's glint returned to his eyes.

Chapter 25
— Sheriff James Walker —

THE PHYSICAL DAMAGE WAS REPAIRED. Doc re-stitched the filleted skin she'd closed once already across my palm. My body had begun to heal from the crushing blows delivered by the Rougarou. My soul? Not so much. I'd given up on healing long ago. It's a badge of honor for cops to be broken. It's stupid, but it comes with the pension.

We rolled into the jammed parking lot at Boudreaux's Catfish House. I tilted my chin and looked over my glasses at her, pleading for somewhere less crowded. Less public.

Instead, she smiled and scooted out the passenger's side.

It was the least I could do. Susan had helped out many times and promised a debriefing after the fifteen-year-old's autopsy. What better place to discuss death than over supper?

Our shoulders brushed as we walked side-by-side toward the restaurant. She pulled her arm firmly against her body when our elbows touched. Her cheeks flushed pink at the contact. When her heel caught in the oyster shell parking lot, she clutched my wrist to steady herself. I turned my chin up toward the crescent moon and threw out a fake howl of pain. She shot a concerned look my way, but laughed and punched my shoulder with her free hand without letting go of my wrist.

She relaxed against me as the thick aroma of fried seafood, stagnant marsh, and hurricane season's humidity blended with the faint floral of her perfume. If only I could ignore the last few days, to breathe in the heady mix of scents and walk in the moonlight. But this wasn't a date. It was business. I stiffened my shoulders as we neared the entrance.

The screen door creaked as patrons left the restaurant laughing and rubbing their bellies over untucked shirts. The yellow iridescent bulb over the barroom entrance cast an eerie haze. The zydeco blasted from inside.

"Who's your new whore, James?" Gaunt, I knew the voice but not her pipe-cleaner frame.

It took a moment for the words to sink in. Doc's hand slipped from my arm as I spun to the shrill voice.

"Anita, you're drunk again." I fiddled with my shirtsleeves, while heat flashed over my body. I tried to change the topic but she postured herself as if ready to pounce on a trembling Susan. I tried to encourage Susan to go inside by nudging her across the lower back. Like a concrete pillar, she couldn't budge.

"You're one hell of a father. Forgot your son's birthday. Screw you, James Walker." She beat her fist into the sticky night air.

I ducked out of range. Some *cooyon* stumbled out of the same rickety barroom exit and took up a wobbly attack stance. Her ride? Not tonight, he wasn't. My guess was that he was going to the hospital. My gut rumbled as my legs steeled for the coming confrontation. "Susan, go inside. Call an ambulance."

Doc's eyes were glued to something she'd probably never experienced: the idiotic behavior that often landed people on her autopsy table.

"An ambulance? You betta call da freak'n cops, cuz I'ma whoop yo ass, son."

As drunk as Anita was, her rolling eyes showed how stupid that sounded coming from her escort, who looked to be trying to help his eyes catch up to their sockets and his ass to the check his mouth couldn't cash.

"Sir, just go back inside," I said. "This doesn't concern you." I was the Sheriff, after all. Then I heard the flimsy screen storm door flap as Susan left us. "Anita, if he comes close, I'm going to drop him." I shook out my hands as they positioned just above my waist.

"Big Johnny, it's okay. Go back inside, baby. I'll just be a second." She threw out her spindly arm to stop the lumbering man, but he steamrolled past her and she planted both hands on her boney hips instead.

His black leather motorcycle boots scuffled into the loose dirt and broken shells. I noticed a heavy metal rope chain hung from his waistband to his pants pocket. Sometimes these dirt bags strap a knife or gun to the other end. I tapped my lower back. The new backup would do. He stood square, like the Jolly Green Giant, with his hands on his hips. The idiot either didn't want to fight, or didn't know how. My eyes flashed over his form. The greasy black denims matched his sleeveless t-shirt. The random tattoos looked home or prison-made.

"I'm going to ask you one last time to walk away. This doesn't involve you, and Anita is okay." I swallowed hard, really hard, trying to be diplomatic. I wasn't going to turn my back on him to walk into the restaurant so this had to end now.

"How you know her name, dickhead?"

"He's my ex, Big Johnny." Anita slurred her words. How far she'd fallen.

"Oh, ya dat azzhole who forgot yo boy birfday," the big buffoon sputtered.

I shot a furious glare at Anita, who threw her hands up. My eyes swiveled back to him and I blanked out with wrath and an immeasurable sorrow. He was missing one tooth just off-center to the right top and two teeth just below that. That was my target.

I'd lowered my right hand, rocked my hip back slightly, balled my fist up along the upward launch and lifted Big Johnny off his feet. I had only intended to hit him once until he spewed that comment about my boy. His strung-out torso wedged between two cars parked in the shadows. She scurried over to pull him by an arm. Big Johnny was out cold. Blood ran from his mouth as he mumbled something stupid. There was no need to check—he'd be missing several other teeth now.

Like I said, I only intended to hit him once. I stepped onto his soft belly to cross over to his right side. Reaching down, I jerked the metal chain from his waistband and pocket. I wasn't going to get ambushed at the table by this jerk. A tattered leather wallet hung loosely from the over-sized ring. No weapon, just a one-dollar bill and a probation & parole identification card: Johnny Paul Chiasson. He'd go on my shit list.

"I hate you," my ex hissed. "Why don't you find who killed our son instead of running around with that whore?"

I dropped his wallet into her lap as she clung to the only shit bag who'd tolerate her, and walked away. Once inside the restaurant, I spotted Susan on the other side of the crowded dining room. Adrenaline pumped through my body, so I eased it with deep breaths, flexing and releasing my shoulders.

The place was smoldering and smoking with sound. A singer on stage scratched fingers across a stainless steel washboard like lightning. I worked my way across the room, stopping for handshakes and hugs until I cleared the dance area. My appetite faded as I noticed my least favorite parish councilman at a booth, in unholy conversation with none other than Chief of Police Tom Roberts.

"Boys." I didn't bother extending my hand to either.

"Walker." Roberts was the only one who'd face me, but he wouldn't look me in the eyes.

"You get you car fixed? I bet Hebert left quiet a dent." Electricity coursed through my veins. Wiping the mist of post-confrontation from my upper lip, I tried to hide the smirk curling at my comment. I would have gladly traded Big Johnny for these two.

"Don't fuck with me, Walker." Roberts said it, but didn't look like he believed it.

My knee dimpled the plastic covering his booth padding as I

leaned into his ear. "Thomas, you've already dug a grave by showing your ass at the governor's town hall meeting." I then switched my attention to his supper companion, who strained to hear what was said.

"Anthony, you want me out of office, and then come after me. Until it happens, keep out of my parking spot or I'll tow and ticket you myself. I'm the Sheriff in this parish, and no small-town cop or part-time politician's going to stop me from honoring my oath."

I was shaking inside. My legs felt like dragging cement across the saw-dusted wooden dance floor. Skin prickling with the *frissons*—I couldn't get to Susan's table quick enough.

"Buck, what just happened? You've the strangest glow across your face." Her mouth twisted with an uncertainty.

"I just made the bravest move of my political career or the dumbest move of my personal life." Holding the menu up to hide my face, I quietly exhaled. Either way, I had maintained my integrity.

"You're a good man, Buck. This parish has been through plenty. We need you to be you." Her smooth fingertips glided over my bruised knuckles.

I slumped against the back wall while facing the front door to survey the dinner, and enjoyed the delicate contact.

"Buck, you're bleeding again. I'm going to end up cutting that darn hand off if you don't behave."

Just then, my phone buzzed in my pocket. "Deal, Doc. Excuse me, I gotta take this call."

Chapter 26
— Deputy Chief Genevieve St. Pierre —

BUCK LOOKED THREADBARE. I hadn't lived his career, but he had to be hurting. This job causes us to suffer, but he was a half step over the razor's edge. More like a wavy shock, his hair was longer than the usual close-cropped style I'd seen for decades. Hunched, slumped shoulders replaced the casual at-attention strut of shoulders—he showed the strain of every one of his fifty-five years.

"Hey Sheriff. Sorry to pull you away from whatever you were enjoying. This is big." I fought the urge to hug him.

"No problem, Genevieve. What now?"

Sensing his agitation, I'd make this quick. "First thing. Anita called to say you attacked her and the latest love interest at Boudreaux's."

"That's why you called me?" he wasn't amused.

"I could care less about Anita—I'm worried about you eating that greasy, fried food." I countered.

His grizzled grin eased my concerns.

"I'll watch the diet soon. Scout's honor." He held up a bloody palm with three fingers in a scout salute. "What's going down? I've got to head out to White Castle soon."

"Remi stopped by earlier. He and Stone are putting this case to bed. They still got the girls so-called parents on ice. Hope they at least fed them. Jail's been notified that they'll be booked on drug and child abuse charges. As if the torture those girls went through wasn't enough, Task Force also discovered an Uncle Roy. Seems he babysat them most of their short lives. He also was the first to molest them. Remi convinced him to set up the crystal meth buy from Diesel in exchange for –"

"For his life." Buck's eyes narrowed, but not before a single tear slipped from the corner of one eye.

Talking about a young child being molested, then murdered, was taking its toll on him. "I'm sorry, Buck. I should've been more aware."

He pressed his lips together and motioned for me to continue.

"They placed a few recorded calls to Diesel. Wired up Uncle Roy and gave him the photocopied undercover buy money. He did as they said. He bought an eight-ball of crank straight from this guy Diesel's cookhouse. Remi's getting the search warrant signed as we speak."

"Diesel? Who the hell is that?" The name clearly meant nothing to him. This parish is close to two hundred thousand folks, after all. A mixed blend of Creoles, Cajuns, physicians, academic, farmers, artist, and oil field hands. Some here for generations, others just passing through.

"We don't know. Could've asked Bobby Hale, but Sergeant Ruiz put that bullet through his skull." I tried bringing him back into the present with another smart-ass comment.

He smiled slightly, and then concern softened his eyes. "How is Ruiz anyways?"

"She's fine. Getting out of the hospital in the morning and re-leased for light duty soon. Ruiz said she appreciated you stopping by every day." I patted his shoulder and felt him release the tension.

Buck was a cop. He loved cops and they appreciated his connec-tion to their sacrifices. They knew he'd walked the walk. I just worried that the voting public wouldn't feel that same connection come election time.

"So this mystery turd just appears and sets up shop. He connects with Bobby Hale to cook his poison after the bikers no longer needed him, and Uncle Roy traded the girls for dope so their parents could stay high?" He pressed his lips together as his eyes wandered across my office. He tipped his head to one side as he weighed the scenario. I caught myself biting the inside of my cheek in anticipation.

The circle seemed connected, but Buck didn't look convinced it was that tidy. I trusted his instinct on dope cases. He'd run Narcotics for years on his way through the ranks. He knew them. He'd lived amongst them in long-term undercover roles. He'd even admitted once that he'd actually become them at some point before drawing himself away. *"Once that weed is planted, it's hard to kill."*

"Remi said it's best to strike at dawn. SWAT's on notice. Briefing here for zero four hundred hours."

"Four o'clock—there goes the White Castle trip. Why not at the Task Force office?"

"Mom, pop and Uncle Roy are still tied up in there."

He frowned. "I hope all that clustering here doesn't alert Diesel." He dug his uncut nails across his cheek stubble while considering the need-to-know details of bringing that many officers together without telegraphing the mission.

"Move it?"

"No. I'll be here."

"Remi also said he had something for your ears only."

Shuffling his worn boots across my stained blue industrial carpet he whispered, "What?"

Wish I could answer. "You know Remi. Your ears only."

— Lieutenant Remi Leblanc —

THE QUIET OF PROFESSIONALS PREPARING for a mission is a silence all its own. The bridled energy is a good sign of competent officers working as a single organism. It was still dark outside as the conference room began to hum with armor-clad SWAT Operators and notebook-toting detectives. Sheriff Walker and I made eye contact.

He'd done my job before I came on. He knew it was time to roll.

"Thank you for being here on time. Let me start by saying Sergeant Ruiz will be released from the hospital this morning. Don't bother her with visits, she still needs the rest." Muffled applause sounded, and then it was back to the briefing.

"Look at your packets for details. All we know about our target is he's called Diesel. He sold hand-to-hand to our snitch from the listed address. It's a shithole meth den. That's why SWAT is going in plastic. They got less than sixty minutes of air, so once their commander gives the go signal, everyone on perimeter be ready to lock down the area."

"Remi, how's your gut on this?" Walker looked tense as he cornered me away from the others. He knew the pressure on me, so I thought it odd that he'd ask that question.

"Sheriff, if it was just a buy/bust, I'd be okay, but we know nothing about this Diesel. It bothers me."

"SWAT got this, Remi. You've done your part." His heavy hand eased the knotted muscles across my shoulder. When Stone walked into the conference room, I waved him over.

"Morning, Sheriff. So, can you believe it?" Stone eagerly blurted.

Shit. I hadn't had a chance to tell Walker yet, but now wasn't the time. The three of us huddled in the corner while Velcro ripped and meshed around us, signaling that everyone else was prepared to head out. I lifted my chin to signal Agent Smith and Agent Jones to hustle everyone out. Walker frowned at Stone and turned to me.

"Sheriff, we learned that Diesel has information about your son's murder." I held my breath and waited for the explosion.

Instead, the Sheriff stumbled back against the wall on rubber legs. "He did it?" He asked in despair.

"No sir, but the snitch said he'd bragged about knowing who did." Stone looked scared shitless.

"You believe him?"

"Yes, sir. The rat told us about another child found killed in Tangipahoa Parish last week. We checked. They'd just recovered an eight-year-old's body."

Relief flooded the hardened man whose emotional river had drained dry years earlier. I nudged Stone toward the door. There were some things a man needed privacy for, and confronting your demons was top of the list. I had more than a clue, but this kid hadn't been around the block enough to relate.

"Buck, if you wanna skip this, no one will know," I said quietly from the doorway. "I'll call you first thing. Smith and Jones will extract Diesel to the warehouse for you."

"Thanks Remi. But it's my job. I'll stay outside the perimeter. Just watch."

I didn't believe him for an instant, but I'd do anything for this man. Anything.

Chapter 27

— Diesel —

"WHY THE FUCK AM I up so early? And where the fuck did all these cops come from?"

I tugged my cap a little lower and drove real casual past the third cop car I'd seen in the last five minutes. Sucking down them pain pills with vodka was gonna knock my ass out fast. I had to get settled back at my place.

Up ahead a ways was some sort of police parade. Soon as they hard broke across the rickety Bayou Rond Pom Pon Bridge, I knew— this ain't no place for me.

I drove on past while they lipped an uncertain right turn near my cookhouse. There was no way in hell I was getting busted. I tried to remember whether I'd left anything linking me to there. Since they'd blasted Billy Hale, I retooled my operation alone.

I eased the old V8 into a patch of brush along the board road. Jumping the rusted pipe swing gate, I crouched along the gravel path in the moist darkness. A marching crew of ballistic-clad army ants spilled from the back of a painted delivery truck, dressed in plastic suits with air packs. Fat lot of good that would do them – that house was so full of fumes, one shot and it'd go up in a fireball. Would serve their asses right. Screw them.

Ignoring the urge to piss, my gut twisted in panic. I told myself there was nothing wrong—the hell it wasn't. Time crawled as the cops fanned out around my place. The neighbors' lights popped on, but they'd never tell. Them wooden houses burn easy and I made sure the neighbors knew it. I waited, shifting from foot to foot, and swatted gnats from my ears and nose.

Shit. Once those cops slipped into the shadows, they were like ghosts. I was a stuck duck. Had to take a closer look, so I jumped back in my ride.

Blood pounded in my ears as I whipped the car back around toward the bridge. No alibi made sense, but I had to know what they were up to. I had to see. After lighting a cigarette, I tucked it loosely between my fingers and pulled my big rust bucket back onto the old state highway. Cop cars crammed into the lane around the house.

Guess it's time to move. Not my property anyways.

Humid air swirled in through my open windows and dampened my smoke. Sucking in another drag of tar, I leaned back onto the vinyl headrest to calm my nerves while coasting across the old Rond Pom Pon's metal grating. Damn road was goose-shit slick in the early mornings.

I locked eyes with a lone cop standing on the opposite side of the bridge. Son of a bitch had my number. "Play it cool, man," I said out loud, nodding in his direction as I passed. The tip of a radio antenna rose to his face.

My legs went weak so I could barely hold down the gas pedal. Cold fear flushed through me, and a tunnel of streaked light filled my vision. It cleared when my car skidded into the opposite guardrail. Damn—my brother sure was gonna be pissed when he saw his car.

A dust and rock cloud rose in my rearview mirror. A pick-up swung onto the highway pointing in my direction, and I righted my car for the escape. If I was hauled in, it would be my third strike—no second place finishes or surrenders.

The rising sun glared through the misty windshield. The wiper blades did nothing but smear. Fuck—the truck was gaining ground. It had to be a cop, but there were no blue lights or sirens. If he was, he looked to be the only one on my tail. Maybe I'd be better off putting a bullet between his eyes.

The road ribboned around every narrow curve. My arms ached from holding the V8 on the pavement. Launching it into the swamp wouldn't help matters.

A lumbering tractor pulled onto the highway from a gravel access road. "Move!" My adrenaline spiked as the headlights closed in behind me. I swerved into the oncoming lane to jut around the farm equipment. I was rocking at over one hundred miles an hour, but the truck never disappeared from my rear view. This guy was a mad man.

Shaking my head to clear the effects of pills and vodka, I tried to slow my breathing. Suddenly my legs cramped and twisting intestines pulled me over the wheel. Dry eyes blinked like a late night yellow caution light. There was a red light up ahead, but hell if I could judge the distance. With the asshole on my tail, no way could I slow down.

I blasted the intersection just before a white sedan hurtled across, almost t-boning the pick-up. No way would this dude keep going at the same pace? Still, he was alone. The long straightaway leading onto the interstate allowed me to stretch my fingers. I shoved the gun under my right leg and felt the humidity covering the grip.

"I gotta end this shit soon. Pull over and pop him. Then hop the interstate and vanish."

I flew along the open road until I got closer to the on-ramp. My heart pounded in my throat. It wasn't easy to kill a man, but it's a hell of a lot easier than being killed. Just around this curve and I'd pull onto the shoulder in the cane field.

"Move, grandma. Get your ass outta the way." I laid on the horn and jerked the wheel hard to the left. Just a little further and this prick was history. Gaining speed around another blind curve, I leaned my shoulders back to the right, yanking the steering wheel with both hands sharp enough to hang in the bend. By the time I saw the tractor it was too late to veer back and out of the way.

"What happened?" It was hard to breathe. I was fading. I looked down at blood and bone coagulating with dirt, rocks and cane stalks.

"You stupid asshole!" Through the debris crammed into my eyes, I saw the guy kneeling over me was him. "Anita's ex?" I mouthed.

"Big Johnny? You're Diesel?" The man's smeared by horror jerked me by the collar.

I was cold—made no sense to have that much damage and feel nothing.

"Johnny, what do you know about my son?" Walker's yelling sounded like I was underwater.

"Fuck you." I needed help. Not questions. "Call ambulance."

"Tell me first, Johnny. Who killed our son?"

"Ya wanna know, call doctor, help me."

"Johnny, I'll get you help, but please. Please tell me who killed our boy."

My mind was going stone blank. I heard my heart's thud turn to a few final thumps.

"Under ya nose." I said.

— Sheriff James Walker —

I WASN'T EVEN SURE WHERE to buy flowers, but I wanted to be there as Sergeant Ruiz was wheeled from the hospital. Soon, thirty members of my staff joined me. I grinned despite Johnny Chiasson's serious injuries that prevented me from interrogating his ass. It was the first and only lead toward solving my son's murder. This agency had come together as a family.

I read the look on Deputy Chief St. Pierre's face to mean she had less than great news and hated to burden me with it. I patted her upper shoulder and thanked her for arranging the flowers.

"You heard the news, Sheriff?" Her eyes darted everywhere but into mine.

"Genevieve, what news you talking about?"

"Big Johnny, aka Diesel, Johnny Chiasson is none other than your best friend's brother." She tried to curl the corners of her mouth, but worry weighed them down.

"My best friend... you mean the councilman? His brother? Who knew 'Up Right' Anthony had family." I knew regardless of their relationship, Tony would hold me accountable.

"Chiasson's on his way here right now." She shifted her weight and stamped her palms together.

"Gen, it's bad enough Diesel looks like he'll survive the crash. I don't want a confrontation with Tony Chiasson as Sergeant Ruiz comes out of the hospital." I felt blood flush up my neck at the thought of the councilman coming to comfort the one responsible for Ruiz taking a bullet into her chest.

"It's covered, Buck. Agents Jones and Smith are assigned to guard the prisoner while he's in surgery. Once Johnny Chiasson is released, they'll ensure he goes straight to prison for booking charges." St. Pierre had all the bases covered.

Remi stood apart from the huddle of anxious officers, his shoulders pulled back unconsciously at attention. "Squeeze him before he passed out?" he asked. Our hands fused together and we spoke in close quarters as warriors do.

"Nothing." I twinged at telling Remi a lie, but it was my revenge, not his.

"Heard he was dating your ex. Sorry bout that." It wasn't an apology, just an acknowledgement.

"Remi, jail said they received the girls' parents. Didn't mention an Uncle Roy."

"Who?" Remi asked. There must've been a more suitable option for the child molester.

"We're going to have to keep eyes on Councilman Chiasson. Diesel's his brother."

Remi raised an eyebrow. "Seriously? That piece of shit was operating just under your nose."

Chapter 28
— Sheriff James Walker —

BREAKFAST AT SPARK'S CAFÉ WAS typical. Businessmen, hung-over college kids and early morning exercise enthusiasts clustered for French toast pancakes. Clanking like rusty pipes, my knotted intestines finally signaled it was time after the last few days to try eating—or at least try holding food down.

The far end table was open. I shuffled through cramped quarters, squeezing hands while struggling to remember names. Finally, I hunched over a long table of old timers. Their dusty eyes dodged mine as a quiet fog settled over the table. Except one.

"I think Walker's done worn out his welcome. Just looking for revenge on whoever killed his boy. Hell, if he'd been home more often instead of playing cop his whole life, maybe the boy'd be here today." My ex-father-in-law never used discretion when it came to running his mouth.

"John, you're entitled to your opinions, but I'd suggest you tend to your daughter," I warned. "Anita needs help, even help from a drunk like you."

Coffee launched over the cup's rim as the life-long alcoholic's weathered hand quaked. The stench of whiskey drifted from the mug as he exhaled. Leathered fists pressed against the metal edge of the table, and his flushed cheeks puffed feebly as the old man struggled to heave the wooden chair over the linoleum flooring.

"Stay down, John. No need to go to jail. Again." I'd grown weary of this idiot after years of him punching his wife and pushing his daughters around. I maintained a death grip on the back of his wooden chair – the only thing keeping me from strangling him once and for all.

"Sheriff, why don't you go bust them Mexicans coming into this here parish?" The youngest at the table, who had to be at least in his mid-sixties, intervened. Stone faced, his gristly body had only known hard labor since birth. His slow, whispered drawl sent a frozen spike into my spine. Emory Ballard was bad news and had no intention of apologizing for it.

"What kinda trouble they causing?" I knew the answer—none.

Hate seethed from Emory Ballard's core. Not the racism of mainstream media bashing for political correctness or profit, but from pure generational bigotry. This kind of loathing respected no one. Forgave no one.

"They ain't white," Ballard spewed, looking past me to a table of mixed race college students.

— *Deputy Chief Genevieve St. Pierre* —

SWEAT BLISTERED ACROSS MY FOREARMS and face. I twisted my torso to allow streams of moisture to trail beneath the bulletproof vest. The roux of baby powder and deodorant exploded from beneath the black nylon vest carrier.

The wind shifted directions and basted me in the odor of death. Covering my mouth beneath the rank aroma of my bulletproof vest became immediately preferable. Gagging, I flipped perspiration from my jostling hairline and moved from downwind.

"Detective Sergeant Brooks, what we know so far?" I was careful not to encroach upon the inner crime scene. The crew of detectives seemed impervious to the heat. Their saturated button-down shirts buzzed by blowflies as hunched backs and knees pressed against the filthy soil. Each meticulously focused on processing the muddy bog.

"Well, she wasn't killed here, but they wanted her found." Emotionless, the older black officer guided me through the subtle clues seasoned detectives spot immediately. "Trying to determine what those symbols knifed into her chest mean." His long arthritic index finger traced the air to mimic the images.

I hadn't noticed the carvings until he directed my attention to the dead woman's naked torso, but once I saw them my head began to swim. Bile burned up my esophagus. My past stint in CID exposed me to the horrid realities of what people did to each other. Solving these crimes was as much gut instinct as learned skill. Vomiting wasn't part of either.

"They?" I managed despite the acid that blistered over my tongue.

"The shoe prints close to the body are mashed together. Tough to tell how many, but look over here." Brooks led me to the edge of the clearing, next to a clump of marsh grass. "Four different sets of prints."

He swiped his forearm across before leaning towards me. "Chief, you okay? Looking green."

"Thanks Brooks. Not sure what's going on this morning. Guess I'm just tired of seeing so many mutilated children lately."

We walked back to my vehicle and I leaned against the front tire's quarter-panel. Running fingers through my matted hair, I struggled to breathe without an invading blowfly darting for my nose or mouth. I'd seen corpses before, worse than her, but there was a vibe in this parish—something bad was going down. It ran deeper than a murder.

This was a message.

I steeled myself, and looked up at the victim's body suspended over the pile of construction site debris. The killers had fashioned a cross from busted two by fours. Shoved it into the pile of dirt and cement. Nailed her palms into the wood. The only mercy was that she was already dead, evident because no blood had run from her wounds.

I turned my face into the mid-morning's glow. Around us in what had once been a swamp, remnants of wildlife and egrets reluctantly surrendered to new residential development. Cypress trees highlighted the marketing potential as out of town home seekers paid premium prices for that authentic Cajun community. Now, it was a killing field.

Susan Lambert eased across the soft terrain, nodding as she passed me. No need for words, her duties lay ahead. Detective Sergeant Brooks peeled his wet and soiled rubber gloves off to greet the coroner before she settled down to examine the body.

Why after twenty-five years am I still one of the first to leap out of bed at the late night wake up calls for the dead? There's no morbid curiosity in seeing dismembered corpses. The burden of all those bodies had taken a toll on my soul.

I scrubbed my face and dug deep to compose myself. I was here to oversee the investigation. Neither my weak stomach nor heavy heart was going to lead to someone paying for what they did.

Shoving my weight from the fender, I marched across the clearing to greet Doctor Lambert.

Chapter 29

— Detective Todd Stone —

GRAZA THREW HIS LOCKER DOOR open and glowered at me while I shrugged out of my civilian shirt. "Stone, who the hell's behind this? There's been five other Hispanic girls raped. Now it's escalated to murder. This is bullshit."

From the way he jerked at every officer who walked through the locker room, the senior detective was one step away from climbing the nearest water tower. Why the hell did I get stuck with this life-sucking cops?

The blanket of tattoos across his shoulders, back, and chest caught my eye. I had just the one ankle tattoo with my fraternity symbol. "Where'd you get all that ink?"

"From my youth. My *vida loca.*" He snapped the yellow cotton dress shirt across his shoulders and turned away.

Crazy life? I worked gel into my spiked haircut and tried not to roll my eyes. No way had this straight arrow ever done anything outside the line.

He angled the cell phone under the dimly lit fluorescent lights over the steam-moistened benches. His brows drew together at a text message, and he shoved the phone into his pocket.

"Strap up, we gotta go."

An artery pulsed down the right side of his neck. An explosion was imminent. Graza slammed his dented metal locker door shut, and then drove his shoulder into my left side as he demanded I hurry up.

"Watch where you going?" I rubbed my throbbing shoulder.

The detective turned in the doorway and glared back at me. "*Gringo*, you ain't gotta come. I doubt you give a shit about this Latina anyway." Both fists were balled tight as he punched the metal grating that covered the wooden locker room door on his way out.

— Detective Sergeant Earl Brooks —

YEA, HER BODY LOOKED LIKE shit, but it ain't my job to mourn them. Somebody enjoyed killing this chick, and now it was time to do what I do best—catch some killers' asses. Too fuckin' bad Deputy Chief St. Pierre felt like shit this morning and decided to stick this Detective Stone with me. He better just stay the fuck outta my way.

"Stone, props on that case with the tiger eating the dude's ass, but this is a different situation. Best you watch your step. These people might be your folk."

By the time we drove across town to the shithole hotel, the kid's grin was history. Detective Graza met us in the breezeway that reeked of urine and booze. Busted glass and condoms littered the ground, but Stone didn't seem to notice. One point for him. Places like this are reserved for the desperate and desolate. I guess every city has at least one. Ours has too many.

"Yo Sarge, you brought that dude? Thought I lost his ass in the locker room." Graza was straight up business, so it was messed up to see his attitude toward Stone. No time to play go-between. We had a vicious ass murder to solve.

"Stone's riding with me on this one. Why we here?" I sensed the problem, but I'd give Graza the benefit of being above it.

"I guess because I'm brown, they think I'm the only one that gives a shit about them. Probably right. Five others raped, and we ain't solved crap."

Graza's shoulders hunched over. It wasn't like him. His lean military fitness was still obvious though he'd been out for several years. He'd been institutionalized in the service, and that's how he operated—all about discipline. He stalked back and forth in the clammy outdoor hallway like a captive panther pacing its enclosure. I watched his frustration over a phone call that looked to not come.

Every few seconds he stole a glance at his cell phone and growled.

Here I am, a black man, who gotta help the Hispanic and white dude get along. How fucking ironic.

Stone, both hands in his pockets, strolled around the hotel's trashed courtyard. Them rookies all act the same—don't want to be bothered with details, just want the action.

"You bored son?" I asked him. "I can find you something to do." Stone smiled and shook his head.

I turned back to the Hispanic officer. "Graza, I'm gonna ask you again—why the fuck're we here? I've still got people at the dump site processing where the body was found, and another greenhorn at an autopsy with a real cop making sure she doesn't go black." I moved closer to him and spoke quietly, out of earshot of Stone.

"Sarge, I appreciate it, but there's some shit happening to my people and I feel like no one cares." His eyes misted.

"Did you know the girl from this morning?" I placed my hand on his rock-solid shoulder and felt the heat steaming through the light-colored button down.

"Officially, I don't know her because she's an illegal and that would mean I was derelict in my duties. Between us? Yes. I knew her and the family back home well."

He looked back down to his cellphone at a new text. "Finally. Room 117." He glanced up at a sign on the spray-painted wall that indicated the room was across the courtyard to the left of the drink machine.

I tightened my fingers on his shoulder. "Hold on son. Before you go running anywhere, let's chill. Fill us in. We're on the same side here."

A feral emptiness in his eyes dragged a shudder up my spine. This cat was on autopilot. It wasn't going to turn out anyway but shitty for whoever's behind this.

"She was last checked into room 117. The dude might still be there. Let's move." His left upper arm was hard as steel as he swung it around like a pitcher on the mound to break my grip on him.

Stone snaked between us with both hands held up. "Dude, chill out, will ya?"

I was still pretty tough for an old guy, but Graza shoved Stone into the brick wall so hard flecks of paint floated off of it.

"Sarge, keep this white bread the fuck out of my face."

Intensity was one thing, but attacking another officer was bullshit and means for dismissal. I swallowed, waiting for the adrenaline to dump. Emotion didn't help when chasing murderers.

Stone folded down to a crouch on the nasty-ass cement floor and blinked a few times.

"Graza, fucking check yourself or beat the street. Who the fuck you think you are, attacking another cop? We gonna catch these people, but not by fighting with each other."

"How the hell you act concerned now Sarge? This is the sixth Mexican girl attacked. Now you care? You don't have a clue what it's like trying to make it in this white man's world."

That damn fool just lost his mind.

"Graza, you're nuts to say that to Sarge." Stone pushed himself back off the ground.

"Why, because I'm black?" I shot Stone a warning look.

"No, because you're the Sergeant."

Naiveté had its good points. I turned back to Graza. "Son, let's walk to 117. Calm down in the process." I patted the back of his neck and we walked.

Chapter 30
— Sheriff James Walker —

COUNCILMAN ANTHONY CHIASSON HAD DISRESPECTED my son's memory, claimed I was the cause of violence in this parish, blamed me for his idiot brother's car crash, and now, was calling for my termination before the parish council.

If only I cared enough to give a crap about the last three. Not so with his comment in the office about my boy—I'd ached since those words spit from his cracked bacon-like lips. The jerk always wreaked of old alcohol and barroom ashtrays. I had the patience of Job, but Chiasson's ignorance had punched his time on life's clock.

Stretching my legs as I slumped onto the painted wooden bench out behind the seafood restaurant, I watched for the alligators to resurface. My face met the sun and I let the sweat roll behind my head and into my ears. I found it hard to concentrate this morning. I needed to escape, to keep my head above water—it wasn't working.

The detectives were still on this morning's murder, but my mind fixed on young Jackson Andrews' body hung upside down from that meat hook. My heart's thumping against its chest was a shallow, deliberate beat. I wouldn't have been surprised if it had stopped.

Alone, I wasn't concerned about being bothered, so I allowed the streams of tears to run from the outside corners of my eyes until they mixed with the sweat already trailing inside my shirt collar. Lost in a mix of broken emotions, the warm air-dried lines of salty residue across my cheeks.

The deep bellowing grew louder with a sound like wood slowly dragged over concrete. Eyes sealed shut toward the sun—I rolled my neck over the back of the green bench and nearly shit myself. An alligator, easily twelve feet long was perched mere feet from my cowhide boots.

He hissed as the trap of teeth cranked open. You wouldn't think an eight hundred pound tank of scale and muscle was quick. You'd be wrong, and dead. I flinched as my palms pressed against the bench's heat and I gently tried pulling my legs away from him. The reptile slowed and groaned—looked like he was steadying to lunge. I knew he'd easily tower over the bench's height, so pulling my feet up wasn't an option. Concern caused my thighs to weigh like cement pillars—I couldn't spring backward if I wanted to, so I eased my left hand behind my back for the revolver.

The bouncing object caught my eye. It obviously caught the gator's attention too. I looked onto the ground and saw about ten giant sized marshmallows laid around my boots. The gator turned for the last marshmallow so I waited to roll off the seat.

"What's the matter, Walker? Almost became a snack?" Tony Chiasson sneered without remorse for the danger he'd placed me in. I still wasn't free to move—otherwise I'd have planted that fat ass on his back.

"Chiasson, be careful what you ask for. You come looking for a fight without a clue who you're screwing with. Big Johnny thought he wanted the same thing and look where he's at." I split vision between the less-threatening gator and the always-dangerous snake.

"We gonna take care of you trying to kill my brother at this week's council meeting. You ain't fit to be Sheriff of this here parish. You fucking worthless James Walker."

I covered my mouth and nose at the stench of the restaurant's garbage dumpster that bathed Chiasson as it fanned into the marsh. He didn't flinch at the smell—actually—he looked like he belonged in the mist of it. Chiasson's fists remained pressed against the gut that poured over his belt. Dulled eyes squinted under sun-bleached eyebrows as his reddened face defied the sun.

"I'm a damn good lawman Chiasson. Just ask your son when he gets outta prison in ten or so years." I stepped inches from his face. Just a short shit, I looked down onto his fat round head waiting for him to react. Anything and I'd bury his ass in the marsh.

"Your days are numbered lawman. You'll be lucky to find a job at all once Tom Roberts gets through with you." He avoided eye contact.

"What's that idiot got to do with this?" My eyes were glued to his hands—*please make one move toward me.*

"Jewel won't be governor forever. Only reason your murdering ass is in that seat." Opening and clinching my fists, a sheen of moisture covered my skin as I felt the heat of my heart rate rising. My chest muscles twitched as anger vibrated through me—the switch was beginning to flip. I had to get a handle on my emotions.

"Tony, you'll be lucky to survive your next election. I'm gonna bury your ass every chance I get." My spine was aflame with fury. I pumped my fist harder while my breathing narrowed. His face reflected he knew it was much more than politics.

"You better cool it Sheriff. You're an out of control maniac." His hands shielded his face from the sun as crow's feet exploded beyond his reddened eyes.

"Cool it? Chiasson, you're disrespect of my son Wyatt was the final straw. I'm done with the diplomacy as far as you're concerned." I still wasn't sure whether I'd just talk or attack. My body pulsed for the latter.

"Angie, hey what time y'all opening?" The female employee then called back to Chiasson from the kitchen's back door. That lucky son of a bitch. I shook my head—how could I've let my anger take control without looking for anyone else in the area? I was a ticking time bomb, *I need help.*

"This isn't over Chiasson. I got your shit bag brother, you're dirt bag son and I'll get you." My tongue scraped across arid lips as I tried calming myself. I wanted to strike him so bad—I could just imagine the fat flesh folding beneath my fist. I backed toward the bench to pick up my cell phone and keys, but never took an eye off him.

"Whatever asshole. You got my son. I got yours. Now take that picture off your bookshelf. It's just damn creepy. The kid is dead." Then he guffawed.

What the hell did that mean?

Hands white knuckled the chipped green paint covering the old wooden bench. It prevented my failing knees from crashing to the concrete. Again, I became aware of the sun's intensity.

Some of the wait staff and kitchen crew walked toward me with hands full of marshmallows as I inhaled through my nose to maintain control—my grin was plastered as they walked past me and to the hissing sounds of a still hungry gator.

Chapter 31
— Sheriff James Walker —

TRICEPS FLEXED TO REPOSITION MY body. Usually comfortable, the executive leather seat provided nothing more than aggravation. Today had been a challenge, and trying to settle behind my desk was not any easier.

A flush of uneasy swept over me as Deputy Chief Genevieve St. Pierre, Sergeant Brooks and Detectives Graza and Stone piled in and jockeyed for position around the conference table. Miss Martha peeked into the office to motion that Doctor Susan Lambert was on the phone.

"Hi Susan. Thanks for calling in. We're all sitting down to start the briefing." I drove my heel into the hard plastic mat under the chair as I realized I referred to her by first name in front of my staff. I caught Genevieve's look as she mouthed *Susan?*

"Brooks, start from the top." Robotic, I felt detached from the others.

"Sure thing boss man. Maria Sanchez, twenty-three years old, illeg.... I mean undocumented worker. Unmarried, no known kids. Unknown family in the States, but lived between hotels and houses." The supervisor was no-nonsense. His correction of illegal caught my attention. There was a nasty tension in the room and it was obviously affecting him.

"Was she a prostitute?" I asked.

Brooks shot a glance to his right, so I slipped a look to Graza. He'd twisted his fingers into knots as his forearms flexed beneath steady streams of exasperated exhales.

"Gunny, you okay?" I asked Graza.

"Yes sir Sheriff. I'm anxious to get back onto the streets and catch these gringos." Disapprovingly, Brooks shook his head at Graza's response. A secret finger across his throat and I knew what the problem was.

"Graza, I've got another assignment for you. Let's have the Sarge and Stone take it from here. If you hear of anything, let the Sarge know. Understand?"

"But sir. You taking me off this shit? Who's going to communicate with my people?" Graza stood up slamming his fists together.

"First off son, I'm going to caution you to watch your language. Next, I just gave you an order." I hated to pull rank, but he was on a violent revenge binge and no way was I allowing anything to get out of control.

"Whatever you say sir."

"Gunny—I trust you and I need you. Brooks and Stone will handle this. I've got a special assignment that requires your skill." His posture snapped back to rigid as he finally made eye contact. "Yes sir. Understood."

The heavy wooden door eased shut and we resumed. "I apologize, but we're not going to have race revenge play a part in this investigation."

"Sheriff, actually we have a suspect and he's not Caucasian." Doctor Lambert's voice sang through the speaker. Brooks' eyes brightened as he nodded in agreement. St. Pierre set her cell phone on the table and now leaned into the loop. Clearing my throat and again shuffling my ass over the leather, I nodded to Brooks.

"Seems our girl was earning extra cash while on extended stay in the U.S. She'd just finished with a customer in room one seventeen and bolted for the ice machine." Brooks' usually colorful descriptions were tempered for the civilian on the hard line, but I got the point.

"What led us to him? Forensics?" I felt myself reattaching to the scenario despite my emotions running wild as I glanced at my son's picture on the bookshelf.

"Ms. Sanchez left with just a t-shirt on. Seems her customer's *seed* landed along the hallway. Since housekeeping is a fantasy in that dive, the CSI techs located the trail. A Rapid DNA Analysis through CODIS confirmed the sample's match with a known offender who'd been through intake at the jail five months ago. Buccal swab got his ass."

"CODIS?" Stone asked.

St. Pierre straightened from her hunched lean, "Todd, it's the FBI's combined DNA index system. I trust you know that everyone processed at the jail is swabbed for a DNA sample. It creates a database." She slung her head in disappointment with the young detective's question.

"Stone, its new technology, but you do need to get up to speed on resources like that. Okay son?" It was no time to gang up on the kid—we had to stick together to solve this mess. His sheepish smile and avoidance of St. Pierre showed me there would be damage to undue later. For now, there was work to do, and Brooks was ahead of the game.

"ATM surveillance from across the highway showed a vehicle matching the one registered to Tommy Chang pull into the hotel's parking lot." Brooks continued.

"How can we be sure it was Chang's vehicle from that distance?" I rubbed my eyes to feel the tracks of sweat and tears from earlier.

"The horney bastard ran across the highway to get cash from the ATM. His missing teeth and tats are all clear as a bell in the camera. Guess he was using his master criminal mind when he checked in by paying cash and using the name John Chang."

"Wraps tight. Thanks." I thought it'd be tougher than this. Patting my palms against both thighs, I rocked to stand up.

"Oh, and he used a stolen debit card to get the cash." Stone added.

"Let's get cuffs on his murdering butt and wrap it up." I was relieved. The council meeting was this week and I didn't need another death hanging over my head.

"Gents and Genevieve. I don't mean to rain on your parade, but we've got a problem. My autopsy shows there were at least four assailants. Unless Chang set her up for the taking, he wasn't the only one. Right off—bite marks and blood typing are leaning to multiple attackers. Sorry, but this isn't over." Doctor Lambert said apologetically.

Brooks bobbed his head as his eyes fluttered. He looked exhausted but not defeated. Around long enough to know the first forty-eight hours' value to solving a homicide, time ticked and I'd just reassigned the most useful resource for breaking the case.

"Sheriff, she wasn't killed in room one seventeen. Sex yes—murder no." Brooks stood to stretch.

"Either way I want this Chang picked up. He's our best lead, so squeeze him till the truth oozes from his credit card stealing ass." They knew their jobs—a nod from me was their cue.

A compression against my insides caused lightheadedness. The ebb and flow of homicide investigations are filled with promises and dead-ends. Coupled with my gator and Chiasson encounter, this day didn't hold promise for anything getting better.

Chapter 32

— *Lieutenant Remi Leblanc* —

NEVER HEARD OF TOMMY CHANG, but if Buck wanted the red dot on his ass, that dude was as good as delivered. My word to Sergeant Brooks was that I'd have him by the end of the day. We went back through the years and spent a few months on the same patrol hitch. Until I disappeared undercover that is.

I pulled the Task Force off a drug surveillance operation to beat the streets until Chang was ours. Just after dark, Agent Blue pinched a street snitch with a dime bag of weed. Typical rats, he rolled over on his homeboy—so much for loyalty.

Seems Chang got into a scrape with some white guys that turned into rounds of bullets exchanged. The snitch claimed Chang was held up in a club safe house until the heat cooled over the shooting. He also said the dude had an arsenal just in case the Arians came knocking. I'd activate SWAT once confirmed.

"Agent Blue, get this rat wired up and ready to go into the hideout. I want conversation with Chang before we apply for a search warrant." I saw the small-framed drug user begin to shiver. Placing my hand on his shoulder and the other under his scabbed chin, I easily craned his head back until he looked me in the eyes. "It's gonna be okay. You ready to do this?" I reassured him.

"Man, fuck you. I ain't getting killed over a dime bag of weed. Fucking Asian Triad is crazy violent. Find another rat and take me to the hole." His body turned to stone as strings of spit bounced off his already bloodied lips.

"I understand your fear, I really do. Jail's not an option for you. See, I made a promise to deliver Tommy Chang by tonight. Promises don't break, but your body will." My hand slid from his shoulder and around his throat. I tightened until he realized his air was becoming scarce. I never blinked—he was scared shitless and for good reason. High stakes permitted collateral damage, and he was expendable. His change of heart was sudden and expected.

"Good decision. You'll be home before you know it. Unless Chang sniffs you out as a snitch." Agent Blue added.

Agent Blue pulled the small electronic device from a hard plastic carrying case. Changing the watch-sized battery, he activated the body wire and tested it to ensure surveillance teams picked up the sound. Agent Blue slid the *bug* into a buttonhole on the snitch's shirt. It was critical to monitor every word of their meeting.

The undercover teams sped away toward the club's hide out. I called Judge Boudreaux and told him to expect a search warrant within the hour. We'd hit the target before the ink dried. The old judge was not enthused, but seemed to be more of a result from his nightly liquor binge than concern for the judicial bench. Poor dude, he'd sign anything I raised my hand and swore to.

Deputy Chief St. Pierre was notified and promised to call Buck. One more call to make. The administrative stuff sucked, but I'd learned the importance of communications from Buck. He also taught me the life and death values of keeping other people's shit secret.

Chapter 33
— Sergeant RJ Ruiz —

IF I HEARD ANOTHER COMMENT about light duty I was gonna throat punch somebody. I didn't spend three tours through the Middle East to sit at home with a stich in my side. Besides, there aren't many female SWAT Operators in this game and I wasn't riding the bench while they snatched a killer.

Biting down on my smile, I forced a facial expression to form a concentrated scowl. My insides pulsated as Remi reached across my shoulder toward the paper map. He pointed out Tommy Chang's location, but all I could do was close my eyes and inhale his scent. Rugged and overworked, Remi didn't metro himself up with colognes or gels. He was natural, and the aroma of *badass* was intoxicating.

A quick shake of my head to refocus and I was back on apprehending Tommy Chang. Remi might've lit my wick, but business was my candle. Hell, I was stuck in the desert with a six hundred soldier fighting battalion and never let one of those troops invade me.

After briefing my unit, I walked away to reflect on the minutest details of the raid. I hadn't realized I'd been picking at a cuticle on my left thumb and caused it to bleed. Maybe I wasn't ready to come back to duty just yet. I licked the spotted trail of blood over my knuckle.

Just covering the bases I calmed myself with that thought—though I knew there was more. I ripped, and then reattached the Velcro straps on my tactical body armor at least a dozen times. Fidgeting with the knobs, it was difficult to manipulate my fingers over the tactical radio.

"Where the hell is that map? Who took the map?" my eyes bounced over the sea of drab olive green battle dress uniforms, black balaclava Nomex hoods and Kevlar. Clearing my throat and swallowing often I sucked in air and began to ask one last time. The slight pressure under my triceps muscles and over my bicep diverted the attention.

"RJ, you okay baby?" Remi's eyes were easy and non-adversarial. His towering figure shadowed my reaction from the others. I wanted to fall into his chest and have him hold me—protect me. Licking my lips, I felt electric near him, though returning to our past together wasn't possible.

From the front passenger's seat of the second panel van, the moist late-night air coated my gloved hand as it rode the wind through the open window. My mind drifted back to a time before this job, before my military deployment—back to a time when I felt confident and protected.

Going to visit grandparents in my daddy's old pickup truck, my small hand would sail through the same humid air as I imagined flying an airplane. Now, I just imagined I'd survive. I pulled my arm back through the window—no time for childish memories.

Placing my palm against the rigid steel trauma plate sitting inside the nylon vest carrier covering my heart, I was thankful Billy Hale's bullet struck it instead of me. Wrenched with most deep breaths, my ribs relived the concussion of the projectile's impact. This was no time to self-assess—team depended on me.

"Three blocks out go stealth." I radioed to the other personnel transports. The cavalry decelerated to a sneak as we turned off Canal Street onto Thomas Drive. The scene changed immediately. I pressed my ear for sounds of dogs barking, tires squealing, guns firing or phones ringing to give away our approach.

"Randy, back off—you're too close to the other van. Why don't you drop the NVG's?" He knew his job, I was clearly nervous.

Each vehicle's kill switch deactivated every light on the unit. Since local gang bangers had shot out most streetlights, we traveled through a murky ink black night. I heard the familiar zing and hum of the night vision activating, and then made out Randy's sheepish grin under the eerie green hue of the goggles.

Throbbing ran through my thighs and into my gut until I was cricked over. Unsure whether I had to crap or was just anxious, I tried making small chatter with the team located in the back of the van. No one was interested in talking. Stopping at Thomas Drive and Crestview, the vehicles silently idled.

"Go left." Remi, in the lead unit suggested from over the radio.

"Negative. Right on Crestview until the left at Mahoney Street." I'd memorized the map.

"Check your scope—armed spotters at three o'clock." I fumbled for the activation switch, but soon eased the second-generation night scope over the lip of the van's window. *Damn, I would'a led us right into an ambush.*

"Good call Remi—go left." Breaths caught in my chest while I swallowed repeatedly after acknowledging him.

"One block out, lock and load." I whispered quickly, and then pressed my toes against the floorboard while cracking my knuckles and rocking back and forth in the cloth covered seat.

"Snipers, report." My focus returned and giving orders became smooth like butter. I was back where I best—where the shit hit the fan.

"Sniper-3, eyes on at one–four corner of the building. One armed target. Smoking right now. Weapon just set on ground. Good time to move." Agent Jones' words were spoken softly. The former Force Recon Marine and Task Force Agent, was also an outstanding SWAT sniper.

"Perimeter units, report out if need to change mission approach." I asked.

"Armed guards on Crestview are in custody." An unknown voice quaked—he sounded shaken by the conflict.

"Ruiz, my team will take foot and down target on smoke break to clear entrance for your unit." Remi's voice never changed in all the years I'd known him. Never stressed or hurried—always under control and soft spoken.

Flipping on the NVG's as I hopped out of the unit, my body moved clumsily as the greenish light led me through the unfamiliar territory. I quickly regained my stealth as the unit of highly skilled SWAT operators silently mustered behind the three bulletproof shields assigned to each squad for the approach to the house.

No longer tense, my mind washed with a thousand different scenarios and tactical decisions if things went wrong. Either way, I was mentally prepared to lead my team through this.

"Sniper-3 to Command-1. Exterior lookout is down. Clear to move." Agent Jones' sharp and sure radio transmission was like a 5k starter's pistol.

"Roger that Sniper-3." I acknowledged.

Without words, I squeezed the Operator in front of me that it was time to execute the mission. Noise discipline was critical.

My thighs singed with lactic acid from the crouched position behind the Alpha Team's point man carrying the ballistic shield. The automatic submachine gun held with muzzle on target, slightly bounced as I cat walked across the uneven, garbage strewn front yard leading to Chang's clubhouse. I felt the gunshot's injury to my chest beginning to ache—adrenaline and purpose would ease this pain.

The boarded up house sat in what was once a quiet residential neighborhood of middle class, single story homes. Original homeowners died off and their kids, uninterested in maintaining the family home, rented to transients or abandoned them all together. What remained was the crap hole we were maneuvering through.

Bravo Team fanned out at a forty-five degree angle from the left side of the front door's fatal funnel. My team angled from the right side of the same door. Operators focused their weapons on assigned windows, corners and perimeter.

Charlie Team slipped up next to the door behind their ballistic shield to adhere an explosive charge to the door's lock.

"Fire in the hole, fire in the hole, fire in the hole." I whispered before mashing the detonation pin. I glanced to see Operators tucking their bodies behind each other. This tactical train was ready to roll and Tommy Chang was its first stop.

A brilliantly violent explosion of light and the crunching of metal losing its ability signaled the next phase. Like magic, an opening appeared into this fortress and we were about to close the curtain. Seamless in motion, an Operator moved to the left side of the opening with the flashbang's pin already pulled.

The heavy metal casing clanked around on the room's floor before the flashbang's concussion of blinding bright light and deafening sound ignited. The bang's effect would temporarily incapacitate anyone in that room. Just enough time for my team to glide into place. Bravo Team flowed through the door without sound to secure it.

"Room clear. Moving." Snapped over the tactical headset.

The sound of two more heavy metal casings and two more violent flashbang explosions signaled Bravo Team was on the move and time for Alpha Team to occupy the first secured room.

"Room clear. Moving." Bravo Team leader sounded.

My team filled in once Bravo Team moved.

"Entering." Charlie Team leader was now inside the target structure. It was a full house of controlled chaos and coordinated motion.

The rhythm of clank, bang, "Moving" continued from room to room until Bravo Team leader radioed, "One in custody–target secured."

"Brooks notified" snuck across the airwave and Remi asked Agent Smith drive the Task Force panel van into the front yard for extraction.

Chapter 34
— Sheriff James Walker —

SLEEPLESS, I GREETED THE DAY shift during their briefing. The Patrol Division lieutenant invited me to join them, though my focus was elsewhere. I sat in the back of the squad room as committed deputies discussed vital assignments, community involvement projects and last night's SWAT raid.

I shuddered my shoulders at the news. I'd forgotten to check my messages. Hands clamped together, I tried avoiding conversation after the briefing. I felt myself sitting unnaturally still with my lips pursed tight. A sense of anxiety was building as I imagined the results of last night's arrest warrant op. Hell, I didn't even know if they'd captured Chang.

Peering through my office windows, I saw Detective Graza's police cruiser pull into the lot. Shoving the chair against the credenza, I slipped past the radio room to intercept him while outside.

"Good morning Detective." His dropped shoulders hitched at my greeting.

"Hello Sheriff. Ya'll break the case yet?" His eyes watered with what looked like an inward focus. He broke eye contact.

"Son, I'm not gonna blow sunshine up your ass. This is the deal— you're not going off on some holy war against white people because this friend of yours got killed. You may not want to admit it, but she was a prostitute. She put herself in a dangerous situation and a horrible thing happened. The Asian guy, Chang was victimizing her also. So drop the race hating and get your mind focused on solving crime and protecting the people—every color of them."

"Sheriff, Chang was her *novio*. She was pregnant for him. They had to sneak to see each other because her family threatened to bring her back to Guadalajara." His head dropped with either disappointment in me, or to spare me seeing his grief. However, I'd possibly screwed this case up.

"Graza, I'm sorry."

I saw the muscles clench along his jaw line as he planted his feet in an exaggerated stance. He inhaled deeply through his nose and his chiseled torso expanded. He extended his right hand, "Thank you Sheriff. Your apology mean everything."

Meeting his grip with equal force I pulled him close. Craning over, I whispered into his ear. I saw the frissons rise along the skin below his ear. He was refocused and I knew he was the man for this mission.

"Chiasson's every move?" He mouthed.

"Every single one. Don't breathe a word to anyone." His alert gaze never broke stare. My chagrin towards Chiasson was obvious, but at this point I didn't give a shit—he'd be made to pay.

I returned to my office to await the detectives briefing.

I SCRUBBED THE BACK OF my aching neck, and then returned to cramming files around my desk while waiting for Detective Stone to arrive. Meanwhile Doctor Lambert's call rang over the desk line, but I wasn't overly anxious to have this discussion with her.

"Good morning Doctor Lambert. I'm waiting on the staff to get together so we can start the homicide briefing." Twisting the coiled phone line around my fingers, I wasn't sure how to breach the topic of her autopsy results.

"Buck, I do something wrong?" Her voice raised an octave—I clamped my teeth together and knew she was aware I knew—she had to be.

"Susan, it's just us on the call. What happened with the autopsy results?" I flexed my fist to squeeze the ballpoint pen I'd been chewing on.

"Oh, the pregnancy?" I arched up unsure of how to take the casualness in her tone.

"Yes Susan. The pregnancy." Filling my lungs with cleansing air, my brow cinched in hopes of an answer that wouldn't ruin my respect for her.

"Not sure, early first trimester, just didn't think it was vital at this point. Because..." *Damn it.* My thumb pressed the ink pen to the point of snapping.

"Because she's an illegal?" I'd blown my cool and spouted what I feared.

"No, because you had a suspect, I still hadn't completed the final report out, and because the stupid detective you sent threw up all over my lab." Slapping my palm against the desk, I'd made an ass of myself with that assumption.

"I'm sorry Susan."

"You should be Sheriff. I thought you knew me better than that. It's very disappointing." I set the handset down after the clanking of her phone rung in my ear.

The rush of humiliation weighed the back of my chair against the credenza. The clock across the office said eight after eight—couldn't be right—they knew my obsession with punctuality. Obsession?

My left hand wound behind to feel the slight bulge of the stainless steel snub-nosed revolver wedged between my back and belt. Working from this desk all these months and I never stopped to really think through what happened that late night.

A prickling across my scalp signaled the flush of emotion bubbling subsurface. Feeling like I wanted to bolt from this chair, I forced myself to stay put and think it through. I glanced at my office door and knew my pasted smile wouldn't fool the deputies who were already late.

Those crazy bastards almost killed me that night—right where I sat between the desk and credenza. How could I have been so careless as to let Gill Gaudet trap my weapon under his shoe? My hand trembled as I struggled to steady it while swiping the moisture that exploded across my forehead. Sitting straight up in the reclined chair, my gut turned over as my heart flipped inside my chest.

I trusted Lucy Bates, and that's why I was blinded to her evil, murdering ass. Hated to put a bullet in her face, but that knife wasn't stopping before it slid right through me.

"Buck, you okay? What the hell you doing?" Deputy Chief St. Pierre's blank expression surprised me. What shocked me more was that I'd unholstered the revolver from behind my back and had it pointed beneath the desk. I was reliving that moment—and never realized it.

"I'm still not over this, am I?" I said as she shook her head side-to-side. Her dark eyes darted to the detectives approaching behind her. Hurriedly, I shoved the revolver under my right hamstring before the investigators entered the office.

Biting my lip to stop the verbal bashing over their being late, I had my own demons to deal with. Punctuality wasn't one of them.

"Brooks, go with what you got." I placed my hands atop my thighs. They quaked uncontrollably.

"Sir, the SWAT raid was clockwork. I'd say we woke up the neighborhood, but they're immune to flash bangs and violence." His usual sturdy posture had sloped while the puffy circles beneath his eyes twitched.

"Good effort from all. Brooks, why don't you get some rest and let the Lieutenant tidy things up." Brooks was the kind of detective who honored his oath and saw rest as a sign of weakness.

"With all due respect Sir, I've got a 10-15 in the holding cell waiting to be processed to the jail. I've been up all night writing the arrest report. This is no time to bring in the second string." The battles with his supervisor had become legendary, but his work ethic was impeccable.

"How about Stone, doesn't he know enough to carry it forward until you get back?"

"Seriously? He's an unsigned free agent. Lucky to make it outta camp." Stone reared up to protest, but Brooks' red eyes eliminated the fight out of anything Stone might have offered.

"I'm going to speak straight to you both and I want you to hear me out." Their eyes wriggled to stay open against the burden of fatigue. "I've got serious doubts this is our man." My body continued to jerk with the anxiety over hiding the revolver beneath my right thigh as the men first entered the room.

"Are you freaking shitting me boss?" Brooks hutched out of his chair. Stone was trapped between indecision and uniformed, so he sat back down. "I busted my ass to crack this kill, and it's a solid case." Brooks protested.

"Brooks, no doubt you did and I'm always proud of your work. I have information that he's not the killer or rapist. He had sex with her, but consensual." My lips were moving, but my brain walked to keep up. "I'm inclined to let Tommy Chang go to be on the safe side."

"Safe side? That fucking guy raped Maria Sanchez and we letting him go?" Detective Stone's immature passion burst across the room. I allowed it to process since I wasn't one hundred percent sure. Though it was the right thing to do.

"Buck, you know the hell you going to catch from the public. Mostly from that prick Tony Chiasson once he hears you set a murdering rapist free into the community?" St. Pierre's concerns already bounced around my head—probably why I'd been up all morning and arrived early. My gut told me it was the right thing to do. Gripping my snub-nose as I tried reassuring the deputies, my heart thumped in grief for the girl and maybe the community. I hope I'm right.

Chapter 35

— *Lieutenant Remi Leblanc* —

THIS WAS THE FIRST TIME Buck had been to the warehouse since taking the interim role as Bayou Parish Sheriff. He'd spent a good part of his career in this dump. His absence was a sign he trusted my work, though he also needed a professional distance from the nontraditional means used by the Task Force in solving cases.

Hearing the echo from his truck's door slamming shut inside the sally port, I hurriedly unlocked the access door to greet him. No words were spoken in this space until entering the isolation of my office.

"Buck, this is a first. Crap must be loaded to hit the fan." It was odd sitting behind what was once his desk, so I slipped around to the old cloth chair next to his.

"Too many irons in the fire Remi. Time to start poking the embers. Putting heat on asses to get them off of mine." He didn't have to explain—only ask.

"You know Big Johnny Chiasson has been patched up and back at the jail? When the time is right, I'll pull him and get more about your boy's murder."

"Remi, thanks. It's torn me up for five years and I don't see ever getting over it. I'm a shell." His hands shook as he switched between wiping them on his jeans and hiding them under his armpits.

"We snatched the guy in the murder case last night, but Chang just doesn't seem like the killing type. Lots of rambling in the van ride over, though nothing said to pin. More *rico sauvé* than a killer. Seems too weak to make that commitment." Wasn't sure what I said, but Buck's torso collapsed onto his elbows that pressed into his thighs.

"That's what I thought too. Graza said Tommy Chang and the girl were engaged. She was pregnant. Lambert confirmed the pregnancy and will match it for paternity." Reaching across the armrest I patted Buck on his forearm, he was ice cold and moisture coated his skin.

"I want this case solved now. I'm releasing Tommy Chang and don't need to set off a firestorm of panic. Chiasson is waiting for the council meeting to blame his brother's injures on me. I don't need him lying about releasing a murderer. Put this thing to bed Remi."

"Letting him walk? What about the stolen credit card?" I wanted to offer him an alternative to release, but avoided insulting him.

"We got bigger fish to fry Remi. Understand me?" The loose skin beneath his jaw shook.

Dropping my eyes, I preferred to not see my boss looking desperate, but what I wouldn't look upon, I couldn't avoid hearing. His voice shook like a nursing home resident. I've known this man my whole life, and I'd never seen him defeated.

"Who do I work with on this? Heard Brooks is doing a good job but fading fast."

"Keep it in house, smallest circle the quickest result. Go off radar— I don't give a shit. Get it done Remi." Ghostly pale, I hated seeing my friend and mentor in this condition.

"Buck, do you trust me?"

"Yes Remi."

"Go home, stash your weapons, and lay your butt on the bed and go to sleep." His fingertips were holding onto the rope that would either pull him through or hang him.

"I'm fine. They need me out there." Buck grunted until coming to an upright stance.

"If you trust me, then listen. You're no good to anyone right now my brother. Heard you played out the Gaudet/Bates shooting this morning. You're not over it yet. We need you whole Buck." He threw his hand up over his shoulder with flippant fingers as he shuffled the soles of his worn leather boots back toward his truck.

"Genevieve run her mouth? I'll address that with her later." He stormed through the narrow hall.

"It's out of concern Buck. We need you—that's all."

"Pull the gate will ya?" he demanded.

I repeated myself over the clanking ching-a-ling as the sally port's metal door clutched open and then closed.

NEVER PLAY YOUR CARDS FOR someone else—unless you owe who you are to that someone. This was gonna suck, and hurt even worse. I'd taken my beatings over past decisions, and knew this would put me back in harms way.

Splashing hot water against my skin wasn't doing the trick. Brushing my palm across the steamed up glass, I blinked at the man avoiding me in the mirror.

Ink needled across my torso read like the road map of my life, my mistakes and my attempts to make things right. There was a long family history of piss poor decisions made. The swastikas were one of them.

My home was way out in the country, and except for the dogs roaming the forty arpents—it was quiet and visitor free. The land had been in the family for generations. Granddad said the original Nova Scotians settled here after exiled during Canada's Great Expulsion and the Seven Years War.

Even the land was cursed it seemed. Parting the blinds in the bathroom, my chest tightened to see the skeletons of the fire pit not far from where the old church once stood. I recall many a night as a young boy watching the congregation of men arrive.

As a child, the blazing fire licked the shadows across the marsh, and was curiously fascinating. My teenage years saw that same flame as power over something I didn't understand, and feared—diversity.

It wasn't until my dad and uncle died I realized the brainwashing. Years back I closed off the property, tried my best to burn down the *church* and used a backhoe to fill the fire pit.

Closing my eyes, the crime scene photographs exploded in my mind. The deep carvings in Maria Sanchez's chest were familiar. My left pectoral muscle flinched as I traced my fingers over the permanent whelps that branded me as a young boy. Her's were the same ritual markings I got the night I finished my initiation into the ring of fire. Try as I might to cover them with tattoos, they still bled through— mostly on the inside.

When did they turn to rape and murder?

"Hello?" the angry voice answering my call resounded through my past.

"Ya'll gone too far." Few words were required, but the point was made.

"Got no control over the Southern Guard. Group on the edge, you know that boy. Where you got your start." He still knew how to inflict pain. Even after my daddy died, this bastard saw to it that I suffer the way he thought real men should.

"We never killed nobody, nor raped. Who's the Guard's leader now? He's got to be stopped." I regretted the words as they escaped over my lips—I knew the code for confidentiality. I also knew the consequences for breaking it.

This old timer didn't know I was there that night he and the White Is Power leadership accused my daddy and his brother of being FBI informants. My father was no angel, but he sure the hell wasn't no rat.

"You there boy? WIP let you walk because ya daddy died with dignity. Don't disgrace him by asking shit like that. You know the consequences." Even now, his voice struck a cold spike through my spine. This man was evil incarnate and I honestly didn't want to fuck with him.

"Dignity? You accused him of something he didn't do, then

whipped him till skin bare. Man lay in bed for weeks with his skeleton exposed until he had the strength to crawl to the gun cabinet and take his own life." I beat my fist against the hot air as the towel dropped from around my waist.

"True son, but he died with his mouth shut. Unlike your uncle."

No apologies from this man were expected, but he should be made to pay for his sins. *Why am I so damn afraid of this devil?*

My breath was cut short and heart pounded as I spoke to him. I tried walking it off, to get some blood flowing maybe. My adrenaline was spiking as childhood memories reigned terror over me.

Walking in front of the closet door's mirror I saw my naked self, exposed for who I was. I was still that chicken-shit little boy peeking over the back of his daddy's truck bed. I'd hidden under the crab traps, but was where I belonged—in the shadows and afraid. Hell, I was even too frightened to say no when they initiated me with that glowing hot cattle branding iron.

"I want whoever raped and murdered Maria Sanchez. You can keep your club in the shadows, but this shit went too far. Someone's gonna pay." I swallowed hard to force those words out. My heart ripped through my chest.

Pinching the wet towel between my toes and lifting it back into my hand, I felt the urge to apologize and hope for the best—but not this time. Screw being afraid. This was for Buck Walker. This was for me, my dad and all the stupid things my family's done.

"Remi?" He baited me with his tone.

"Yes sir?"

"You and Walker better watch your backs." Click.

Chapter 36
— Sheriff James Walker —

THE ROOM WAS PITCH EXCEPT for the lax light peeking through the open window's blind. Running my hands along the wall I froze on the light switch. Just thinking about entering the office snarled my stomach. Lost gazing at the desk, my feet felt cemented to the floor. I opted for the conference room instead.

"Buck, what'cha doing in here? I'm sorry, never mind. We got troubles." St. Pierre looked drained.

"What now Genevieve?" Her lips parted, and head nodded with a thumb jabbing over her shoulder.

"Looks like half the town is out front. Calling for your job. Media vans rolling across the highway, got traffic all backed up." Her shoulders slumped and arms crossed, words seemed to compete with swallowed breaths for space.

"Well, no ones talking to the media, so they can just go on back to the station." I'd had more than enough of the false accusations, but the court of public opinion was no place to try this case.

"You might not talk to them but Anita, Councilman Chiasson and get this—Emory Ballard are at the tip of the spear." Disgust, contempt and dread avalanched over me as I caved back into the thinly padded conference room chair.

"This shit ends right now. Get Remi LeBlanc on the phone."

Chapter 37
— Sheriff James Walker —

"WYATT CASH WALKER." THERE I said it.

The name hadn't crossed my lips in nearly five years. Clammy, cold skin felt on fire. Kind of concerned me. I knew my days were numbered until I either accepted my son's murder, or I punished the world because of it. My mind wouldn't suppress it much longer.

A misty haze off the bog allowed a reprieve from the day's coming heat. I sensed a force pressing my spirit. It drove me from sleep before dawn. It led me here. Shaded by a cluster of oak trees, Spanish moss danced in the slight breeze, so I closed my eyes.

Running my hand over the treated wood tree house, I could still hear his laughter. Lifting my unshaven face to the green and grey canopy of tree cover, I pressed to picture his smile. Time reduced the vivid facial details to a silhouette. I squeezed my eyelids harder. Still, only his shock of curly hair and a red t-shirt with shorts were all I mustered.

Rubbing my hand over the blackened left thumbnail, I tried to smile about the time we dragged lumber out here to build his fort. Compassionate, Wyatt loved nature. He even kissed the thumb I smashed with that hammer. I'd give ten smashed fingers to have one small kiss again.

Pressing both hands into my eyes I couldn't stop the flood of grief. The lumber gave way to the railings on his fort as my reddening fists struck them. My screams remained without sound.

Why God? Why'd you allow this? I hate you!

Pushing off the platform, I fell the five feet. The earth was soft. My knees buckled, leaving me planted into the soil. My right hand slipped against the dew-covered blades of grass. Taking a moment to catch my breath, the wetness seeped through my jeans. My head hung closer to the ground without the burden of life pulling me back up to my feet.

I sensed the same spirit that roused me from bed come over me again. The child-like voice said, "Stay. Don't go yet."

"Wyatt?" I knew better, but my body tingled with hope. Eyes scanned along the level of the fog in hopes of seeing movement, anything.

"Don't go. Stay." The voice was crystal clear. Unafraid or disbelieving, remaining on all fours connected me to a peace I'd forgotten over the years.

"Wyatt Cash, is that you son? Daddy's here." Tears washed away any notion of feeling foolish. Cool drops fell and soaked the same ground he used to walk on as he struggled up the knotted rope ladder that hung from the giant limb over his treehouse.

"Wyatt is okay. Says he loves you." I sucked for air until the sobbing turned to dry heaves. My chest rocked against its spine as I tried to form the words to say I love you too, son. I began to believe it wasn't a dream.

"Oh God, please let me see my baby one more time. I need this, Lord—need to see his face. To know he has peace."

My shoulders shook with an icy cold shutter. Paralyzed by fear as I fought to raise my face, I sought him through the haze. There was no struggle, just surrender to the small quiet voice, "He loves you."

Chapter 38
— Lieutenant Remi LeBlanc —

"GEN, I'M NOT HERE TO give a shit about the parish council. Buck is my concern. The media will soon find something else to feed off." She and I had worked together long enough to not bullshit each other.

"Remi, I care about Buck too, but if we don't appease the council with something soon, Buck may be a goner." Her eyes flinched at that statement. She looked desperate.

"What's going on with everyone lately? We've been through hell and back before without batting an eye. All of a sudden, we gotta kiss the council's ass." I wasn't the diplomatic type.

I paced St. Pierre's office like a caged animal. My gut turned flips realizing our operations were being put on ice. No way had Buck authorized this.

"Remi, just lay low and try keeping a lid on things for a bit. I'm hoping Brooks and Stone will break this murder case. They just have to." She didn't realize it, but her head shook no as she said that.

"That doesn't sound hopeful. You're putting a lot of faith in a hope so. This is Buck's ass on the line, Genevieve. He goes, we go too." Smashing one fist into my palm, I bit my top lip. No need arguing with her. Buck had already given me marching orders—Do whatever it takes.

"Right now, it's all we got." Yeah, she was on the down slope of desperate.

Unlike some of the other deputies, I wasn't sliming out the side door. This picketing of the Sheriff's Office had gone on long enough. These idiots didn't have a clue as to the truth of this case. Although, I still wondered if Buck should've kept Tommy Chang on ice for the stolen credit card just to keep things quiet.

The small corridor leading into the parking lot was deafening with the echoes of a handful of faithfully ignorant protestors. They'd shown up every day and remained until the lobby closed at six o'clock. I recognized some as members of White Is Power, and others probably on the payroll for Councilman Chiasson and Johnny Jones. Didn't matter—the media arrived to tight shot the small group for sensationalizing the daily buzz feed.

"Remi, how the hell can you work for a killer like Buck Walker?" Caught off guard by the tightness of her grip, anger fueled her.

"Anita, you both lost a son. This won't bring Wyatt back. I'm so disappointed in you." I whispered in her ear—the truth was meant only for her. The effects of the methamphetamine her boyfriend Big Johnny Chiasson had hooked her onto concealed her surface emotions. Her wet eyes glistened with sadness over the reality of her loss. She knew better.

Righting myself from the whisper, I spun to escape the breezeway but was jolted backward. The shoulder purposefully driven into my chest was draped in a black satin shirt with pearl buttons. Swallowing more than usual, I felt a barb of hot hatred jack its way through my veins.

"Do it." Johnny Jones never blinked as he dared me to punch him. His breath reeked like the mist of hell. Brown cigarette tar stains dotted his teeth, except for the pitted gold ones. The left side of his mouth quivered, though I don't think he realized his fear manifested itself through his cleft lips.

Mashing the inside of my cheeks, I sucked back the words. The sun silhouetted his frame, but I still locked onto the dead stare of Emory Ballard's hollowed black eyes. He said nothing. I said nothing. Suddenly, I pressed my shoulder blades together as a frigid snap bit through my spine. *Pure evil.*

Escaping the outside hallway and media, I stomped the accelerator, creating as much distance from that place as possible. Sergeant Brooks agreed to meet at the warehouse. It was time to team up and put this chaos to bed by solving this murder.

I spotted Brooks' unmarked vehicle after easing around the sharp curve that led to the dead-end. Activating the remote control, a smaller sally port door jerked its way to open. I squeezed my steering wheel and cursed aloud—who the hell else is in the car with Brooks?

"One welcome. One unknown." Trying to alert Agent Smith over the encrypted Task Force radio before granting further access into the secure perimeter—wasn't sure if I'd made it. The microphone cracked inaudible.

Idling at the entrance, I hit my high beams to illuminate Brooks' passenger. The chicken coop hatch slid open from the highest point inside the warehouse. The flicker of glass from the sniper scope alerted me that Agent Jones had it covered.

"Brooks driver. Graza passenger." Agent Jones' growls signaled trouble. The popping of iridescent bulbs overhead burst the giant bay area into a trap of blinding white light. Though Brooks and Graza would be unable to see him, Agent Smith had taken a cover position with his sub-compact machine gun through a loophole in the main wall to keep eyes on both occupants.

[Y Graza] I crushed the keys to text Brooks.

[Info 4U] Brooks replied immediately.

Testosterone flooded the conference room. Mistrust, though, was the dominant vibe. Hunched over in his chair, Detective Jose Graza snorted long breaths through his nostrils. Unsure whether he was going to charge at me or offer what he knew, my patience had run thin.

"Let's get to the point. Why's he here?" Looking around the table, I saw blank looks on everyone's faces. Reminded me of the way we looked after working the endless hours once Hurricane Katrina whipped our ass.

"Heard you in the Klan?" Graza countered. I watched the muscles in his forearms surface and disappear as he flexed his hands in tension. A quick look to Agent Smith and Agent Blue—they also saw it.

"Was. Not gonna lie to you. Not proud of it. I was a child—a victim of ignorant circumstances." I'd not publicly confessed that fact to anyone, much less in a room with minorities. Graza was a good man, and deserved my truth.

"Jumped out?" He rose while speaking. Agent Blue and Agent Smith edged in.

"Yeah. Two days till found, two weeks in hospital." Reliving the beating in my mind made it real yet again.

"Me too." Graza's eyes watered—his thin grizzled hand opened wide to take mine. He clasped onto me. I sensed life's sorrow drain from his spirit.

"Understood. Now let's bust somebody's ass for Maria Sanchez." He nodded.

Officers settled around the old mechanic shop table like knights in Camelot. Sergeant Brooks laid everything they knew out to the small group. No need to pledge secrecy. It was always unspoken.

"Graza's already assigned another black bag mission, so what you heard today didn't come from him." Sergeant Brooks gave that one last warning before everyone dispersed with new leads and information.

Chapter 39
— *Sheriff James Walker* —

BACK TURNED TO THE DOOR, I heard the crumpling rattle of paper. Her hand shook while setting it on my desk. Miss Martha's relaxed disposition had been unsettled by the constant attacks on this administration. Forcing a smile to reassure her, she knew me well enough.

"Parish Council's agenda for tonight. You're on it Sheriff."

"What now?" Signing papers without glancing up.

Already weakened, her voice escaped in breathless whispers. I looked up to hear her and saw her chest heaving as she fingered the hem of her modest blouse. It took two hands to pick up and steady the council agenda—causing the paper to shake more vigorously.

"Agenda item one is to remove James Walker from the interim position of Sheriff in Bayou Parish, Louisiana." Breathing like a sprinter's finish, she hesitated.

"Not surprising." Dropping my head to finish going over the paperwork, she coughed trying to clear her throat. Her exhales took longer between each and grew deeper—more frantic.

"Agenda item number two is to appoint current Chief of Police Tom Roberts as the permanent Sheriff of Bayou Parish until such time that a regular election is held in three years' time." Bright red flashes of panic rushed over her otherwise pale skin.

"That is a surprise." The strength fled from my hands as the ballpoint pen hit the desk, and then slowly rolled onto the floor. Silence, except for the sound of her body rumpling to the floor. I sprang across the desk just in time to cradle her head before it met the coffee table's sharp edge.

"Call 911, Martha's having a heart attack," Beads of sweat blistered my lip. "Somebody help. Call 911."

Patting Genevieve around her shoulders, I'd become lost in the moment as the ambulance sped away. Doctor Lambert called to say she was on her way to the emergency room. I trusted her to care for Miss Martha.

"Gen, this stuff is out of hand. I've got to make a move to end this scenario. Playing the politics is making me soft." My lips puckered to say more, but it was best to remain quiet. We spun away from the late afternoon's sun and back into the building. I had to prepare for tonight's parish council meeting.

"Buck, you've got to get things straight inside. I know you're worried about tonight, but Wyatt's death is shredding you to pieces. And what the hell was that the other day when you had your pistol pointed beneath your desk?" She continued without taking a breath, "The crap with Gaudet and Bates is still eating at you. Drive north of New Orleans and see a shrink." Her words landed softly on my bruised ego. Looking around the parking lot, she avoided my response by staring at her polished patent leather shoes.

Jamming a hand into my pants pocket, I yanked the vibrating cell phone out to see it was Remi. That gave us both the escape needed. I nodded to her while pressing the cell to my ear. St. Pierre placed her fingers to her ear and mouth and said she would call from the hospital.

Between the protesting chants in the front of the building and the rumbling air conditioning units at the rear, it was difficult to make out what Lieutenant Leblanc was saying. We'd meet in person.

Unusually quiet for an early evening, the Willow Café served hot coffee and no intruding wait staff. The three people already seated had their heads in books or taking advantage of the free Wi-Fi access.

I spotted my usual seat in the corner furthest from the front door. Turning the heavy chair to face the entrance, I stretched my back side to side. The chime of the door opening grabbed my attention. A familiarly tall figure muscled the old led crystal door open.

His gaze scanned across the open space, looking for threats. Remi's shoulders looked comfortably rounded and his body relaxed for reacting quickly. Reflecting, I grinned—many cops try dominating the space they occupy. The burden of police work returned upon my chest and I rapped fingers across the tabletop. Every door a cop enters is a tactical exercise. The simplest acts like walking through a door create unimaginable danger for us. We become targets of deadly attacks simply by breaching the gap between spaces. *Avoid the fatal funnel.* Remi knew to flow within it.

Remi snapped his chin as he watched the hallway leading to the kitchen area. Pressing my stressed leather boot against the base of the table I slapped my thigh. I peeked back over my right shoulder. I'd not cleared it first. I had to unclutter my mind—get my edge back.

"Son, you look mighty paranoid of late." I greeted him with a full, strong handshake as we always do. He squatted into the white wicker high back chair. Pushing the table off to the side, he stretched his legs across the floor.

"Thanks Sheriff, but you seem to be forgetting your tactics. Office life making you soft?" Jabbing his thumb over his shoulder and back toward the kitchen area, he smirked. I winced—he had no idea how painful that comment was.

"You know, to tell you the truth it is. It's about time I get out of that chair and find James Walker. We'll start by catching the killers." I half-heartedly smiled because I knew it was the truth. "And, since you dragged me out here, you can buy."

"Sheriff, we got a big shit pot of troubles brewing. It's gonna get messy. Maybe even bloody, but it got to get done." His face flattened into a blank stare—voice dropped below an octave. Dipping his head, he blinked his eyes as moisture crowded the corners of them.

"Remi, I've never seen you like this. Whatever it is, we'll handle it. Trust me." Feeling like I'd swallowed hot coals, intestines twisted while my quavering arm patted him on the shoulder.

"It's my past Buck—gonna have to face it. Maybe even kill it. Might mean the end of me too." Ruddy faced, Remi was too young for the sagging, dark bags under his eyes. His posture bent as his eyes fluttered between determination and tears.

"Son, don't give up just yet. We're in this together. We've come through worse. These a-holes operate outside the law."

"So have we, Buck." His eyes burned hot like hell.

"But we're the law. It's ours to bend. You still okay with that?" Pausing, I could hear his teeth grinding and saw the taut muscles in his jaw flex and pop.

"Is what we doing the right thing?" His watering big brown eyes looked like my son's. I nearly lost it.

"That's a question you gotta ask yourself, Remi. Some crack quicker than others. When you get out, there's no retaliation. Just the *Code*—don't break it." His shoulders shook beneath the flannel shirt. He wrung his hands and wrist until they bruised purple.

"Remi, I know it hits close to home, why don't you sit this one out. I'll handle things. Time for me to stop acting like some leashed monkey performing to please nine politicians." I gulped the last of my coffee, and then signaled the waitress's attention.

"Ain't happening boss. Owe you for who I am—don't blame you for who I was." Pressing sunglasses across the bridge of his crooked nose before the waitress arrived, he mouthed, "Thank you."

I dug the tattered leather wallet from my back pocket. Pulled out a twenty dollar bill and thanked the waitress for giving us the privacy. Smiling as I thumbed the small metal handcuff key I kept hidden in the billfold. My grandfather, Sheriff at the time I graduated the academy gave it too me. I could still see his smile and hear his words.

Never know when you might need to escape your own cuffs son. Keep it till you need it.

Staring at my watch, I had about twenty minutes until the parish council circus began. "Okay, what mess do we have and how we gonna clean it up?"

"Ain't shit'n you, I met with Graza today. Brooks drove him to the warehouse." He must've saw my torso arching up in agitation over Graza disobeying orders to steer clear, but he powered on. "Word is these attacks are initiation rights for new WIP members." Remi explained. His appearance was gaunt, looked robbed of life. Remi tried sitting up in his café chair, but the strength looked to escape him with those words.

"Ain't never heard of them doing shit like that. Petty crimes, fighting, booze, but never rape and sure not murder." I forced the fresh coffee between my lips—hot, but I was too shocked to care.

"Had a witness." Remi removed the sunglasses and rubbed his eyes as he spoke. Looking at me through parted fingers, he heaved out a breath before continuing.

"Had?" I leaned in.

"Seems Lonny Tucker actually witnessed a gang rape just down from the Tiger Roar Truck Stop and Casino."

"The trucker fucker?" My eyes spun in their sockets as the implication of what he just said struck me. "You don't mean..."

"Dead ass Jacque Hebert and Johnny Jones set Tucker up for the tiger's attack." His mouth turned down. "Buck, I know what we do ain't popular, but it's the right thing. Trust me, I'm solid and will take care of Johnny Jones."

"Remi, we're the shepherds my brother. We'll pay for our sins eventually, but hopefully God will forgive us by then. Did Graza know who murdered Maria Sanchez?" I assured my young charge.

The calendar reminder buzzed on my phone—time to walk down to the council chambers.

"No clue, but we know where they picked up the other prostitutes before raping them. Undercover op and set a plant out on the strip. Bait them bastards, then filet 'em." Remi's look extended far beyond the café's walls. His mind had already worked out the details. He just needed my blessing.

"Keep a small circle in house. Make 'em hurt." I rubbed my wrist and then patted it.

I struggled to escape the chair's low-bottomed seat. He helped me upright as I gathered paperwork for the parish council meeting.

"Going to council—make dem hurt too." It wounded me to smile at Remi. I knew the damage I'd done to his already fractured soul. I was all he had left, so I nodded, "Will do, son."

Chapter 40
— Lieutenant Remi LeBlanc —

SERGEANT RJ RUIZ WAS BABBLING as the pitch in her usually mono-tone voice jerked octaves in mid-sentence. Shaking her hands out, she swallowed repeatedly. Agent Blue tried to settle her nerves. He had a knack for communications—nice and not so nice.

Agent Smith and Agent Jones sipped coffee across the room with Sergeant Brooks, while Detective Stone fumbled over his cell phone. Everyone appeared disconnected. That's the danger of bringing in outsiders to help with undercover operations.

Dusk melded into the night, dark and humid—time to troll for Johns. My gut flipped as I began the operational briefing.

"Pay attention. Put your phones away until I'm done." Stone's lack luster attitude was about to piss me off. "Street surveillance teams radioed in. Boulevard is crawling with tricks and treats. This ain't no regular prostitution sting. Looking for the a-holes targeting Hispanic females. Possibly young white males. WIP initiation." I was sweating buckshot—my nerves tingled as I grappled to say that name.

"WIP? What the hell's that?" My liking of Stone was about to end. The way he raised his lip looked like a smart ass Elvis impersonator.

"White Is Power, or WIP is an offshoot of the old Southern Guard. This group was the Klan's enforcers going back to the Reconstruction Era after the Civil War. Got too dangerous for the mainstream racists, so they broke off about fifty years ago." Tension, fear and regret combined in a gumbo of mixed emotions.

Why do I still feel like I'm betraying them?

"How you know so much about this WIP, Remi?" Stone was slung so low across his chair that his knuckles drug the ground. He'd pushed my patience.

"Stone, shut the fuck up or get your ass outta here. You realize what's at stake?" My eyes bolted across the conference table to lock looks with Sergeant Brooks as he put the rookie detective in check. His heaving chest and flexing forearms showed he was more fed up than I was. Earl Brooks was old school. Despite race or other's ignorance, he had a job to do—he was blue before all else.

"Wasting time. Stone you in or out? This is serious shit, no weak links you understand?" He nodded yes, but Agent Blue's head shook no. My breath felt like it was cut short as I spoke incomplete sentences. My voice quivered. It had been years since they jumped me out of WIP, why was I still so nervous?

"Agent Jones, take the details from here please. Gotta reply to this text." Forging a grin to the group probably illustrated my apprehension more than confidence.

"Boys, the only thing you better make sure of is that Sergeant RJ Ruiz is protected. Everyone understand?" Agent Jones' emotionless expression looked like an undertaker had processed it. I responded to Buck's text but watched every deputy nod yes. They were refocused.

"Read your assignment sheets and ask questions right now before we roll out. Street surveillance teams radioed in again. Activity on the strip is fever pitched. It's time to head out." Agent Jones was the perfect deputy commander—loyal, experienced and a no-nonsense terminator when it came to protecting another cop.

"Ruiz, what's the arrest signal?" I tried catching her off guard. Standing in her ripped fishnet stockings that bunched just below the tattered cut off denims, and knot-tied flannel top, she was anything but vulnerable.

"*Winnebago*. They try buying my ass for sex, and I give the code word."

"Ruiz, never, ever get in the car with a suspect. Just say *Winnebago* and walk away." I tossed my cell phone onto the wooden table as I pressed my fists against it—inches from her face. The smeared purple make-up gave the appearance she'd been battered by her pimp—the perfect target. The giant circle of green and blue across her chest showed the impact of the bullet she'd taken during the meth-lab raid.

"Understood Lieutenant. Nowhere to hide a gun anyways. No chances taken." She crossed her arms over her exposed cleavage, and rolled her head from side to side. Breathing quick shots of air. Her pupils were dilated—she had to calm down soon.

Dropping my chin into my heaving chest, my eyes softened with her in them. I had to hide my smile—she knew I loved her.

"Mount up. Guys get your butts into position before Ruiz goes on foot. She won't wander from the corner in front of Crazy Two Times Liquor Store. Lighting is good there. Agent Blue, please check the signal on her body microphone before we drive to the drop off location."

"About time, let's kick some hooker ass." Stone's cocky arrogance didn't register with me. He'd always been a levelheaded young officer.

"Stone, come see." I placed my hand between his heart and left shoulder. Just above the bulletproof vest as I offered unimportant advice—I didn't detect any whelped skin.

This shit don't register.

Chapter 41
— Sheriff James Walker —

THE SUCTION OF COOL AIR popped behind the closed parish council door as I yanked it to enter. Creaking as the hydraulic pins designed to control the motion struggled against the force of my pull, each of the nine elected officials momentarily jerked their heads up. Only Anthony Chiasson would maintain eye contact.

Usually a low turnout, bodies compressed into the open space's well-lit meeting room. Circus had come to town and ringmaster Chiasson looked hungry to feed the lions.

Adrenaline rattled my hand against my chest during the pledge of allegiance. I felt the pounding heart beat and struggled to recite the words through lips barren of moisture. Staring at the pole mounted American flag, my scowl veered onto the back of Chiasson's balding skull.

Why am I reacting like this?

The council president's voice quaked as she invited everyone to be seated—tension was contagious. Seemed everyone knew something bad was about to go down, and didn't want to miss it. Scanning the fifty-person capacity room, there were no seats available. Doctor Susan Lambert twisted back to motion her seat if I wanted it. Unable to crack my face to smile for her gesture, I shook my head no.

I shuffled the large accordion folder between hands. My knees felt like jackhammers pelting both boots into the ground. Never one to run from a fight, this wasn't my typical arena—it was Chiasson's. The gavel rapped the mahogany bench.

"Agenda item number 1 – The removal of James Walker from the interim position of Sheriff in Bayou Parish, Louisiana." Stiff lipped, the council clerk announced the issue. She guzzled water from a paper cup, and then wriggled to lift the plastic pitcher to refill it.

"This item is open to public discussion. Anyone in the audience?" Eyes roaming the room like a reluctant predator, the council president asked with anticipation.

Clearing my throat, every head spun to the back of the room—to me. The thudding drumbeat in my ears forced me to lean forward trying to determine if someone had spoken to me. I crinkled my right eye and turned that ear toward the audience. Nothing heard, just heavy confrontational breathing.

The sound of a bouncing plastic seat ricocheted from the front of the gallery. Juddering my attention toward the sound, the seat next to Doctor Lambert was vacant. The older gentleman strolled slowly to the podium. The business suit looked tailored and expensive.

Pressing my shoulders against the eggshell colored wall, exhausted eyes rolled toward the ceiling. A gut-twisting knot grinded inside and I felt the dread of a hired gun brought in to attack me. Chiasson sat up taller than the others in what looked like anxious anticipation of the slaughter. Me on the other hand, had this stupid folder full of nothing significant.

Quiet occupied the space nervous chatter once consumed. Throats bobbed with repeated swallows while bodies shifted in their plastic auditorium style seats. Even the council president's elderly torso stiffened, as the distinguished looking man adjusted the microphone to his mouth.

"Sir, please state your name for the council." Madam president said in a low, broken whisper.

"Alcede Gautreaux." His voice was soft, but the name resounded like cannon fire.

"Mr. Gautreaux, I can only imagine you're here for agenda item number one. Thank you and I sure feel the same way you do about getting the current Sheriff removed from that position. I know the honorable Chief of Police Tom Roberts is anxious to begin the tough job of turning that cesspool around." Chiasson said.

Refusing to watch Chiasson's face, my look caught Roberts sitting overly tall in his reserved seat on the first row. I felt out of body as the words launched like rockets while I stood there—a big, helpless target.

"Thank you Councilman Chiasson, it will be an honor to serve Bayou Parish as your next Sheriff." Roberts' dress uniform crunched as he rose and then sat after playing his part in this orchestrated charade. Alcede Gautreaux relaxed against the podium while the two displayed their intentions.

"Thank you for your willingness to serve Chief Roberts. Mr. Gautreaux, as you were saying." Chiasson's lips covered the microphone's tip. His bulk spilled over the mahogany tabletop as he leaned toward the audience on both forearms.

"Thank you councilman. Madam President and the remaining seven duly elected parish officials—it is my honor to address you. I am indeed here in regards to the first agenda item. Mr. Chiasson, while my purpose is to address the council as a whole, I will also address you individually. No disrespect to the council of course." Gautreaux's slight chin nodded.

Mr. Gautreaux's presence cast a spell over the audience. The wavy locks of silvered hair rose and fell with each facial expression. He easily probed the room with piercing ice-blue eyes. His gaze was impossible to break away from. I felt defenseless against his mystique.

The paper folder now felt as heavy as cement. I let it slide along my leg until it landed on the carpeted floor. Mr. Gautreaux's words slipped easily between his lips—a snake charmer. I flinched for the bite.

"Go right ahead." Chiasson had cozied himself against the long countertop as his orbed cheeks rested within both thick palms.

"Mr. Chiasson, I represent the honorable Eleanor Jewel, Governor of the great state of Louisiana. I have with me a certified copy of her proclamation declaring the office of the Sheriff for Bayou Parish to be held by Mr. James Walker until such time that the parish council decides to either extend the term of office the remaining three and a half years or host, at their expense, a special election to vote in a permanent Sheriff.

"Any action initiated to violate this official order shall be deemed a direct breach. It is declared that any violation shall be investigated for criminal prosecution by the State's Attorney General's office." Stunned, but mostly confused by the intoxicating double-talk of legalese and veiled threats—silent slurring murmured throughout the room. Chiasson slumped into an angry pile of defeat and disbelief.

"You, Anthony Chiasson are hereby served notice of violation for contempt of Governor Jewels' official resolution appointing Mr. James Walker as Bayou Parish's Sheriff." The gentile Southern lawyer suddenly bolstered his words and his posture, and then nodded to the council president with a brilliant white smile.

Shocked, I pressed against the wall to straighten myself in case Chiasson's dull eyes sought me out. Looking for an ally, I noticed Doctor Lambert next to the still empty seat. She slid down into her chair, eased around to look over her shoulder and mouthed, "You're welcome."

Chapter 42
— *Lieutenant Remi LeBlanc* —

STEAM DRIFTED OFF THE HOT asphalt after the peppering of rain. Girls covered their heads with soggy Times-Picayune newspapers. They clattered between drops to approach cars like fish drawn to the hook.

"RJ you don't have to stand in it, get back in until the arrest units are in position." I offered. Her already smeared makeup rained streaks toward her defined jawline. She always looked beautiful and innocent, but I knew better.

"That's cool. Gotta look the part." Her smile mangled across perfectly aligned white teeth. My heart lightened with her courage. There'd not been many women I'd been attracted to—she'd been one of them. Careers meant more to both at the time.

"Task Force 5 to Task Force 1. All units are set. Ready to roll." Agent Blue's knack for covert operations rang through with confidence in his voice. Most of us realized these types of undercover stings meant lots of ramp up time in the preparation, long periods of tedious waiting, and only seconds of heart-stopping excitement. The detectives were not used to this roller coaster—that was my concern.

Ruiz jumped at the crackle of the radio's volume. Pushing away from the passenger's side window she expelled deep breaths. Then turned to walk away.

"Sergeant." I called through the rain-pelted window's opening.

"Yes Remi?" Palms up, her hands caught the rain and my attention. No time to coddle her, she was more than capable.

"Radio check one more time. Give a *testing, testing, Winnebago.*"
She unloosened one more button on her tied up flannel shirt, and dipped her head toward the microphone concealed in her bra. "Testing, testing. Winnebago." A playfully sarcastic smile followed the tilting of her head, and double-thumbs up. She was off across the boulevard.

I peered into my rearview mirror to remind myself of the fool who let her get away. Unable to smile at the man I saw, it was time to focus on the present—not our past.

"Task Force 5, I got the prize. All units – eyes open. Busy times." Agent Blue had the primary observation point directly across the highway from the liquor store's corner.

Cutting a quick U-turn, I idled down Sullivan Boulevard. Agent Smith, on foot, took a position across an old bench under a pile of papers and a saturated sleeping bag. Agent Jones, disguised as a crack cocaine dealer, settled just north of Ruiz. I smirked watching him run off a group of crack heads—what a surprise they'd get.

Sergeant Brooks was one block down from Sullivan Boulevard, sitting on East 9th Street. He'd serve as a back up take down unit, or surveillance team if we called out a potential target. Meanwhile, Detective Stone parked his unmarked police vehicle west of the intersection of Sullivan and West 11th. He had an eye on Ruiz, and would also be able to hear her over the hidden microphone.

Two blocks out were multiple vehicles with two-officer arrest teams. They'd sit still until Agent Blue gave descriptions or Ruiz's arrest signal. Shaking my head in the mirror again, I saw a line of traffic behind me. They looked to be lining up to go fishing for sex.

Fast Jake's Gun and Pawn was closed for the night—I backed into the darkest corner of the parking lot. Buck taught me it was a waiting game. Patience was the key. Most officers begin to drive around, or hit their brake lights while parked. Even listening to their favorite radio stations. Any of these gave away surveillance locations and scared off potential targets.

I learned to focus on the undercover agent's voice for subtle clues while they engaged in negotiations for illegal acts with the criminal. Propping my binoculars against the steering wheel, R.J. Ruiz had never looked more beautiful—or sexy.

"You Mexican baby?" His voice was barley audible over the loud music coming from the inside of the full size truck. Squeezing both eyes closed, I heard multiple voices over her microphone. My mind's eye pictured young white males. Pulse quickening, I began to press Agent Blue for details.

Wasn't anyone paying attention?

"Units hold positions. Blue Ford truck. Occupied multiple times." Agent Blue was on the ball of course—I had to check my personal feelings.

"*Si, yo hombres gustan Latina?*" Her voice was calm, almost flirtatious as she asked the men if they liked Hispanic females.

"Fuck no. We hate Spic whores?" Shouted an occupant. I was relieved in one sense, but realized it meant more waiting. The truck fishtailed away from the corner.

"Units hold. No go." Agent Blue's voice wasn't so flirtatious. He had little tolerance for ignorance. That truck was full of it.

Lightning cracked a brilliant, blinding light across the night sky. Rain emptied the clouds. The prostitutes ran for shelter—Ruiz stood at a steady attention. The soldier in her became obvious. Unfortunately, we needed her to portray a hooker, not an MP.

A slight twist of my wiper controls kept them just below full speed to intermittently swipe the flood of water from the windshield. Street lamps, liquor store and approaching vehicle lights blurred into dynamic streams of colorful chaos.

"Task Force 1 to Task Force 3 – eyes on?"

"Negative Task Force 1. Lost eye on after ducking into bus shelter." Apologetic, Agent Jones delivered the daunting news.

Fist tightening across my radio's microphone I called for Agent Smith.

"10-4 Units. Sleeping bag drenched, and so is Ruiz. She's code 4 on the corner. Should I tell her to get out of the rain?" Agent Smith eased my fear.

"Negative, let it ride. Stone, what you see?" I felt the heat rising beneath my bulletproof vest while waiting for Stone to answer. The music was so loud once Stone keyed up his microphone, I couldn't make out his reply. "Stone, turn that fucking radio down and pay attention." It was an encrypted police radio channel, but that was the nicest thing I could say.

"Heads up, new line of targets." Agent Blue called out over my tirade against Stone. I hit the windshield wiper control to try erasing the blinding blur of mingled lights.

"This is Ruiz – I think Agent Jones is having an issue with some street dealers. Sounds like they arguing over him being on their corner. I can hear them yelling." My hand clutched the gear shifter to roll over to him, but I knew he was capable of resolving it.

"Everyone hold tight. Sergeant Brooks—roll up from your position and see if you can help him." Agent Blue was the coordinator. I refocused attention on Ruiz as I saw the flash of headlights speeding up East 9th Street to Sullivan.

"Shit," I shouted out as the lightning flashed just above our position. Maybe we should call it a night, or wait out this rain. Scrunching into my seat, my eyes shot heavenward at another flash of heat. That one was close—had my heart racing.

Besides the weather, shit was getting out of hand on the ground. I still wasn't sure if Agent Jones had run those crack dealers off.

"Agent Blue, let's wrap this up for now. We can't see anything through this storm." It was his op, but I had to make the call.

"10-4 boss. Had to get two thugs off of the Sarge's ass. Them dudes went nuts when the lightning struck." My gut sunk.

"You took eyes off?"

"Stone got clear sight." Agent Blue's voice lacked confidence.

"Stone." I called.

"Detective Stone." I demanded.

"Todd Stone." I yelled.

"What'cha want Remi?" I saw the light of a cell phone screen pressed against Stone's head through the back window of his vehicle.

She was gone.

Chapter 43
— Sheriff James Walker —

EASING THROUGH THE KNOTTED ROOTS supporting a cluster of ancient oaks, my eyes narrowed to focus on the muddy trails. My flashlight sliced the night as I was drawn back to Wyatt's tree house. Crying out his name, I sloshed through slippery grass until resting my bone soaked hands across the lumber.

"God, I know you're here. Today's been a tough one, but it began out here. Please let Wyatt speak to me. I'm doing all I can to hold it together. Just a break please." My eyes batted against the falling rain.

The foliage canopy interrupted an immediate downfall of water. Rhythmic dripping gave way to the crush of rain. The crash of lightning slashed the sky's fabric. Shaking my head and closing my eyes, I bathed in the turmoil. Cold entombed me—I tried to call out again. My throat was thick, and feeling light-headed, I stumbled backward over a cypress stump.

Lying prone on the earth's floor, my arms flailed out to either side. The deluge of water forced my eyes and mouth closed again. Mud splashed into my ears. My body vibrated with each thunderous clap. I thought the ground might open up to consume me right then. I listened through the raging sky. Listened for Wyatt.

God, why bring me out here if you're going to drown me in sorrow?

Rising ground water licked the corners of my mouth. Pressing lips together, I couldn't pray out loud. I lay there listening. The beat of thunder, followed by lightning, steady rapping of rain and the flood current beating against my body. I couldn't move.

A twinkling of light caused my head to jerk to the right. Squinting, my eye partially open against the muck, it slashed through the night again. I rolled onto my right side and grabbed the snub nose revolver from the rear of my waistband.

The swinging beam continued to encroach. No way would someone stalk me out here—this was my own damn property. Motionless, my breathing shallowed. I watched, waited and listened for a clue as to who it might be.

Plodding carelessly through the same trails of mud I had just traversed an hour earlier, the intruder was heading too fast to be unfamiliar with this area. With mere feet separating us, I lurched up and shoved my body behind the solid oak. The high-powered flashlight shined in the figure's direction. My weapon perched right beneath my beam.

"You're trespassing." Spitting water and mud from my cold, bluing lips.

"Buck, its Remi. We got trouble." Gasping for air, his voice shuddered on the verge of panic.

"Tell me on the way to the house." We both slipped along the way, but the sense of urgency seemed to give additional traction. Soon, the lights under my back porch became clear. "Who's that?" Still shielding my eyes from the downpour.

"Genevieve and Graza. No time to waste questioning him coming along—I pulled him off the Chiasson case."

"Who gave you the authority?" Grabbing his arm before we made it to the house. Exhausted from the run, I wanted answers. "Chiasson is priority damn it."

"No, Ruiz is our priority right now." I saw his wide eyes spilling tears through the rain. His chin began to quiver as he fought over his next sentence. "I fucked up, they took her."

"Remi, we'll get her back. Graza and anyone else needed. We *will* get her back." Lungs filling with moist marsh air, my chest swole with determination. The very switch I feared to flip was what I needed at this moment.

"Buck, sorry about this. Got Agent Blue on the way along with Sergeant Brooks. Jones and Smith are beating the streets with the rest of the Task Force. They'll report wherever you say." Spoken without hesitation, Genevieve's words assured me she was on the right side of this operation. Though I trusted her, she'd never been exposed to the hell of police work.

Toweling myself off, I slipped out of my clothes and then into dry underwear and jeans. Genevieve didn't take notice—this wasn't junior high. I was dressed and ready.

"Graza what you got?" The intensity in his eyes hypnotized me.

"I know you put me onto Chiasson. This is related boss."

"It's okay that you're here. I'd have it no other way. Now go." Placing my palm on his shoulder, I felt the flex of his torso relax.

"You know Johnny Jones and Jacque Hebert led Lonny Tucker into that tiger's cage because Lonny witnessed a rape?" My eyes blinked and I nodded my head for him to continue.

"Councilman Chiasson is connected to Jones obviously through politics and supporting his casino, which in turn funds Chiasson's campaigns. Both introduced by a guy named Emory Ballard. Never heard of him though." Graza's hands bobbed up and down in question.

Rain pounding against the sheet metal tin roof, made hearing near impossible. Remi heard him though.

Remi's eyes slammed shut and his shoulders jerked him backward into the rain. I knew his dilemma, because I had the same frigid spear hammering its way through me. Ballard was pure fucking evil. Neither one of us wanted to confront the inevitable. "Go on, Jose." I anxiously encouraged.

"Jones was given permission to revive the Southern Guard. I thought it was a private security business, but once my Mexican-ass started asking question about it, I realized it was something different."

Graza spoke without fear. Had he known the peril he'd placed himself in, I doubt he'd still care. This soldier was rock solid. "But how does Ballard fit?"

His wet leather motorcycle boots scuffled back onto the cement. Remi shook the wetness from his jeans and shirt. Eyes glued to the picnic table, he cleared his throat several times before speaking.

"Emery Ballard is WIP's grand wizard. He raised me after he killed my father and uncle. He's the devil. Honestly, I don't know that I could kill him if I had to." Remi unsnapped each pearl button on his western style shirt. Pulling it back over his left shoulder, he exposed the branded whelps of skin between his heart and shoulder. Covered in crimson red and death black tattoo ink, it still clearly showed the swastikas.

"Remi, maybe you should sit this one out. Agent Blue will handle the interview, we'll handle the rescue," Genevieve offered as she pulled the wet shirt back across Remi's chest.

"I'm solid. Ruiz is more important than old scars." Remi's glazed look showed the conflict stirring inside. I knew he'd do the right thing when it counted.

Headlamps shot light across the back yard as tires crunched onto the mixture of gravel and oyster shells. Two doors slammed and footsteps jolted straight beneath the porch. The two lawmen had been through the shit before, but this was going to make Hurricane Katrina look like an afternoon shower. Sergeant Brooks and Agent Blue were more than capable.

Rain spilling over the gutters and slapping the cement echoed the sound. We huddled close avoiding the spray. No one blinked. Once I gave the orders, each nodded silently—no need for words, there was work to be done. Quick, violent work.

Digging into my back pocket, I looked at the gold badge. Rubbing my fingers across the embossed lettering, SHERIFF, I tossed it onto the wooden picnic table. Five other shields joined it.

"For Ruiz."

Chapter 44
— *Lieutenant Remi LeBlanc* —

KILLING EMORY BALLARD WOULD DRAW less public attention than Johnny Jones. A loner, he isolated himself on a compound protected by cameras, guards and German Shepherds.

Driving along Sullivan Boulevard to meet Agents Jones and Smith, I slowed up before the corner liquor store. White knuckles gripped the steering wheel and I'd expected, actually hoped, to see Ruiz back, standing at attention in the rain. I knew better.

Approaching the two hunched shadows just before the alley, I looked again into the rearview mirror. "God please keep Ruiz safe. I'll do anything for her if You give me another chance. Even quit this job." Pain came with those words. I looked away from my image.

Both agents slid across the back seat with their heads concealed until the interior dome light dimmed. "Be sure to kill that light before we get there, Remi." Jones said.

"Agent Blue's gathering supplies. He'll meet us at the target location once we clear a path." Both agents acknowledged, but appeared sullen. I recognized their moods, but feared they were feeding off my emotions.

Feeling the hard metal against my shoulder, I reached up with my right hand to accept both of their badges. One of them patted my other shoulder. "We're with ya."

The eight-mile drive to Emory Ballard's compound took us beyond the oil tank batteries, matrix of pipelines and an alligator farm.

Endless sugarcane fields lined the rural parish highway. Cutting a trail of dust and slop through the moonless sky, my mind replayed the layout. I knew the anti-intruder obstacles because I'd helped build them—we'd be there quick. Still, my ass clinched as we drew close.

"One mile out." I repeatedly flexed and relaxed my fingers over the hard plastic steering wheel. Eyes itched—I'd not blinked once since we left Sullivan Boulevard. I struggled with the desire to flee this mission—fight or flight in full out conflict. Breathing deep but strained, I knew my fears were irrational—I wasn't that boy anymore.

The click and whirl of night vision goggles hummed from the back seat. "Boss, lights out."

I fumbled to locate the switch until I fingered the button to kill all lights on my truck. Immediately, I dropped the binocular NVG's into place. A dim green hue occupied the cab.

The large truck tires ate the mixture of mud and gravel while it crept along the road until a break in the cane field appeared. The headland would make for our departure point. Slipping through the rear window to avoid the sounds of closing doors, we helped each other navigate the move.

"Boss, you okay?" Agent Smith must've noticed me rubbing both hands against my pants repeatedly although they were covered in Nomex tactical gloves.

"Not gonna bullshit you boys, I'm scared to death. Ballard has this control thing going over my mind. I know it sounds stupid, but when you've been a victim long enough, you begin to depend on your abuser. That bastard raised me while he kicked the shit out of me daily. I should want to kill him for what he did—not sure I have the heart for it." Stuttering, I stumbled over that confession. The team needed to know where my head was.

"Boss, you okay when we encounter others?" Agent Smith placed his hand over my shoulder. I saw his mouth parted under the light of the night-vision goggles. "I owe them nothing. This is about rescuing Ruiz."

"Remi, try keeping emotion out of this for now. We know how you feel about her, but anger will only lead to mistakes. This has to be precise—not personal. They'll kill all of us if any of this slips out." Agent Jones' words pierced my soul. He was right—the stakes were higher than ever before.

"Agent Blue asked for an ETA. Waiting at the oil tanks." Tapping his watch, Agent Smith suggested we move. "Tell him about thirty tops," I said.

Plugging through the muddy cane field headlands was slowing us down—thirty minutes would be a miracle. The rain had stopped, and the lack of moonlight or lightning played to our advantage. The darker, the better. Humidity was at an all time high though—I couldn't stop sweating.

I heard Agent Smith breathing fast and heavy. His feet kept slipping off the uneven row headers that paralleled each line of stalks. The cane was about eight feet high and blocked any chance of wind.

"Fence twenty yards out." Agent Smith gasped through his microphone.

We crouched, covering each other with our compact submachine guns held at ready fire positions. Stretching my eyes wide open to increase visibility through the goggles, I remained behind the others to provide rear guard security.

"Remi, taking cutters from your pack." Agent Smith easily snipped the barbed wire fence. He tapped my shoulder to signal we were again moving.

"Perimeter motion sensors to your left and right. Both about thirty yards either way." I felt smooth as my mind processed the system I tested and sometimes attempted to escape from as a kid.

I watched Agent Smith's shoulders heave up and down as he fought to catch his breath. He laid eyes across the open field. I turned my back to the unit to again watch our six. Agent Jones silently shot out both sensors with his silenced twenty-two-caliber rifle.

Sliding through the hole in the fence, we spread out along a straight line about ten yards apart and slithered in zig-zagged patterns until reaching an old barn. The barking never stopped from within the kennel. The yelping would help cover our movements as we closed in. Agent Smith crawled to the front gate and wrapped a chained padlock around the remote control bailout on the dogs' door.

Two figures moved across the shadow breaks. The light from their cigarette tips glowing made both easy targets. Agent Jones swapped his small caliber weapon for his silenced 308-sniper rifle. Kneeling, he nodded for us to begin our approach. My belly scraped across the mixture of muddy grass, broken branches and jagged stones.

Pressing my lips together and emptying my lungs quietly, I prepared both mind and body for what was about to occur. There would be no arrests tonight. "Hold," came softly over my tactical headset. Watching through his rifle's scope, Agent Jones had a better view than we did. Our heads were pressed against the dirt—motionless, we waited on his signal.

"Move. Ten yards out."

Ten yards until I kill another human being. I was totally okay with it.

"Slow. Five yards out. Both targets together. Hold." Agent Jones directed.

Grinding in my stomach was a fluttery, empty feeling. I felt the tickle across my exposed forearms—red fire ants. My heart rate elevated with the flush of panic running through the back of my neck and into my ears. Holding breaths to minimize my body's movement became impossible as I felt hundreds of legs prickling across the under side of my bicep and into my armpits.

Come the hell on Jones. What's taking so long?

Chapter 45

— *Lieutenant Remi LeBlanc* —

"TARGET HUNG UP HIS CALL. Both turned away. Move now."

I'd imagined a push up off the dirt and a quick lunge onto my target. The spring in both legs was gone. Agent Smith had already wrapped the cutting cord around his target's throat—he was fast in the process of ending that life. Stumbling, I leapt to tackle my target as he turned to aim his rifle at Agent Smith.

The man was thin as a meth-addicted rail, but his strength was unnatural. He spun from his belly, onto his back by swiping the rifle across my face. I felt the cold exposure as a gash along my eye opened up. Blood gushed from my brow to cover my ant-eaten arms and his chest.

Grunting, my NVG's were knocked across the dirt path, so I concentrated on disarming him. Pressing the magazine release button on his rifle's frame, the thirty round clip fell from its receiver. He tried jerking the barrel of his rifle back to the right side, but I leaned forward and caught it between my ribs and triceps.

His shaking eyes opened wide with panic, but the dilated pupils signaled he was drugged and fearless. He growled. I shoved the knife into the hollow spot between his Adam's apple and breastplate. He groaned. I pushed the blade through until I heard it crunch gravel on the backside. He was dead.

"Let's move," I radioed to the unit.

"Boss, your blood?" Agent Smith asked.

"Think so. That fucker's rifle caught me pretty good." A handful of Quickclot was pressed against my temple to seal the injury. "Remi, we can't have your blood left out here. No traces of us at all. It'll sting for a bit. Ready to move?" Agent Smith was on autopilot. Agent Jones never flinched as he maintained an over-watch position through the massive sniper scope.

We continued toward the main house at an increased pace. The soft grass and ink black sky silenced our movements. "Hold. Two at main entrance." Agent Smith and I held positions to each side of Agent Jones. He crouched into a supported squat position. I could hear his breathing pattern change, and knew he was coming closer to eliminating them both.

Plink. Plink. "Clear to move." We continued until stepping over both corpses.

I peeked through the large bay windows and saw Emory Ballard seated in his chair watching television. I shook my head to clear the doubts. He looked so normal—like an everyday dad resting after a hard day at work.

What am I doing back here? I can't do this to him. He made me who I am. To kill him is to kill me.

"Remi, focus. I know it's tough. Why don't you keep watch outside?" Agent Smith's mouth pressed against my ear. I bit the insides of my mouth while exhaling through my nose. Lowering my eyes off target, a stream of hot tears seeped along the bridge of my nose until falling onto the knee of my pants.

How many nights did I spend at this very spot? Waiting for Emory to fall asleep in that chair. All I wanted to do was sneak back in the house for a few hours of rest. That bastard took pleasure in forcing me back into the yard like an animal—I'd slept outside more than I did in the comfort of a bed.

"Remi, we gotta move." Agent Jones demanded.

"Around the other side, follow me. There's a way in." Breaking in betrayal, my heart shattered—it'd all be over soon. "Message Agent

Blue to be ready to roll. Same path."

It went easy. The interior was empty, except for Ballard and an unexpected eight-year-old boy. Unchaining him from the concrete floor he lay sleeping on, I told him it'd be okay—just stay in the room. His eyes were hollow and dark—they blinked and he tucked his hands beneath his head and went back to sleep.

Averting my gaze from the child, I was wretched over as my stomach churned with bile. I swallowed hard as I shoved my fist against my mouth. Cheeks puffing out, I felt empty—as thought looking at myself years ago. "He'll be okay in here Remi, let's go." Cringing away from the door, I knew Buck had to know this soon. It complicated and possibly solved plenty.

I leaned against the hallway as the agents spoke with Ballard. I heard the crumpling walk of Agent Blue covered in a plastic Tyvek biohazard suit. The heavy leather bag crashed onto the hardwood floor with the clanking of metals inside.

"Think you bother me in that stupid space suit. Fuck off. Where's Remi?" Ballard nervously smirked.

There was no response from Agent Blue. I watched his face through the thin plastic shield covering his head. Mechanical, he'd learned this trade through years of application in countries foreign and distant to ours. Torture made Americans uncomfortable, unsafe. Agent Blue's education came from cultures taking pride in their ability to sustain life through even the most unthinkable pain.

"You know who you fucking with, son? My militia will overrun this place and destroy every one of you and your families. You got kids? They're already dead." Ballard's face red, spewed curses he knew he could deliver.

Weak, I hid against the wall listening to his rant. Licking sticky lips, sweat bubbled from my hairline to trace across my face. Ballard would never break—he was pure hate. You can't stop it. Only kill it.

"Mr. Ballard. I will ask only one question. Please answer truthfully the first time." Agent Blue's low, even-toned voice was muffled inside his protective suit, but it rang clear as a bell.

"Fuck off." Ballard bucked against the duct tape wrapped around his wrists and ankles. His face drained white as the plastic was rolled out on the floor. Agents Jones and Smith assisted by leaning Ballard's wooden chair to each side so the roll of material slid beneath it.

"Mr. Ballard, are you prepared to answer my one simple question?"

Chapter 46
— *Lieutenant Remi LeBlanc* —

"GO TO HELL." BALLARD'S SPIT landed just below Agent Blue's face shield. The grey plastic crumpled as he reached into the thick leather bag. He concealed an object in his hand and asked Ballard again. He got the same stubborn reply.

I moved closer but still out of Ballard's view. Agent Blue stretched a length of tape from the roll and pressed it against Ballard's right forearm just below his elbow. Ballard's skin turned purple between the two pieces of tape that locked his arm down at the wrist and elbow.

"Mr. Ballard, where is Sergeant RJ Ruiz?" The question hung in the air—it seemed like an eternity had passed. Frozen, we all watched Ballard's body wrangle against his constraints.

Please Emory, just answer the man.

"Fuck you." Ballard's violent red face became distorted.

A swooshing broke the silence. The meat cleaver divided his right forearm into two pieces. His severed wrist and hand still wiggled until the nerves realized they were dead. Ballard's unholy howl sent shock waves through my temples. He convulsed against the chair, but his nub was secured to it.

I grabbed my stomach and throat as vomit raced up behind my teeth. Dropping to my knees, the wall supported my weight while I tried capturing my breath.

Agent Blue stood motionless. He eased down after a bit to grab something else from his leather satchel. He smashed styptic powder into Ballard's open wound to control the bleeding. He was no good to us dead.

"Mr. Ballard, where is Sergeant RJ Ruiz?" Agent Blue repeated himself with the same emotionless tone of voice. He wiped blood from the blade. I assumed it was to prevent wall spatter on his next swing.

"I'm not afraid. I'm going to kill you when this is done." Ballard was one tough old bird, but this was inhumane. Finally pulling myself off the floor, I had to empty the puke from my mouth without leaving my DNA in the place. I peeked in the boy's room on the way to the crapper. Still asleep—definitely drugged.

"Mr. Ballard, where is Sergeant RJ Ruiz?" I heard Agent Blue asking him again as I shuffled rubber legs back down the hall. Stopping before reentering the room, I clinched my fist and pounded the top of both thighs. My instinct told me to end this torture—my heart screamed. It was the only way to save Ruiz.

"Ain't saying shit. Chop it off. That spick whore be dead by the time my boys finish raping her." Ballard inhaled deep breaths. Snorting through flared nostrils, he trembled like an animal readying for the attack.

The blade's speed caused it to sink deeper into the wooden chair. Ballard screamed unlike the first one—more of a whimper. His face shook with the profane color of vibrant crimson. Beads of sweat mixed with tears just below both eyes. It ran off his narrow jawline and into the coagulating pools of blood.

I grit my teeth watching Agent Blue wiping the spray of Ballard's blood from his plastic suit's face guard. Shoulders curling over my chest, I struggled to form the words to beg Emory to just talk. To save himself, and mostly Ruiz. Agent Jones glared at me. I knew it wasn't the right time to interfere.

Spit flew from Ballard's purple lips. A maze of bluish blood vessels burst beneath his red skin. Anguish from the torture twisted his face until he was no longer recognizable.

"You're a madman." His words fading like his life—defiant until the end. "Remi, get your ass in here. Face me like the man I made." He taunted.

"Mr. Ballard, where is Sergeant RJ Ruiz?"

Oh, Lord no. Not that question again. I'd reached my moral limit.

I peeked around the corner with a corded neck. Sorrow filled my eyes. I saw Emory hyperventilating—he knew what was coming, just not which limb.

Agent Blue knelt down and rammed tape around Emory's shin about four inches below the right knee. Wiping off the meat cleaver, he set it inside a sheath and laid it back in the leather bag.

A protracted hacksaw was removed and Agent Blue smeared the jagged blade with a lubricant. Emory's torso quaked violently. Completely separated from his body, both hands and wrist remained duct taped to the chair's arms. He jerked both stubs back and forth with what strength remained. The thick tape wouldn't surrender their grip on his upper forearms. His mouth tore open, but nothing escaped.

"This is going to take some effort." Agent Blue warned as he kneeled before Emory.

"I'll ask you one last time. Mr. Ballard, where is Sergeant RJ Ruiz?"

Chapter 47
— Sheriff James Walker —

TUGGING AT MY COLLAR, THE heat of fury was ignited by Remi's phone call. His pleas to wait for him before moving out hunched a knot into my gut. I knew better than to allow his emotions to enter the equation. Though, there would be no SWAT activation—his rage may be just what evened the odds.

"Gen, get Sergeant Brooks and Graza over here. Once Remi arrives we roll." I knew my appearance was ragged, but I ignored the profuse perspiration as I began to mentally prepare for our rescue.

"Sheriff, you ready?" Brooks was solid. Graza sprinted up behind him. His chest expanding with each attempt to catch his breathe. His stare chilled my spirit. I knew these men were right for this mission.

"Remi's on his way," I said. "Agents are sanitizing the first location. Graza, get the boat ready to sneak across Turtle Bayou. Seems these fuckers are holding Ruiz in a fishing camp along the marsh."

Shoving both hands into my pants pockets, I stared at the tips of my leather boots. I chewed the inside of my mouth, debating whether to ask St. Pierre a question.

"Buck, is there something wrong?" Genevieve asked. "What can I do?" Her shoulders were drawn back in a best effort to mirror her inner strength.

"Gen, this is going to be like nothing you've experienced. If we survive the battle, you might not survive the after effects. I've struggled for decades with the vile shit I've done in the name of justice.

Honestly, it's just as criminal—my badge is the only thing saying it ain't." I rocked back onto my heels as the heart palpitations drove a flash of regret through my body. She'd hate me.

"Thanks for thinking of me. I'm not a child who needs to be shielded from the bogeymen of this world. I've dealt with my share over twenty-five years. Ruiz is my friend as well as another female cop. It's my duty as an officer and a woman." She nodded as her head tilted back to lock looks. "Really, thanks for caring enough to ask." Her shaking hand wrapped around my elbow as she forced an awkward smile. Her command voice snapped, "I'll rally the team at the boat launch."

Raised in the swamp, Remi was a natural at silently piloting the boat across Turtle Bayou. The dawn's light would race to expose us. My foot pressed against the aluminum hull, but the idle remained consistent. Graza navigated using the GPS coordinates punched into Remi's cell phone.

"We bout ten minutes out. You'll see the camp around this bend. Brooks, I need you over the bow with a long gun just in case." Remi said. His face remained tight but his eyes looked more relaxed in his normal environment. I think he was beginning to believe we could rescue Ruiz.

Graza's face was lit by Remi's cell phone screen. A look pulled tight across his brow as he lifted the cell closer. He rotated his back to Remi and I saw his mouth moving as he read something. A single drop of water fell from his eye. It splashed on the glass screen.

Placing my hand on his shoulder, I mouthed, "You okay?"

Graza swiped a free hand between his mouth and nose to clear the accumulated tears and snot. Slung low, his head shook to signal *no*.

"Five minutes out—stay sharp. We can do this." Remi showed the first grin since this began. Squinting against the faintest hint of a pink sunrise, he leaned onto the windshield.

I saw Brooks adjust his prone position. He was ready to engage. St. Pierre dangled her fingers in the water's mist. Graza's arched torso pulsated and he pressed his palm against his face as it jerked in despair. I slid onto both knees and placed my mouth next to his ear.

"Son, what's with you?" He turned Remi's cell phone face down and slipped it into my hand.

Shielding the light from giving away our approach, I thumbed through the sequence of text messages to Remi from Agent Jones.

[Remi call Blue]

[Do NOT go in camp. Call Blue asap]

[Smith found 2-way surveillance system in house]

[Remi – call NOW]

[shit brother answer cell. Call blue or me]

[Camp has video system. Ballard watch gang rape girls. On dvr n house]

[gang watched bastard rape the boy]

[remi, fucking call me. Don't go in camp]

[gang watched Blue kill ballard.]

[got ID on all 5. Gone from camp]

[remi CalL call me now. U OK. All on videotape]

[Remi – plz call me. Ruiz dead. Taped to chair like ballard. Please no go n]

Dropping my head, the wrenching of my gut knocked me on my ass. The boat rocked unexpectedly. "Hold still." Remi snapped back over his shoulder.

Pressing my palms against watering eyes I asked, "God, why?" The grief was too much. "God save me from myself." I gripped the back strap of my Glock 9mm and unsnapped the holster. I couldn't bear what I'd caused to another innocent soul—I looked down into the barrel.

Daddy. Cold air blew across my face.

Wyatt?

Be careful, dad. I glanced across Turtle Bayou and into the haze of another creole morning.

I love you, son.

Love you too dad. Shaking, my hand slipped the gun back into the holster and snapped it shut.

"Remi, stop the boat." My voice rasped above the engine. Remi spun with an agitated expression and his finger pressed against his lips. Graza folded into the aft. St. Pierre wiped her hand on a towel and knelt next to me—her eyes showed a depth of understanding. She began to weep.

"Remi. Stop the boat. Now."

Brooks glanced back over his shoulder. "Sheriff, everything okay?"

"Suspects are gone." I had everyone's attention.

"They moved RJ?" Remi gritted his teeth.

"Just stop the boat." I pleaded.

"Where is she?" He demanded, pushing up his sleeves and arching his spine.

"Inside."

Chapter 48
— Sheriff James Walker —

THE SKY OPENED.

The beauty of standing in the driving rain is that tears hide within the streams. Other than my heaving chest pulling both shoulders forward and jerking my vertebrae like a whip, I thought I'd make it. Fighting the urge to faint—I focused on my duties.

"Sheriff, once the music fades, just walk over." The deputy's instruction was clear enough.

Quaking so violently, my body caused the razor-sharp uniform trousers to shake. It caught Deputy Chief St. Pierre's attention. "Buck, time to be strong." Her hand pressed firmly against my back. The slight rub and patting across my shoulders eased the burden. It didn't relieve my pain—or responsibility.

This is my fault. Another innocent person who trusted me has been brutally murdered. I've been such a failure.

The haunting sound of the bugle's Taps faded into the crackling of lightening's vicious demands for attention. No one flinched. Lightheadedness overtook me. Closed eyes only tempted me to surrender to the reality. Feeling my body's swaying become over extended in both directions, St. Pierre's hand now tugged at the tail of my Class "A" dress uniform jacket.

"We all need Sheriff Walker right now. Do this for them." St. Pierre's words, though whispered, jackhammered into my ear. She was right—I could fall apart later.

Deep breaths helped straighten my torso. The jacket unrumpled. Medals and ribbons earned through the years for valor, marksmanship, outstanding service, injuries on duty and having stood the line in the face of Hurricane Katrina's wrath now laid directly below the polished gold Sheriff's badge. Four gold stars rested across both shoulders as I arched my back in a broad display of respect for the moment. The ten seniority hash marks sewn up the jacket's left sleeve exploded in a brilliant golden display of time dedicated to serving Bayou Parish.

"Thank you Genevieve." My words shook, but were only meant for her.

Detective Todd Stone moved mechanically toward me. His highly polished Honor Guard uniform was pressed until its sharp creases became deadly. Stiff bodied—the click, click, click of his mirror bright parade dress uniform shoes, shuffle stepped toward me.

Wetness squeezed between my eyelids. Holding my left palm up and my right palm about six inches over it, Detective Stone slipped the folded American flag between them. Pressing against the spongy canvas, I looked at Stone's void expression, "Thank you son."

"Dr. and Misses Ruiz, I am so sorry for the loss of your daughter. We are indebted to your family for her service. She was like a daughter to me."

Bending in front of her parents, I rocked on the balls of my feet. Mustering remaining strength, the words fell from my lips without first considering their affect. Vacant stares pierced me.

"Sheriff Walker, we hold you personally responsible." RJ's mother said through wrinkled lips that trembled as she verbalized what I already knew. "Yes mam. I'm sorry." I said while placing the flag atop her jittering lap. "I know."

The first round of three resonated throughout the church. Sergeant Ruiz's parents jumped. The civilians in the church flinched, and the screams of grieving sorrow poured through the pews.

The seven riflemen shouldered their weapons and unleashed another deafening blast of seven shots fired. Her mother fell limp into her father's chest—he squeezed her while pressing his craggy cheek against her forehead.

Members of the United States Army and Bayou Parish Sheriff's Office combined as a seamlessly operational Honor Guard unit. They flowed with a rigid precision to deliver the final round of their twenty-one gun salute.

Déjà vu—shaking my head, it washed over my spirit. This was the second funeral where I'd honored the loss of a young life. The second one I was asked to stay away from the church reception following the burial.

Wonder who'll show up for my funeral?

— *Lieutenant Remi LeBlanc* —

"WHAT THE FUCK YOU LOOKING at?" I swiped my hand across smacking lips. The guy could have been alone, or with one or two more. Shaking my head to clear the cobwebs, I drew both shoulders back, arching my chest. Slamming my eyelids shut and then reopening helped to clear the vision. This sucker was alone—and his ass was mine.

"Boy, maybe you'd better move it along. Seems you've had enough to drink." The stranger said. He raised his hands in a sign of surrender, or attack.

"Keep your hands off me. Unless you want me to saw them off." I slurred. Rolling my shoulder forward, I swung in wild, big arcs at the man's head. I didn't cringe when my left hand struck the solid wood countertop. Streams of tears rivered down my face—I didn't give a shit that I was making an ass out of myself. Someone was going to feel my pain.

"Okay cowboy, you've had enough. Hit the road." Another man, taller than the first spun me around toward the door.

"I said, nobody touch me." Reaching into my waistband, I ripped out the 9mm. My hand trembling, it swung back and forth across the old biker bar. The last thing I recall was the smack of a pool stick across my forearm, and then the swarm of leather clad bruisers piling on top of me.

There was no need explaining to Buck what happened the night before. He looked like his own demons had been kicking the shit out of him too. Slumped in the old cloth chair across from my desk I watched his shoulders rise and fall in the regret of having to cope.

"When do the others get here?" he asked.

"I told them to be in before noon. Best not to push 'em right now. Too much emotion." Playing the role of supervisor was getting more difficult—I fucked up. Who was I to lead anyone?

"Remi, this gotta get fixed before we get to grieve. I know it's hard, but I've waited five years to cry for Wyatt Cash. It's what keeps me focused. Angry." Walker's words floored me, but I knew without a doubt they were true.

I pressed my forehead against the handcrafted oak conference table. It was just us, but it felt like the world was watching. The flashing red light turned my attention. My gut knotted as I saw Agent Blue's unmarked vehicle slip into the secured sally port. I turned off the closed circuit television monitor. Knowing he was only doing his job, I hadn't faced him since the night he butchered Emory Ballard.

"Remi, you okay son? Your face got mighty red real quick." Buck's observation was right, but I didn't understand why. Feeling like it was on fire, I fanned my cheeks with an old manila folder centered on the table.

"Buck, I'm okay. Just tired, and a lotta sore. I'm sure you'll hear about if you ain't already. I might'a pulled my gun out on the crowd last night inside the Iron Horse Saloon." Gingerly, I pressed against my swollen cheek and closed right eye.

"What'cha talking about? You go screwing with them bikers again, hell Remi, I thought y'all made peace." Buck walked over to buzz open the interior metal door for Agent Blue. I felt a jolt of hate ram through me.

"Morning." Agent Blue waved as he crossed the threshold. I was overcome.

Grabbing him by the shirt collar with both hands, I jerked him up onto his toes, "What the shit you mean good morning? You fucking devil, you sawed a man to pieces. How can you live with yourself?" I saw my spittle fling onto the bridge of his nose and chin. His hands remained by his side.

"Just doing my job boss man." Agent Jones clutched me by my shoulders. He startled me—I'd not seen him come in. Agent Blue walked off. I tried going down the hall after him, but Agent Jones and Walker blocked my path.

"Remi, settle down or go home. Tough times right now, don't need internal cracks." Buck stood nose to nose with me. My beer breath bathed his face.

"He's right, Remi. We got business to handle before we break." Agent Jones lingered to make sure it was okay. "We all lost something—don't blame him or us for doing the job." The former Force Recon Marine's presence always lent a presence of intensity to each situation—today Agents Jones provided calm.

A rare moment alone. A soft rap against my office door—I ignored it. Laying my head back against the chair, I tried processing the hell I witnessed. Breathing became labored, stomach twisted and my throated wretched until I'd found my face inside the plastic lined trash basket. Each heave brought watered eyes and promises to quit.

"Remi you alright son?" Buck asked through the door.

"Give me a minute." He had a key, but respected my privacy.

"Take what you need. Brooks, Graza, and Deputy Chief St. Pierre are here. We'll wait in the conference room." I heard footfalls distancing from the door.

The computer screen's glow lit the ink black office. Absent external windows, the fortified environment served the Task Force mission well. It also entombed each of us with the realities of this life—and death.

Watching our team assemble through the surveillance monitor, I straightened myself up and dabbed at my face with a napkin from last week's pizza run. We each had to be strong for the other. I knew that meant sometimes falling apart—this space was for that. Outside these walls there could be no weakness.

The small frame caught my attention. Pressing my eyes inches from the computer's screen, they narrowed to focus on the motion activating the camera. My neck stretched across the keyboard before my life's air escaped. It was him.

Chapter 49

— *Sheriff James Walker* —

"I'M NOT SURE HOW TO begin. I need for each of you to understand how serious this is. Our isolated parish is about to become overrun with media, mafia and misinformation. It's just a matter of time till everything breaks. The people in this room are most trusted with the duty to maintain the peace. I will count on each of you to be strong when the enemy rages against us." I paced along the wall as I spoke. It wasn't prepared—came from my heart.

"Sheriff, what's the plan? There are five monsters roaming this parish. Do we kill 'em or capture 'em?" Sergeant Brooks pressed his forearms across the conference table. His eyes deflecting from me, to visually query each of the others. Everyone else's heads sought refuge from the reality of his question.

"Earl, I thought about this. The answer's not an easy one, but it's one I've faced before. Can't put y'all in that predicament again. It's best we brief here and get everything out on the table. Go back to the daily business of law enforcement. Trust that they'll get their due." Unable to lock his look, I scanned the room for a bobbing head. None.

A quieted hush sucked the confrontation from the room. Blood-shot from tears and sleeplessness, all eyes looked past me. Rubbing my chin, the *freesons* covered my skin—I felt an innocent presence close by.

Standing outside the door, in the hallway, Detective Todd Stone's muscular hands rested gently across the frightened looking little boy's shoulders. In his small, scarred hands he held police patches and a tee shirt that read, "Bayou Parish Sheriff." His crooked smirk pierced my heart—he looked like my boy.

Waving back at him, the rush of grief swelled in my stomach until crashing through my eyes. Spinning away from the glass door, tears flooded my face. I wasn't supposed to show emotion this morning. I was going to be strong. Be brave for them.

No one spoke. Remi heaved over in his chair—back shaking as he buried his face into his palms. He charged out the door. Genevieve St. Pierre reached for him. She tugged at his shirttail—he was too strong—too determined to not show us his frailty. Her eyes moist, she sought a silent answer from me. I had none.

Agent Smith nodded and exited the rear door. Detached from the emotional churn, I trusted him to refocus Remi. Their mission would be simple—kill five.

Agent Jones, leaning against the rear wall, patted a fist on his bent knee and tapped his watch. Running my hand between my mouth and nose to swipe the snot of sadness, I coughed to clear my throat.

"Sheriff, can I ask why Stone's here?" Graza's body stiffened, he looked unsure about the participants. I knew he had concerns about the young detective.

The remaining officers keyed into my answer, "He's only here to sit with the boy until we contact the child advocacy center for a specialist to debrief him. God knows Duncan has gone through enough—no need causing more damage questioning him like a suspect."

"Still, you got that asshole sitting with him?" Genevieve nodded in agreement with Graza.

"Buck, let Duncan stay with me. Remi has serious concerns about Stone. He'll probably feel safer with a woman. God knows what Emory Ballard did to that angel." She dabbed at tears and gently shook her head yes.

"Okay, but do not allow the parents near this child. I've been told they traded him to Ballard." I demanded.

"Traded for what?" Sergeant Brooks stood up to stretch out.

"A twelve pack of beer." Saying the words sickened me. "Team, do you understand the crap we're dealing with?" Standing erect, focus filled me—time to respond to this filth. Everyone looked straight into my eyes, and then past me as Remi, Agent Jones and Agent Blue returned to the meeting.

"Sheriff, we're here for you. It's more than our job—it's our oath." Remi held out his hand. I pulled him close to me. "Thank you son." The spirit of oneness bathed that moment, and I felt the sense of commitment that it'd take to avenge Ruiz's murder.

"Okay, Agent Smith says we've jobs to do. Task Force, you have you're assignment. Gen—you and Duncan lay low around the office until the advocacy specialist contacts you. Brooks, I know these bastards murdered one of ours, but they also killed Maria Sanchez. Work that case to clear Tommy Chang, and worst case scenario, if one survives—we need to be ready to arrest for murder." I spit out instructions and the team looked ready to execute them.

"On my honor, no one will survive." Remi's low growl hushed my instructions. I grinned at his reassurance.

"Graza, I want Councilman Anthony Chiasson's investigation made top priority. Go to the state violent crimes task force if you have to. I expect Duncan's help will point his way. Now that we know there were videos made of the children's torture and murder—find those videos." Grinding my teeth into my tongue, shock jolted my body to realize there might be a video of my son's death.

"All except one Sheriff. I'll recover all but one." Graza gripped my bicep. I pulled him into a hug. His military rigidity loosened for the embrace. "Thank you Jose."

Sitting in my truck waiting for the clanking sally port's door to free me—my chest heaved while looking through the rearview mirror. Remi shoved Stone out the building's door. The sun shown bright and glare bouncing off the dashboard made much sight difficult. I was sure though that these two had gotten into it after all.

Releasing my foot from the brake, I sighed—I'd let the bucks settle their differences without my interference. Turning the corner to enter the highway, I knew it wouldn't end here—I just hoped it wouldn't end deadly.

Chapter 50

— *Lieutenant Remi LeBlanc* —

STUCK IN A CLUTCH BETWEEN anger to kill and desperate to quit, I was unsure what would happen next. Had it just been a week since we sat in the idling boat, just yards away from the marsh camp where RJ's dismembered body sat strapped inside? I'd steeled my mind and body for the *black bag* operations, but that satchel had been ripped open. I'd do this job for Ruiz—then I'd find another profession.

"How you wanna go about it boss?" Agent Jones' slow southern drawl intimidated most. The chunk of tobacco shoved between his teeth smacked constantly. He meshed back into the seats with the other two Agents caught in this chaos. Agent Blue sat with his wiry arms folded—his gaze cast down, I feared he thought I hated him.

"Blue, I don't blame you. Yeah I'm freaked out by the shit I saw, but I don't judge. It's what you do. I trust you." Rising out of the chair, my legs were tight as I unconsciously moved around the desk to extend my hand. We finally made eye contact, though no emotional connection stirred.

"What's up with Stone? Saw y'all getting into it pretty heavy out back. Pissed you off?" Agent Jones exposed something I thought I'd address on my own. Turning back to my chair, I chewed the inside of my mouth to keep quiet.

This wasn't the time for secrets or mongering panic, "I gotta feed from him—it ain't good." Twisting my torso side to side behind the desk to relieve the aches from last night's barroom mishap, I had to get it out there. "Stone had the last eye-ball on Ruiz before she went missing. Kinda odd the way everyone just so happened to get distracted right before she disappeared. I also think he's a member of WIP. He's not branded but he's got the attitude." Sucking in a deep breath through my swollen nose, I felt like a weight was lifted.

"Wanna put a tail on him?" Agent Smith eagerly offered. My eyes narrowed on the eulogy card from the funeral home—rage bubbled in my gut.

"I need you three on the five."

"Five?" Agent Jones's crinkled brow leaned forward.

"Five. The five corpses I'd better see soon." Both hands pressed against the glass top of my worn oak desk. Pressing away from the desk, I bounced back against the chair. I'd been cursed with taking life, but I'd never ordered it done—it felt hollower than imagined.

"Rules of engagement boss?" Questions asked by capable men tend to intimidate others—Agent Blue was that man.

"Nothing public." I spun to lean my face into the computer's keyboard. These men read lives for a living. My dread of sealing the fate of five men I didn't know, but hated, stirred a wicked storm in my soul. They'd pick up on that conflict—they had a job to do.

"Boss, don't quit us over this." Rarely compassionate, Agent Smith's voice whispered what was on my heart.

"I'm sorry, just can't promise that."

— Detective Jose Graza —

SPOTS OF LIGHT DULLED THE locked room's walls. Saving others the horror, volume ran through my earbuds. The stack of videos seized from Ballard's ranch shamed my laptop. Their words would never be unheard, but I couldn't chance missing a name or recognizing a voice. Still, the small screen had no help limiting the damage done to my mind—sick mutha'fuckers.

Walking through the hallways, I felt dirty—violated. Entombed in the windowless complex, flickering overhead lights haunted the rear bathroom. I needed to decompress. This closet-sized shitter was the place. Stinging bruises exploded on both fists as I slammed them against the painted cinder-block wall. I fell against the porcelain basin—tears streamed from eyes barren for decades.

"Okay in there?" Someone banged on the metal door.

Violently, my cheeks grew swollen with puke. Pressing a hand hard against my lips, both eyes shot wide open in the water-spotted mirror. I swung my head to the left and dropped to a knee. The force of backsplash speckled my cotton button down.

"All good. Bad lunch." I spit through the bile.

Dabbing at the shirt stains while making my way into Deputy Chief St. Pierre's office, I tried burying the emotion. Kicking the angled rubber doorstopper against the wall, I collapsed in the leather chair while the door eased shut.

"Jose, you look grey. You okay?" She reached across the desk to hand a bottle of water.

"How's the kid—Duncan?"

She shielded her eyes with the paperwork already in hand. Sentiments ran raw before the click of the door connected with its frame. "Not good. I think he's lost. This community will have hell to pay if he decides to act out on his rage once old enough to channel it." She leaned back and lifted her eyes to the light. Blinking back tears, her chest slowly rose and fell.

"Deputy Chief, combat tours can't prep a man for what I just watched. Whoever did this shit has to die. No place in prison—as long as the fucker's mind is free, these kids won't rest in peace." The hard plastic CD case snapped between my iron-fisted grip. Sweat blistered across my brow—heart racing.

"The boy's been through some serious stuff Graza. Physical abuse and unthinkable emotional reprogramming. Shrink's not sure how much of what he says is the truth or his mind shutting down to protect itself." St. Pierre patted beneath her eyes, and then drew a deep gulp of air.

Erecting herself behind the dark cherry-stained desk, she looked directly into my face. "Crying over it won't bring justice Jose. Forgive me—I was just wondering if Remi had gone through the same hell under Ballard's control." She couldn't stop the stream of grief.

Hollowed inside from watching pure evil, I'd thought the same thing. I was too ashamed to express it. Skin prickled with a desire to apologize to Remi for gaining a glimpse into his past. It was sinister—not sure if I could face him again.

"Graza, gain anything from those videos? A name, voice, location, anything?" Her voice became monotone. Remaining void of humanity would be the only way to investigate this.

"Nothing yet. Trying to digest it, but I'll watch again. Every frame."

"I intercepted a call for Buck earlier. Seems Big Johnny is feeling better and wants to talk. Still claims to know who's behind the killing. He wants out of jail." St. Pierre offered.

"Did he give you names?" My back tightened as scenarios began to form in my mind.

"No, he's not stupid. It's his only shot at avoiding a life sentence. He holds the cards and knows it. Hell, he holds the entire deck if he's telling the truth." She thumbed through her written notes. Puffy eyes scanning back and forth as pages flipped.

"Was he on a protected line or a payphone in general population?" It struck me like lightening. My fingers wrapped the edges of her desk and I pressed up and out of the chair. "He may be in danger."

St. Pierre's expression erased earlier resolve. Clutching her hands together, she fumbled for the desk phone. The hard plastic receiver banged on the credenza before falling to the floor dangled by the coiled cord. She thumbed through sticky notes looking for an extension number to the jail—eyes narrowed on the one.

"Deputy Chief St. Pierre, who am I speaking with?" Finger impatiently tapping her teeth. "Hi Deputy Adams, I'm trying to get a status on inmate Johnny Chiasson. Which cell block is he being housed?"

A pinkish hue flushed blood red as her lips parted without sound. Her tongue rested just on the inside of her mouth as a humming sound escaped—her eyes glassed over.

"When was he transferred from the parish detention center to the city jail? Who authorized this?" Slamming the office phone against its cradle, her head hung heavily without movement.

"Getting deep Deputy Chief?" Easing my grip from the polished wood's edge, I flopped my body to drop back into the cool padded leather. It would be my only comfort.

"Why would Police Chief Tom Roberts have Johnny transferred to his facility?" The muscles along her forearms bounced as she tapped fingers across her jaw. Eyes cut up to the left, reality would soon strike.

"Anthony Chiasson." Stating the obvious.

"By now Roberts has listened to everything Johnny and I said over the prisoner monitoring system. Our time is draining Graza—better get moving. I'll update Walker."

I snapped from the comfort of the executive office chair—I almost saluted her as I vaulted from the office.

Chapter 51

— Sheriff James Walker —

SEATED IN THE OFFICE, MY body jittered—this wasn't the place to right the wrongs. I needed to be back on the street. Swigging another splash of bottled water, I tried focusing on the administrative tasks of being the law enforcement CEO. The temporary worker at Miss Martha's desk tried her best, but was no replacement. Heck, I'd not visited her since released from the hospital.

Maybe I'm not cut out to be the office exec. I'm just a street cop after all—but a damn good one.

The young girl stepped into my doorway and stood waiting for acknowledgement. Looking over my reading glasses I noticed her hands fidgeting as she bit her bottom lip.

"Devin, can I help you with something?" Recently graduated from high school, I appreciated her work effort—just not her lurking.

"Sir, Doctor Susan Lambert is on the phone for you. Can I patch her through?" A thumbs up and she spun smiling as she bounced back to her desk. I guess she didn't know there was an intercom to save her making the trips.

"Hi Susan, how are you?" Finally allowing myself to ease back against the chair.

"Buck, I'm fine. Something you may be interested in." Her voice never reached casual. Springing up in the seat, I plopped my elbow on the desk.

"What now Doc?"

"Sheriff Gaston Breaux in Jean Laffite Parish called this morning. Seems an old gator trapper pulled in a monster catch at daybreak. Dang thing had trouble swallowing the chicken baited hook." Agitated I waited for the punch line.

"You a veterinarian now?" Squeezing the receiver between my jaw and shoulder, I stared at the e-mails flooding my inbox.

"The problem was that it had half a body caught in his throat."

"How's that my problem Doc? One of my voters?" I rubbed a hand over my mouth and decided to avoid further sarcasm. Devin was back in my door—standing—waiting. "Excuse me Doc. Devin, can I help you?"

"Sir, may I be excused? I have to meet my guidance counselor to register for college." Her face lit with the fear and the promise of a bright future. "Yes, that's fine. Close my door please."

"Any idea who it belonged to?" My brow crunched as I lay my forehead into my moistened palm.

"Not yet, my staff is coordinating with Sergeant Caroline St. Claire on recovering more information. And body pieces." Her conversational stream was difficult to decipher—was she suggesting something? I leaned closer into the handheld phone.

"I know Caroline. Thought she was working undercover?" I asked more hypothetical.

"Anyway, this wasn't an alligator attack—the parts we've recovered so far were dismembered. Some with a scalpel clean through, others hacked. Same body though, just different methods to separate the parts." Her clinical voice detailed her observations.

My thoughts flipped through scenarios and possibilities. "Any idea who?" I pushed the receiver away from my mouth as I blasted a breath from my faltering lungs. Rapping my knuckles along the credenza, her replies drug on.

"I'll know later. We're checking on missing persons, welfare concerns, and etcetera within the region. Makes it easier if we have a positive identification to work toward." Shaking my head, I had to escape the accusations I only assumed she cast.

"Good luck Susan, I know how horrible these cases can become."

"Thanks Buck. I've not seen you since the funeral. It's so horrible the way RJ was murdered. It's another reason I called, but we can discuss later."

"What Susan?" My words pressed aggressive—unintentional.

"Buck, two bodies dismembered, I'm not stupid. You know exactly who was the alligator's breakfast..." Her directness tumbled me back against the leather chair.

"We can talk later. In person." Slapping my hand against my forehead.

Running my finger inside the hallway's cinderblock mortar as I made my way toward the bathroom, raised voices just outside the radio communications caused me to pause.

"Todd you're insane, why would you say something like that?" I recognized Deputy Debi Benoit's shrill voice. I pressed against the wall and backed up a step.

"Why do you care? You didn't like her anyway. Thought she was badass. Fucking spick should'a stayed in Mexico or the Army where they train 'em to behave." Stone's voice carried through the hall. Was he that insensitive or just cracking from the pressure of this case?

"Word is you ought to get your ass suspended or fired for screwing up surveillance during the undercover deal." Benoit wasn't backing down despite her five-foot frame.

"Who cares? Fuck this place. Things were better under Sheriff Martin. Hell for that matter, Gil Gaudet was better than this hack." Stone said while laughing.

Rolling both shoulders, I rocked my head side to side as I clinched my fists. Canting my torso to sweep around the corner, steam had to whistle from my ears. The hand pressed over my right shoulder pulled me off balance and backward.

Into Genevieve's office Remi pressed a finger over his lips. Shaking his head, he cupped a hand to his ear. Genevieve wore ear buds while listening to the two deputies' conversation over the video surveillance system. Shaking her head, a pencil jotted notes and phrases.

Leaning over her shoulder, I watched the monitor of Benoit wagging her finger in Stone's face. Storming past her, he smashed his right shoulder into her left side. Benoit fell back against the corner near the women's bathroom. My back arched in rage as I sprung up from the chair to head out after Stone.

"Check it out Buck," Genevieve said—Benoit looked straight into the fish-eye lens camera mounted above the hallway. She unleashed a giant smile. "Remi's got a gut feeling and Benoit's agreed vet him out if he double-crossed us."

"Remi, you thinking Stone set up Ruiz's kidnapping?" The seriousness of my question caused my insides to quiver over the answer. I'd brought Stone into the detective bureau. His failures would be my responsibility.

"Buck, he don't have the branding whelps, but these WIP turds are mainstreaming themselves." Remi's right hand glided over his left shoulder and chest without thought. I'd seen him do it often—almost a habit or twitch. Those scars haunted him often, possibly always.

"You sure Remi? That'll cause serious rip in this agency. Especially since Buck promoted Stone over more senior and qualified candidates for CID." Genevieve asked.

"What the hell Gen?" Had she just thrown me under the bus?

"Sorry Buck, not what I meant. You saw something special in the boy, gave him a chance. Now it may bite you in the ass. I think it'd be better to handle it quietly for now." Genevieve's expression never flinched—always serious though genuine. Dipping my head with a slight nod, I agreed.

She'll make a great Sheriff one day.

"Buck, let me handle this. It's my mistake in the first place. Ruiz was my responsibility—I failed her. Failed her twice." The world's burden was cast upon Remi's shoulders.

The tall rangy Cajun, who'd served me without hesitation or emotion, fell onto the corner of the desk. Face buried between shaking hands, his pushed back mane of uncombed hair falling forward to conceal the sorrow. Gen moved to place her hand across his quivering back. It heaved with each shudder of the deepest kind of grief—regret.

"Come on now mai cha, we all a part of dis Remi. Don't be blaming yourself." Her natural motherly Creole accent soothed the young man. She pet his back and his body began to rock with each stroke. Pressing a curled hand across my lips, I choked back the reality of the moment.

She was the closet he had to a mom. This case had torn his moral fiber to shreds. The horror he knew as a child, became the evil he fought as a man. In Genevieve's swaying arms I saw the end of both.

Chapter 52
— Detective Jose Graza —

THE INTERSTATE WAS SPOTTED WITH purposeful speeders and reluctant travelers. Unfortunately they blended across lane lines making for hazardous travel returning from Baton Rouge. I swerved off I-10 to run the blue highways back home through Plaquemines, White Castle and Pierre Part.

Clicking over to Bluetooth, Sheriff Walker's voice quivered, "Graza where are we on this case?"

"Sheriff, the Attorney General's Violent Crimes Task Force sends their regards over Sergeant Ruiz. They are highly motivated to resolve this serial killing and believe Ruiz's murder is connected." Restating what we both already believed, my mind reeled from the information shared.

"Chiasson. How's Councilman Chiasson involved in this?" Walker's tone became terse. I sensed the desperation.

"They're not a hundred percent sure he's the killer. They've reviewed the video stash I sent them from Ballard's ranch, and...."

"What? You didn't tell them where the tapes came from did you?" This was the first time I'd ever heard Walker raise his voice. Maybe this conversation was better suited face to face. I smashed the gas pedal.

"Never. I did as you said sir."

"I didn't mean to snap. I trust you Jose."

"They do believe he's at the least is a co-conspirator. They're meeting with the Attorney General about subpoenaing him into a grand jury." Biting my lip, hoping that appeased him for now.

"Okay, that's a start. Get back here soon, we gotta talk to Big Johnny. I hear he wants to trade the killer's name for a taste of freedom." Optimism sprung into Walker's voice.

"Thanks Sir. Did you get him returned?"

"Returned?" Walker spewed.

"Didn't you know? He was moved into the city jail two days ago. Chief Roberts authorized the transfer." White knuckled grip on the steering wheel, I braced for his explosion.

Silence—click.

Chapter 53

— *Sheriff James Walker* —

SURPRISED TO SEE REMI'S TRUCK parked outside the warehouse, I called to speak with Agent Smith. While I trusted the entire Task Force unit, I gravitated closest to him next to Remi. I think Remi did too. He needed to know the entire situation if Remi decided to up and quit.

Unable to pull my truck all the way through the back sally port arena, I stopped just short of a series of metal and wooden contraptions. Agent Blue, concealed behind a welding shield, wielded the torch's flame with purpose. His head lifted as I approached, but I waved him off—I'd rather not know the specifics.

"Smith, where's Remi?" Usually stoic, the grappler's grip lacked the usual crushing connection.

"Not sure Sheriff. Said he'd go on foot. No tracks or trails." Agent Smith's rugged face crunched as he brushed the hair from his eyes. His long goatee was braided and the series of rubber bands lent a sinister look.

"Was he armed?"

"Seriously sir?" Kicking a pile of cut rusted rebar, I tried hiding a grin. "What was I thinking? You're right Smith."

"His cell is on the desk too. Not sure what he's planning, but in the event he returns with a rabbit, Blue here is constructing a cage." Motioning his hand to the center of the giant cement slab, he smiled.

"Just make sure that rabbit tells us who killed my son before you skin it." Slapping him on the shoulder, I thanked him for being loyal to Remi and skipped around Agent Blue's creation to climb back in my truck.

Back onto the highway, my cell showed a text from Genevieve, *[call asap]*.

"Gen, what's up now?" Ramming my foot into the accelerator, I felt the need to get back to the office immediately. This stop at the warehouse had taken me through the swamp and out of the way.

"Got paperwork from the state. Gonna crack open a whole new can of worms." St. Pierre emphasized.

"E-mail it to me. No time to wait—it'll take me a while to get back there." Zipping around blind corners would do me no good if I got killed getting there. Gripping the steering wheel while roaring through the marsh, I suddenly mashed the brakes before hitting the Bayou Rond Pom Pon Bridge.

Shit Buck, focus.

Flashing back to the SWAT raid out here and chasing Big Johnny Chiasson until he crashed caused my body to respond the same way that morning. Sweating and short of breath I narrowed my eyes along the roadway.

"Big Johnny? Oh hell, Johnny's in the city jail. How'd I forget to take care of that?" Grabbing my cell to call Police Chief Tom Roberts, I saw St. Pierre's e-mail. Waiting for the attachment to open, I found a clear shoulder to pull off the highway.

Thumbing through the digital pages of legal documents attached, I finally saw the order from the Louisiana Attorney General's Office. It was an order for my office to serve Anthony Paul Chiasson with the official subpoena to appear before a special grand jury convened by the State of Louisiana.

"Hell yeah. About time that asshole gets what he deserves." I screamed so loud inside my truck the egrets and nutria panicked. My fist beat the air—revenge was close. My heart pounded out of control and again my breathing constricted. Weeks without this health issue—I had to will myself to settle down.

Light began to speckle and explode behind my eyelids—I clutched my chest as it wrapped itself around my heart. The truck began creeping toward the marsh. Both feet stomped against the floorboard to hit the brake pedal, but I didn't have the strength to mash it. My hand wouldn't release to grab the cell phone—or the police radio microphone.

"Oh God, save me. Don't let me go without solving Wyatt's murder. It's all I live for." I bargained. I begged. I saw the front of the truck easing forward into the marsh. "God—help me."

"Daddy?" Afraid, I looked to the passenger's seat.

"Daddy what's the matter? I'm scared." His face was unclear but the sun streaming through the glass silhouetted the shock of curly blonde hair.

"Son, it's okay. Daddy's not feeling good today. I'm alright baby." I struggled to reach him, but my arm was welded to my chest.

The truck lurched. I leaned against the steering wheel to turn the tires left, but it was like rubbing soapy hands together. I couldn't torque my body that far. I began to panic, but I knew Wyatt was watching. Had to keep him calm.

"Daddy, are we gonna die? Should I go now?" His little hand stretched across the large padded console. "You coming with me this time?"

My eyes exploded with tears. It took all my will to stay conscious. Forcing the stiffening tendons in my neck to give way, I caught a glimpse of him. Face still fuzzy, I felt peace about passing.

"Yes baby boy, dad's going with you this time." I closed my eyes and felt the crushing compression on my heart begin to smother my light. An easy grin followed thoughts of Wyatt Cash in the tree house. *Thank you Lord.*

"Daddy?"

"What sweetheart?" My body relaxed as the speckled splashes turned into a steady stream of welcoming light.

"Will the bad men come too?" My chin trembled.

Forcing my eyes to reopen, I saw the horizon leveling off through the windshield. Chest ached like the devil danced upon it. My gummy eyelids were willed to reject the stream of white light. Looking toward my feet, I still couldn't strike the brake.

"Wyatt, daddy needs your help baby. Can you be a big boy and do what I ask?"

"Sure." He sat up tall. His shadowy outline looked confident.

Fighting to jar my right arm free from my curled over chest, I pointed to the stick shift. "Push it up Wyatt. Help daddy." The cab dropped further along the decline, I scrambled my legs as hard as I could to push back against the seat. Wyatt's body never moved—he hovered on the padded seat.

Jerking to a stop, the truck teetered.

Exhaling as the sweat subsided, my body still wretched against itself, "Thank you baby." Enough slack to lean my head against my right shoulder—I shared a smile with him. Wyatt Cash was gone.

Blinking my eyes to clear the fog clouding them, I rolled down the window to get fresh air. I peeked out to see my rear wheels still contacting the ground. I jammed it into reverse and slammed my foot against the gas pedal. A roux of rock, mud and grass rattled the undercarriage.

"Thank you baby boy. Daddy will never let the bad men come after you again."

"Genevieve, have that subpoena ready for me. I'll serve it myself at the parish council meeting tonight." I mashed the end call button just as Doctor Lambert's call was coming in.

"Hi Susan."

"Buck, please meet me today, we need to discuss the body found in the alligator." I'd just escaped death thanks to my son's spirit—this corpse wasn't going to sink me.

Did I just think that?

"Doc, I gotta make a quick stop at the parish council this evening and then I'm all yours." Looking across the cab, hoping for a sign of Wyatt. Anything to prove he was there.

"Okay Buck, but it must be today. I'm not risking my career. Sheriff Breaux keeps calling for information, and I don't know what to say to hold him off."

"Don't worry about Gaston—he's just looking for a press conference to feed his ego. Susan, can I ask you a personal question?"

"Sure Buck, anything." Her voice dropped an octave.

"Do you believe in ghost or spirits?" I cringed as soon as the question left my lips. Squinting my eyes against the highway's glare, I didn't wait for her reply, "Never mind, we can discuss tonight."

"Buck, promise me you will get with me after your council meeting."

"Sure."

Chapter 54

— *Lieutenant Remi LeBlanc* —

TRUDGING THROUGH THE MARSH HAD taken longer than anticipated to reach the boat launch. My informant told me one of the five would return to the camp where Ruiz was butchered. They were scattered and running scared. This one, the youngest had no safe house or cash—those limit your ability to hide. The snitch said Jed had a few handguns and a fishing pole—he'd try to survive off the land until things cooled. Neither of those options would become possibilities for Jed.

Paddling the pirogue along Turtle Bayou's outline meant navigating a huge lake and numerous barrier islands. The afternoon sun bounced off the murky water, and a constant crosswind crested small waves against the side. Spotting the camp about a quarter mile through the marsh, my heart sunk.

I heard Ruiz's cries echoing through the cypress canopy of grey hues. Beams of light breached the cover of foliage leading up to the small porch. My hands trembled laying the paddle inside the boat. A combination of muscular fatigue and returning to this place caused my entire body to jerk. Forcing air into my lungs, the swim would drain the rest of my reserves.

I lay across the inside of the rickety pirogue to steady the sway and to scan the area. There was no boat out front—he could have been dropped off. Tying my boat off to an ageless cypress knee, I slipped into the brackish backwater. My feet didn't touch—shit, I was hoping to wade there.

I'd trapped this areas my whole life. My arms pulled smoothly threw the water while my eyes set just above the surface. The trashing alerted me too more deadly predators than me. My bare feet curled after each kick stroke—I knew what lurked in this shaded area. No need dangling a limb to lose.

Finally under the wooded cabin, I held onto a series of sunken pilings that supported the makeshift structure. Struggling to control my breathing, the effort against the constant wave action took its toll on my already exhausted body. Creases between the wooden slat floors allowed peeks into the room. No movement. I'd slip in through the rear opening.

I crouched on the floor and positioned the sheet hanging over the front opening to allow for a view. The old plywood was warped and full of nail holes. My fists pressed against it and I saw the dark stains saturating the cheap porous surface. My gut wretched to hurl, but I fought to remain silent. Human sound travels through the wetland.

Breeze blows cooler this deep in the swamp—the centuries old ecosystem gives life a chance to bloom under their constant watch. The stained pink cloth nailed above the front window began to whip as winds tried erasing the pungent odor of dried blood. I knelt into the corner as the whirl of a small outboard trawling motor became more pronounced.

Fingers shaking as I lipped the bottom edge to eye a jo-boat approaching. There were no guns in this shack, so I figured he had them with him. My knees quaked balancing on just toes. I cringed at the thought of touching the same spot where the love of my life had been dissected. I raged at the thought of ending one of the killers' lives.

The motor cut and I heard the water lapping against its aluminum hull as it coasted to the small porch. A slight bump, and then the rub of thin metal against wood signaled Jed arrived.

Pressing my body deep into the northeast corner of the cramped space, I had to avoid him seeing me until he entered. Nowhere to hide.

Just enough to surprise before killing him. Holding my breath to quiet my pounding heart, I felt the pulse in each finger. Without a plan, I'd arrived here on emotion—emotion gets you killed. True for one of us that would be.

I peeked over the ledge as a gust of air ploughed through the tattered lace curtain. Slamming my eyelids shut, the image of Ruiz strapped in that chair, staring at this same curtain, through the same window. Seeking, hoping, pleading someone would rescue her. Me, it was my responsibility to be here for her.

I fucking failed her.

My eyes exploded open, my fists steeled against the rotting floor and my spine arched with a bolt of fury I couldn't control.

I sprung up to see Jed bent over tying off the boat. Ripping the serrated blade from its leather sheath I squeezed the wrapped handle until blood drained out of each finger. Filling my lungs with the bayou's breeze and Ruiz's blood remnants, I screamed like a mad man. Yanking the hollow core door back, Jed turned around. Fear etched across his unwrinkled face. He couldn't have been more than seventeen years old.

His body quivered as both palms spread open, and void of weapons. He tried to mouth something as I charged him. Driving my left shoulder between his chest and chin, I heard the clamp of his mouth jarring shut—teeth breaking.

The cold water must have revived him as he struggled wildly under the surface. I had the benefit of lungs full of air. He didn't. Brackish water teemed with life around us. Everything seemed to panic in efforts to escape. Except me—I was what caused the panic.

Shoving the long blade through Jed, the resistance beneath the tide slowed my attack. Visibility less than a foot, I saw his eyes spring wide open with the second entry. Bubbles of blood and air rose between us—his.

Breaking the surface, he gasped for air, "Please."

He thrashed. Arms flailing to stay above the water. Too deep to touch bottom. His exertions only caused blood to pump faster—in saving himself—he was killing himself.

"Please?" My voice quieted by the fatigue.

"Please sir." Fear raped this boy of the brutal facade he tried to portray.

"Fuck you." Again I stuffed the twelve-inch blade through his torso. I didn't know where but it went in—deep. His mouth opened and hands sunk to cover the wound. I smashed my forehead into his face just before he sunk.

Holding onto the porch, I kicked around until feeling his corpse below the surface. Getting him into the camp was difficult, but I drug his dead ass square in the center of the room. Untying his small boat, I pushed away from the camp as the fire began to rage. There'd be no fire department to respond. The estuary would reclaim its peace once the materials were consumed.

I hope he burns in hell.

Chapter 55
— Sheriff James Walker —

THE PARISH COUNCIL'S AGENDA WAS minimal. The room was scattered with a few contractors waiting on bid approvals, elderly citizens who enjoyed the process of government and a newspaper reporter. Perfect.

"Your honor, if I may address the council." Feeling the heat from Anthony Chiasson's stare, I focused directly on the council's president. Clearing her throat, the elderly lady's loose neck skin waggled as she looked back and forth to each elected official.

"Sheriff, this is highly irregular as you're not on the agenda. Can it wait until the public discussion session?" She stretched a strained smile across dingy teeth. The others muttered, but Chiasson stiffened—braced for the unknown.

"Madam President, I appreciate that, but I have an urgent official order." Hesitating, I rotated back to face the audience. Actually, just to face the reporter. Her pen to paper.

"The State of Louisiana's Attorney General has ordered me to serve this subpoena without hesitation or delay to one Anthony Paul Chiasson. He is to appear as demanded to answer questions in regard to his involvement and knowledge of multiple murders involving under age victims." I added that last part in there for affect—it obviously worked. The council clerk had to dial 9-1-1 after the president passed out.

I approached the red-faced councilman. His shoulders rumbled and shaking hands reverberated over the room's loudspeaker system. I smiled nearing him across the elevated bench. Slapping the subpoena across the mahogany countertop, his other notes fluttered in the gust created.

"You Anthony Paul Chiasson have been officially served."

I nodded to the reporter—she'd meet in the hall. Walking out that room felt good, damn good. About time.

Dim lights cast a minimal glow across the black top parking lot. The light turned off behind the window and the front door crept open. Susan Lambert peeked behind the screen door. Her smile bloomed as I waved through my open window. She really was a beautiful woman—naturally greying hair swept back and forth across her angular jawline, as she seemed to skip to the truck.

"Hi Susan, you're looking great, good to see you." Feeling re-deemed after the council meeting, I might have come on a bit too friendly. Her hand set upon the open window's frame, "Buck, is that you?" She looked confused.

Leaning over to push the door open, Susan stretched a long leg onto the seat. Her smile tentative, but warm. "Where to Buck?"

"You requested the meeting, where'd you like to go?" Smiling at each other, the cab's dome light dimmed until only her silhouette appeared where Wyatt once was. Shaking my head, a tear welled in the darkness. "Ok, I'll just pick a spot."

Lightly, her fingers tapped my forearm. I dropped the cell phone back into the cup holder. I wasn't interested in reading Anita's novel of text messages. She was on another rant about how horrible of a father I was and that she hated me. What's new? Her attitude would have to wait.

"Buck, let me get this out before we get to wherever you chose. Would you turn off your police radio just to be sure?" I must've misread what I thought was flirting—her tone was serious. Deadly serious. My fingers quickly switched the receiver to off. "There now, secure." I laid my forearm back on the center console in hopes of more contact.

"I'm not going to play around here Buck. You know whose body that was Sheriff Breaux located. I'm not going to be another one of your pawns." Her arms crossed, she stared straight ahead. A quick glance and I saw her biting her bottom lip.

"Susan..." I bumbled.

"I'm not finished. You asked that I keep Sergeant Ruiz's condition quiet and I agreed. I can understand the heinous nature and what it would do to her family and this community, but now another hacked corpse? What the fuck!" The cell phone popped out of the cup holder after her left hand slammed against the console. Heavy exhales and I saw her body jerk as she began to cry.

"Susan, it's spiraling out of control and there's such evil forces at work here you don't want to get mixed up in them." My eyes scanned the jet black horizon, and my rearview mirror for any signs of being followed. I'd still not shaken that suspicion.

"I can take care of myself, thank you." She jutted her chin up as the curl of her lip faded into a scowl.

"Susan, no time to get macho. Look what these bastards did to Ruiz."

"Buck, look what the hell y'all did to Emory Ballard. Who's worse? You're the damn law Buck—what gives you the right to do this shit?" Scratching for the seatbelt latch, she bucked wildly, "Stop this truck and let me out."

"Susan, Honey, we're in the middle of nowhere. I can't let you out in the middle of a cane field." I'd eased up on the gas pedal in case she tried to hop out of the truck. My heart raced watching her reaction. I'd never heard her use a curse word before—stress had claimed another victim.

"Honey? Buck, have you lost your mind? Don't patronize me. I've been your friend through everything. You never even acknowledged the help I gave you at that parish council meeting by calling in Alcede Gautreaux. So don't Honey me Buck Walker." Finally she freed herself from the metal clamp. It clanked off the passenger window as she fought to jerk the door handle.

She stumbled in the Cajun Inn's oyster shell parking lot, "Just stay away from me." Marching into the darkness, she never turned back.

Do I go after her? Crap, this wasn't the way I wanted the night to go.

Maybe I shouldn't have, but after about fifteen minutes, I spun out of that parking lot and headed home. After all, she's a big girl—I wasn't going to chase her like a dog after a bone.

Twisting through the countryside, I zeroed my focus on the winding roadways leading back home. Tucked out of the way, I needed the quiet—needed to think through today's miracle of seeing Wyatt Cash.

Headlights out before the last turn onto my property, I noticed the motion sensors had activated the exterior lights. Braked on the shoulder and watched. *What the hell had set them off?*

It was quiet. The call of frogs and crickets created a backbeat buzz contrasting the dead still of night. Blinking my eyes several times I either saw movement or shadows breaking in the breeze. The engine's hum muffled, so I pressed my ear out the window for anything upsetting the natural balance of the environment.

The click of a revolver's hammer cocking is distinctive. It's also upsetting to the natural balance of my environment. Sliding my right hand over the police radio's microphone, I hit the emergency distress call button.

"Don't move or I'll blow your stupid skull off." I was one step ahead, though my eyes had already cut into the driver's side mirror. All I saw was barrel.

"No problem mister. No need to cock that hammer, I'm no threat to you." Calming him was my first priority, calming myself would come later.

There was no response signal to my mashing the orange emergency button. Chewing my top lip, I debated another attempt. Gravel crunched under the man's shoes—I knew he was closing in, so I mashed it again. The cavalry should be on their way.

"You're no threat to me, but you are a pain in the ass to Councilman Chiasson. Recall that grand jury subpoena or life as you know it ends." His voice was anonymous but familiar—obviously disguised. The moonless night graced him with cover, but the mirror's reflection shared his black glove steadying the silver revolver. Cloaked in a duck hunter's camouflage, his face concealed by a black balaclava only shown wide eyes.

A drop gun? He's planning to kill me and toss the pistol aside.

Screw it, my thighs tensed and hands pumped blood through them. Stealing a glance at the police radio, I recalled turning it off while talking with Susan. The distress call button wasn't activated. No one was coming.

"Okay mister, anything you say. Just be careful with that pistol." Angry, I tried manipulating my voice to sound soothing—non-threatening. If this punk only knew what a danger I was to his life.

"I got a message from a friend." The camo ghost said, the barrel was pressed against my left ear.

"What's your message son?" nudging my right hand against the holster—could I outdraw his trigger pull?

"Chief Roberts says he found a gig pole at Belle Cove Plantation."

"So what?" My fists clinched, and shoulders curled forward. If he had that, he had me by the balls.

"So what? Chief said you'd be an asshole. He also lifted a nice bloody handprint. Wouldn't be yours now would it?" I detected youth in his comments. He had to be one of Ruiz's killers.

Stay calm, keep him talking, focus on him. What's the connection to Ballard, Roberts, Chiasson and murders?

"Roberts told you this? How does a young punk like you know the chief of police?" My face reddened as he pushed the tip of the revolver harder against my skull. Angry, I forced my head back against it.

"Punk? Who you calling a punk old man? Tom's done more for keeping this place pure than your crooked ass." He struck me with the barrel's cold steal—I'd had enough. I also knew the connection—WIP.

It was too late by the time he heard the zip of the polymer exiting through the padded leather. My body dropped—twisting onto the center console as I drove the Glock 9mm toward him.

His bullet exploded in a brilliant spark of light, followed by the booming of glass and metal. Anticipating his retreat, I pulled the trigger, hurling bullet after bullet through the rear window. Unable to see or hear as the rip of led launched inside the encased cab muted me—I felt the thump of flesh rock the truck.

Reloading by feel, my eyes opened wide trying to salvage sight. The barrel swept across the seat scanning for him. Headlights skidded. Slamming in my rear bumper—I was impaled by the steering wheel and radio control knobs. I scrambled to recover. The weapon had landed somewhere in the truck's interior.

Footsteps slowly dragged through the gravel and I heard the crunching grow louder as a shadow emerged. I swiped the back up revolver from the rear of my pants and trained the sights center mass of the open driver's side window.

The hammer clicked back quietly and my index finger held tension against the custom trigger.

"Buck, where are you?" I heard the screaming. Dropping the hammer, "Susan?"

Her silver hair bounced against the lightless sky. Panic etched across her face as she reached through the opening. "Buck, I'm so sorry, I had no idea."

"Susan, you alone?" Wedging myself from between the seats and dashboard, I kept sweeping my free hand for the Glock 9mm.

Where did he go?

Had this been a movie, he would've appeared behind Susan and I'd be forced to take him out with a headshot. This wasn't a movie. Her hopping and screams signaled she'd just discovered him—one of Ruiz's killers. Dead at her feet.

The driver's door was crushed—I climbed out the passenger's side. Susan had dashed across the headlights to meet me. Jumping in my arms, she pressed her head against my bruised chest. Our bodies melted into one. It'd been so long for me, the warmth of her body startled me.

I kissed her.

Chapter 56
— Detective Jose Graza —

"HOLD ON BUDDY, CAN I help you?" Who let this bum roam around the office—crap, he smelled like sewage. Approaching the vagrant, I was cautious. The tall rangy figure had his back turned toward me in only denim shorts and a soaking wet wife beater's undershirt. Hand on my Taser, I asked again.

"Graza, I'm tired and need a ride back to the warehouse, don't fuck with me."

"Remi?"

"Will you help me or not?" I recognized his face once confronting me, but I didn't know him. The empty, thousand yard stare and low growl showed a man lost.

"Brother, you need help. Are you okay Remi?" His mangled hair strewn across his ruddy face made reading him further more difficult. His hallow, empty eyes scanned over my head and into the Squad Room.

"Where's Stone?" he barked. The combat blade was slung from the leather sheath. His hand bounced from it to his waist, his eyes remained fixed on nothing.

"Probably gone for the night. Let us handle this Remi, you need to let your mind rest before it cracks." I put both hands up, palms facing him patting the air.

His eyes engaged with wrath behind them, "You saying I'm crazy Jose?" He snatched my wrist with his left hand—his grip was powerful.

I couldn't break it. I twisted my arm to break free, but he had me solid as his right hand eased toward the sheath.

"Remi let him go or I'll blow your head off." My eyes caught the barrel of her service weapon aimed along the outside of my left shoulder. I turned away and tucked my chin.

"Genevieve you don't wanna get involved in my hell." Remi never flinched.

"Remi, you don't want to get involved with my detective." St. Pierre didn't flinch either—outsized over a foot and a half, she was a rock. "Let him go."

He dropped my arm. Damn that dude is strong.

"Where's Stone? I'm taking out all the trash before I go." Remi looked wild, desperate, but focused.

"Remi, let me take care of Stone. You go get Ruiz's killers." She negotiated.

"Stone's the one who set her up. He's responsible." Stone? Confirmation—I knew he was a racist prick from the second Maria Sanchez's murder broke. He wanted nothing to do with solving her case because she was Hispanic.

I chewed on the inside of my cheek debating on turning this madman loose on that young idiot, "Stone is staying at the Gator Bait Inn, room one-ten." Screw him.

"Graza?" St. Pierre's mouth pinched as she peered at me.

"I heard him on the phone earlier from my cubicle. Thinks people are after him. Heard the Asian Triad were cruising the streets because of the way Tommy Chang was handled." I added, rubbing the purple whelps on my wrist.

"Let us handle this Remi. Please." St. Pierre ordered.

"Y'all have done nothing so far. Am I supposed to wait for a court to decide who killed Ruiz?" Remi stalked the small area wiping his face and grunting.

"No, Buck called earlier, seems there are only three left to find." I cringed hearing the callousness at which St. Pierre delivered her news.

"Two." Remi corrected.

"Two?" I jumped in.

"Called warehouse, Agent Blue was busing skinning the third. We'll have the others very soon." Remi smashed his fist into his palm.

St. Pierre's look mirrored mine—disgust and relief.

"Guys, please. Let me handle Stone. You both need to focus on other shit. Stone disrespected my people, let me have a talk with him." I had no intention of harming the man, but I did want answers.

"Remi, I'll drive you to the warehouse, then I have to pick up Buck. Something about his truck getting smashed in the attack." St. Pierre calmed the giant ball of fury enough to walk him out the side door.

"You can drive me, but once the scores have been settled, I quit." Remi's bombshell caught me off guard—St. Pierre didn't show it if it hit her too.

Walking back into CID straightening my tie, I told Sergeant Brooks where I was heading. Just not why. Rubbing reddened eyes, he only nodded. He'd lost the edge of late. These events pressed us all against the jagged brink. It was up to hardened men like us to keep the secrets and the peace.

Back onto Sullivan Boulevard my mind raced back through the claps of thundering lighting streaks. I replayed every moment that led up to Ruiz's abduction. It wasn't possible—unless Stone set up the distractions. He had the primary eyeball during the fighting with the agents.

Slamming my palm against the steering wheel as I zipped through yellow lights, I had to escape the memory—the guilt. The hell if I wanted to get stuck in some random car jacking or witness a robbery. This part of the city was a throw away. Under Chief Roberts' jurisdiction, the city police department seldom patrolled the area. Probably because it was mostly minority stacked.

My head jerked around the area before slipping the police cruiser into a narrow slot outside the dive's eight-foot wall. Throwing an old windbreaker over my sidearm, I tapped my right heel against my left calf—back up revolver where it should be. The cloudless sky just seemed rainy. I know it was the memory of the last night we were out here. The darkness remained the same—only emptier.

Slipping toward the dimly let entrance I hesitated. I surveyed the interior to spot room one-ten. Stone's cruiser was parked directly in front of the door. *Stupid rookie mistake. Not much good for hiding himself.*

I pulled the cell phone from my slacks pocket to document the strange characters spray painted along the wall at the Gator Bait Inn's entrance. Recognizing the style as Asian lettering, my deployments into the Orient didn't allow for learning the language.

My gut wouldn't allow my first breach between the walls. An evil presence filled the abyss. Stone's unit was the only one inside. Squinting for other signs of life, all the tattered curtains were pressed closed. I was sure the other occupants probably spent more time walking the streets corners. Not much need for motor transportation.

Curling around the wall, I stayed in the shadows beyond the yellow anti-mosquito lighting. It reeked of piss and booze. The broken glass and busted condoms crushed beneath the soles of my polished duty shoes. I made it to the awning that led about ten doors to Stone's room. Silent—dead silent.

Squeezing against the thin brick column between rickety green-painted door and the cigarette smoke-stained plate glass window, I tapped on the door. No sound. The curtains caught my attention, but moved only because of the strip of air conditioning unit activated.

I knocked louder, but whispered, "Stone, it's me Jose Graza."

"Get lost."

"Dude, I'm on your side. Just talk to me." Shrugging my shoulders, I wasn't even sure why I was there, much less why I lied about being on his side.

What am I going to do if he opens the door? Punch him, arrest him, be his Hispanic friend? This is stupid.

Stepping back from the wall, I leapt across the door so he wouldn't see my shadow crossing in front of his door. Dialing St. Pierre to let her know I found him, the door flung open. A barrel breached the threshold.

"Get in here."

I froze. No way I'd outdraw him, his gun was just inches from my head.

"Don't make me say it again Mexican."

Chapter 57
— Sheriff James Walker —

"THANKS FOR THE RIDE GEN. I hated to ask one of these detectives to drive me. They need to focus on this investigation."

"Anytime, after all you're the boss." Her feigned smile failed to conceal the concern engraved deep in her round face. Both hands on the steering wheel, she handled everything the same way—with stability.

"That's true—also part of why I wanted you to come pick me up— so we could talk."

"Sure Buck, but you didn't have to trick me by totaling your truck. By the way, Sergeant Brooks said he'd get with you tomorrow to take a full statement. He said he'd also call Remi. Two to go as I understand it." Smiling had become very difficult for her after that statement. We all suffered the strain of these last months.

Glancing away as cars approached in the narrow opposing lane of traffic, she eased off the accelerator. We were only heading to the motor pool for a replacement vehicle. No need to hurry.

"So, what was it that you wanted to talk about Buck?"

"Devin e-mailed me a passed resolution from the parish council meeting."

"Devin?" Her lips pinched as eyes scrapped away from the high-way. "Who?" she shrugged both shoulders.

"The temp taking Miss Martha's place." I nudged her and tried to laugh. I swallowed harder than usual and felt like my Adams' apple was the size of a pumpkin.

"Oh, her. I'm sorry. Too much on my mind to recall her name."

"Anyway, the e-mail had an attachment. Seems the parish council passed a resolution once her majesty the president was whisked away by Acadia Ambulance." Feeling my chest begin to tighten again, I arched my back by unbuckling the seatbelt.

"Lemme guess, Councilman Chiasson, the council vice-chair pushed it through?" She unconsciously accelerated, though I didn't mind arriving sooner.

"Exactly. Payback for being called to grand jury. That piece of crap ain't gonna quit. Anyway, they passed a resolution calling for a special election for the Office of Sheriff." There, I said it. Hitting me like a ton of bricks, I'd not known how vested I'd become in the job.

"You mean they going to say screw Governor Jewel? She warned them. She sent her attorney..." She reached into her shirt pocket to stop the ringing cell, "I'm sorry Buck, it's Graza."

"Sure Gen." I leaned back to breath deep and release the tension coursing through my frame.

"Hello."

"Hello?"

"Graza, this is St. Pierre. Hello." Her face squeezed into a pointed focus.

"Everything okay Gen?" Her other hand left the wheel to press a finger against her lips. She sat the cell on the console—hit the speaker-phone button and then the mute.

"Stone what you gonna do with that gun, shoot me?" We both leaned toward the center console.

"Should've minded your own business Graza. Had nothing to do with you." Genevieve mouthed – "That's Stone."

"Now it does, so what you gonna do?" Graza was pushing Stone's buttons—he'd better play it cool. The boy sounded ragged.

"You forced me into this shit. You wanted your Spick girlfriend investigated. You had to know who killed her, didn't you?" I knew the rookie detective's voice. He'd gone over the edge.

"Did you hole up in room one-ten to hide? Your damn police car is right outside. You don't think they gonna find you?" Graza relayed information.

"You giving directions, you fucking brown skin devil? Give me your weapon. And your phone." The phone died.

St. Pierre's wooden expression remained strong, "Buck, he's at the Gator Bait Inn. You heard it—room one-ten. He was going to confront Stone on setting up Ruiz."

"Why the fuck did you let him do that Genevieve?" Slamming my fist against the center console, I felt the hinge of pain from the crash.

"Because if he hadn't, Remi would have. You know what would have happened then?" She glanced at my fist with her mouth twisted in the upper right corner—she wasn't impressed.

"Activate SWAT." I pressed back against the seat fighting the compression forming around my lungs—was it happening again?

"I was already dialing it." She held the glowing screen up to show the call dialed. I saw satisfaction in her capabilities.

"Genevieve?" I rolled my neck, and then took a huge swig from the water bottle I'd thrown in my go-bag.

"Yes Buck, I said I've activated SWAT."

"That's not it."

"I'm sorry." Dropping the cell phone into the plastic cup holder, she laid her hand gently upon my wrist.

"May God be between you and the harm in all the empty places you walk." I offered as I placed my right hand over hers.

"Buck, what are you talking about, I'm confused." Her eyes glistened.

"It's your time Genevieve. I'm not going to run for Sheriff."

Chapter 58

— Agent Jones —

WHORES AND JOHNS ESCAPED FROM behind busted wooden doors. Scattering across the parking lot scurrying for cover, I heard the scuffling of old work boots harmonizing with the click clack of cheap plastic high-heels.

"Blue, let me know once it clears. I need a sit-rep."

The smoky manager's office served as a makeshift operational command post. Dingy colored orange curtains cracked to reveal a pothole filled parking lot full of torn fishnets, over-spilling fake leather purses and beer cans strewn across it by the crowd of cheap sex thrill seekers.

"Sir, everyone's evacuated. Room one-ten is the target. Door and curtains closed." Agent Blue's quiet tone wasn't from worry. He'd been and beaten hell back on more than a few occasions. Stoically, he reported the situation as high-stakes operators do—void of emotion.

"Perimeter?" I asked while leaning closer into the sliver between stained laced-cloth.

"Secure. Patrol officers positioned on outside of walls. No rear windows, no escape. Flat roof, no attic or crawl spaces. He's trapped." Agent Blue rattled off.

"So is Graza." I squeezed the ink pen in my fist while straining to monitor the tactical radio channel. The close-quarters of the Gator Bait Inn made for hushed communications.

"Sheriff Walker's here sir." Agent Blue's ruddy complexion deepened to a purplish grey. Extreme fatigue hit us both days ago. He was fond of saying sleep was for the week, but he was human too. It showed.

Snapping up from the tattered cloth chair, I greeted Sheriff Walker and Deputy Chief St. Pierre. The room cramped quickly. St. Pierre stepped back, but Agent Blue stiffened his body and slid past her without making eye contact.

"What's with him?" St. Pierre said, her eyes rolling with an exaggerated exhale.

"He's got a thing about touching a woman. Said they defile him." Palm pressed against my teeth, wishing I could retrieve those words.

"Probably best, he scares the crap out of me." Her hand cupped over tight lips. Her eyes darted out the door watching for his return.

"What we got Jones?" Walker looked frail. His long frame craned over the hotel manager's desk. A single finger eased the cloth to peer through the curtain's opening.

"Well, Sheriff good going on dropping the second target." St. Pierre stiffened at my words as though a guarded secret had gone badly. Walker nodded his head without breaking his gaze, "What we got?" He repeated.

"Hotel perimeter locked down, all rooms confirmed evac, snipers on one-two and one-four corners and Stone has Graza held up in room one-ten. Negotiators dialing the room phone but no answer. SWAT occupying one room on either side of target." Then I gulped stale air.

"That's it?" His head jerked back to the left as his eyes cut an unimpressed gaze. He righted himself and reached into the thick plastic go-box. "Where's the risk assessment charts? Let's ramp this up and resolve it quick." He flipped the spiral-bound chart over his knuckles and then yanked his fingers back. The plastic coated book bounced off the metal desktop and onto the grime covered linoleum floor.

"Here you go Buck, everything okay?" St. Pierre's face flushed crimson as she retrieved the spiral book. Her eyes sliced a path as it was laid on the desk. Printed on the binder was the name – Sergeant RJ Ruiz.

This was the first SWAT op without her in command.

"Fast is slow." Buck's glistening eyes reflected the redness surrounding his naturally light colored pupils. His crooked finger traced the page until a single teardrop struck it.

"Sir?" I asked.

"Fast is slow. I always told Ruiz that about SWAT maneuvers. Never rush in." His pointy finger jabbed at the corner of both eyes, "I'm sorry Jones—I should just let you handle this. You got it under control." He gently lifted the commander's notebook and laid it back into the case.

Quick peeks through the suffocated quarters and Agent Blue returned. I opened the plastic binder and pressed my hand next to Ruiz's written notes. Blue's smile was rare, but his message was clear— in her honor.

"Progress with calling room phone?" I pressed, now refocused.

"He ripped it out of the wall. We've drilled pinhole cameras through both sidewalls—got eyes on everything he's doing. Guys lost it." Agent Blue had become slightly animated in his briefings.

"How's Graza?" I questioned.

"Handcuffed. Back against the door. To prevent us from bum rushing I guess." Agent Blue laughed, "Dude watches too much TV."

"Get a throw phone up there. We need to establish comms with him quick. He might be a rookie detective, but he's been on the job a few years." My gut clinched racing over tactical scenarios—worse of all, another cop getting murdered.

Not on my watch.

Shadows broke as six armor-clad Operators whished along the interior complex wall. Floodlights focused on the door and window of room one-ten—all other lighting was disconnected. The heavy Kevlar bulletproof shield raised as the team neared the target's door. Submachine guns blanketed both sides of it. Crouched atop each other, the Operators' feet tipped soundlessly on the balls of their soles. Movement slowed.

Two Operators handled the negotiator's throw-phone. The rear guard protected the unit's 6. Almost ghostly, the unit appeared in front of the door, delivered the hard plastic case carrying a rugged one-way communications telephone, and disappeared—mission accomplished.

Sergeant Earl Brooks stood by in the mobile command post vehicle parked along Sullivan Boulevard to assist the Negotiations Unit. I'd just begun working around him, but felt I could rely on him. Crisis situations require keeping those most trusted the closet.

"Jones, the door's opening." Agent Blue grabbed my sleeve.

"Keep an eye out brother—I'm dialing into the phone's channel. Wanna hear what bullshit this punk got to say." I patted him on the shoulder as I struggled with the maze of knobs and wires.

"He's got the phone."

"Got'cha, I hear him clicking in." Eyes pressed, I blocked out my surroundings. Temples veiny, I tuned into his first words. They're the most telling of intentions.

"Everybody leave me alone." Stone said unremarkably.

"Todd, you know that's not possible. Why don't you come on out and lets talk." The negotiator said.

"I can't forgive myself for what I did. I deserve to die—tonight."

"Todd, no one deserves to die. Forgiveness comes in time." The negotiator's voice was soothing—I followed his leading of Stone's conversation. Pressing the earphone to my head, I tensed for the next words.

"I killed Ruiz. It's my fault. They made me. They held Walker's son over my head." Stone's shattered voice infused with regret and sobbing. My head spun with his frank admissions. I searched for Walker—he had to hear this.

"Blue, get Walker in here." His eyes blinked. Handing me the extra set of earphones as his lean musculature cruised toward the hotel's lobby.

"Todd, what did they hold over your head?" The negotiator focused on that statement. It was off track—he should've focused on Stone's surrender, not his crimes.

"I know who killed Wyatt Cash." Stone's blubbering made the words difficult to understand. Walker understood them—his tall frame collapsed onto both knees. Agent Blue laid his palm across the shoulders of this rock. Heaving, his lungs rocked his entire torso. Walker was silent as he pressed his body up, his ears filling with the confessions of a coward.

"Todd, you can use that information for good. Don't let it burden you son." The negotiator sounded off script. Signaling to Agent Blue, SWAT had better be ready to respond.

"It's too late. They're too powerful." Stone declared.

Three gunshots splintered the door from within room one-ten.

"Units stand ready." On my command, tactical squads filling hotel rooms on either side of the target room exited their doors—ready to force entry to confront Stone.

"Sniper One—no movement detected." His tone low—focused.

"Graza still okay." Radioed the SWAT tech monitoring the hidden cameras drilled through each wall of Stone's room.

"Todd, no more shots please. Let's just talk this out. Who has you so afraid? We'll protect you." Balling my fist at the negotiator's use of the word "afraid" I sensed it was going downhill fast. So did Walker.

"Give me that microphone." Walker threw the headphones onto the dirty tile floor and spun to squeeze through the doorway. The paper Mache decorations hung across the threshold caught onto his ear and dangled as he forged through the tiny office.

Both palms facing up, Agent Blue shrugged his shoulders. Retrieving the headset, I nodded side to side, "Leave him be."

"Stone, this is Sheriff Walker. I want to know who killed my son. Please." My gaze burned through to the outside parking lot. Sergeant Earl Brooks stood helpless next to the mobile command vehicle looking back at me.

"Sheriff, I'm so sorry 'bout all this. You trusted me. I failed. I'll tell you—I gotta make this right." Rubbing my chin with a free hand, my brow crinkled and eyes narrowed in on the parking lot. Intuition screamed something was wrong.

"Good boy Todd. Come on out of that room. Meet me in the parking lot and let's talk." The Sheriff's voice lacked tension. It was a setup. Sergeant Brooks still had eyes on me through the lobby's window. Shaking my head violently, I waved my fingers below my chin. Brooks shot me a thumb up, and then scrambled to intercept Walker as he exited the command vehicle.

I sure wish Remi was here.

"Coming out." Snapped a sniper over the radio. I fell over the cluttered metal desktop and jerked the curtain back.

"No sign of Graza." Yelled a SWAT operator.

"Blue, go help Earl hold onto Walker. This shit ain't going down right." Panic gripped me. Things were moving too fast. Too out of sync.

"Eyes on, can't see his hands." A sniper radioed.

"Same traffic." Echoed another sniper.

"Tac Team Alpha. Target has hands concealed. Deploy Taser?" Distracted, I watched the struggle outside the lobby door. St. Pierre tried helping the others, but Walker was too determined.

"Room door left open, eye on Graza. Not moving." The sniper's information fetched me back to focus—sent a spike through my gut. "Tac Team Bravo enter room. Secure Graza." I saw the tactical unit sweep into room one-ten. The Tactical Emergency Medic began to treat Graza while other Operators sat behind a ballistic shield to watch Stone's advance across the uneven surface.

Everything was happening so fast, yet felt like slow motion.

Stone scrapped his feet across the rock and gravel parking lot. "Sheriff where are you?" Calling out, his hands remained hidden.

Glancing between the parking lot and outside the lobby door, I

watched as a man desperate for answers shoved three trusted employ-
ees. He bolted through the high-walled entrance. Tripping across the
darkness atop the water-filled holes in the open surface, Sheriff Walker
began to approach Stone. Arms wide open—unarmed.

"Hands hidden. Watch the hands." Barked a sniper.

"Movement." An unknown voice interrupted.

One shot rang out. Detective Todd Stone's body crumpled.

Chapter 59
— *Sheriff James Walker* —

TWO DAYS HAD BEEN LOST. Unsure where they'd escaped to, but I was on the brink of just not giving a rat's ass. I needed a release—unsure where to look, I headed back toward the abandoned tank batteries off of Highway 307. Susan warned me against returning there, but until those responsible for Wyatt Cash's murder were found, I'd have no peace.

The old highway was unusually quiet this morning. Oilfield workers and fishermen had already settled at their locations, and with school back in session the yellow stream of transportation had delivered cargoes safely.

It was way too early to have a drink, much less a pint—but I wasn't making the best choices of late. Problem was I was caring less and less about making those decisions.

Twisting the cap off the bottle of bourbon I raised it to my lips. Closing my eyes to inhale the sharp odor—the stinging aroma rocked my head. My skull pined as it fell back against the headrest. I slammed both eyes harder to dull the agony. The clatter of the railroad cars whizzing mere feet from my truck almost lulled me to sleep. The force of the motion rhythmically swayed my truck as the generated breeze wafted through the open window.

My foot slipped off the brake. I felt the front bumper strike the lowered crossing arm. Eyes ripped open in panic, the train's fury roared even closer. I slammed on the brake and threw the truck into park.

What the hell am I doing?

Backing off the train track incline, I tossed that glass bottle as deep into the sugarcane field as I could. The pity party would have to wait.

"Sheriff Walker calling for Deputy Chief St. Pierre." Dispatch punched me right through. Wiping the sweat from my hairline, I exhaled repeatedly while gazing wide-eyed into the rearview mirror. I cranked the A/C up to max cool.

"Hi Buck. Getting worried about you. Devin said she'd not heard from you at all." Genevieve's voice eased with relief from knowing I was okay.

"Who?" My lips pressed.

"Devin, the temp worker. You hired her Buck." Gen almost sounded like she way being playful in her admonishment. She sounded like everything was normal—that's the quality of her steady leadership. Looking into the rearview mirror, mixed emotions stirred— I knew she was the right person to take over as Sheriff. I just wasn't sure why I wasn't.

"Gen, any reply from Chief Roberts? I want to know why Big Johnny Chiasson's still in the city's jail." My chest clutched—Roberts' arrogance enraged me. I mashed the accelerator to make my next stop. Just in case there was a repeat from the other day—I had no intention of driving off into the marsh. Again.

"Buck, I've called and even sent Warden Boudreaux over there personally. Chief Roberts had the nerve to say it was confidential. He strongly suggested the Warden leave his facility."

"It's high time I pay a visit to the Police Chief. He's got something of mine, and he's gonna to return it." Opening and closing my fist, a slight mist began to form above my lip.

"Shall I have Devin schedule an appointment?" Gen questioned with curiosity in her quiet tone.

"Not that type of visit."

The quick exit off the dirt road snuck up on me. Turning left while hard braking, my body hurdled off the seat as I bounced along the gravel path through the woods. With a quick text message, the corrugated metal sally port door jerked its way until open.

His snarled figure looked consumed by fury—I barely recognized him. I feared this case would expose Remi's deepest scars—I just didn't know they'd destroy him. Agent Smith closed the door behind us. He returned to the bay area to join Agent Blue. Seems the third target we hunted for killing Ruiz was more resistant than they anticipated.

"Remi, I'm not sure what to say." I stood by the door. The usual handshake wasn't extended—his back was bent emptying desk drawers into an old cardboard box. "Son, I failed you. Put too much on you at once." I strained to see his face against the computer's glow in the dim office.

"Too much at once? I've been nothing but your bitch since I came to the Task Force. You're go-to for cleaning up fuck ups. Never a thank you or how you fucking doing Remi. Nothing. Like a damn yard dog." His hair, oily and unkempt swung side to side as he reached deeper into each drawer to empty items long hidden.

"I don't know what to say son. I failed you too. Been so blinded by finding Wyatt Cash's killer that I didn't see the damage I was doing to others." Leaning toward him, I withdrew my hand—he wasn't in a state to be startled.

"You used me Buck. Just like Emory Ballard. You monsters are cut from the same cloth." Spinning toward me, my eyes shot down to the pistol in his right hand. A strong grip caused muscle fibers to flex and pop along his forearm. Rivers of bright blue veins exploded from beneath the thin layer of skin shrink-wrapped around the long gangly limb.

"Remi, now put that down son." I held both palms open to show I wasn't armed. I was, but no way I'd outdraw him. My chest tightening, the all-to familiar speckles of light streaked behind my eyelids. My knees unhinged. "Whoa Remi, I'm just gonna sit a bit. Not feeling well."

He reduced his long frame into a ball and lingered above me. I heard the smack of the metal revolver against the tile floor. "You okay Buck?"

"Just let me lay down, I need air." I blinked at the yellowed fluorescent lighting as my body stretched into the hallway. Shadowed figures hovered, creating waves of stale air to brush across my face and chest.

"Buck, an ambulance is coming. We gotta move you to the front section away from our operations. Just hang on." The arteries tracing through Remi's temples guided rivers of sweat that ended up bouncing off my face and neck.

"It'll be okay son." I fought to push the words between thickening lips.

"I'm sorry I caused this Buck." His sopping mop of hair lay across my chest. I could feel his weeping through my soul.

"Gig pole. Need it from Roberts." I whispered.

"Okay." He said, "I'll call Gen."

Flashes of hot and cold rushed through my body. Impossible to get comfortable, I pressed my eyes shut. The sirens steady wailing contrasted the jerking of the medical bus' box end. I heard the young medics' stream of foreign jargon. Confused by what they were saying, I tried to drown out their voices by humming a melody.

"Sheriff, you allergic to aspirin?" I'd stopped humming and began passing in and out of consciousness. "Not sure," I tried speaking against the tug across my lips—words came unsure. Body flexed as my mouth began to burn with a tingling sensation. I fought to sit up in the gurney. The medic placed a hand across my sternum, "Sheriff, it's just the nitroglycerin—if it's burning, it's working."

He readjusted the oxygen tube running beneath my nose—I'd pulled it loose struggling to sit up. "Sheriff, you've got to relax. Lay back down sir. Please, we'll be in the ER soon." His young eyes suddenly steeled. They glanced away in absolute focus—I felt the pinch of the IV needle breach my vein. Dropping my head back, I listened to the broken pattern of the ECG monitor.

Wyatt Cash, are you here son?

Crashing of wooden doors and the zipping of glass accesses antici-pating entries. The bright white of hallway lights sealed eyelids shut. The unsteady rattle and bump of the ride through the emergency room landed me in an ice-cold box for a room. Attendants jerked the sheet across an offset pairing, causing me to flinch in agony as I struck the stiff mattress.

"Buck, its Susan. You're going to be okay." The ceiling lights blurred her image but I recognized her voice. I smiled—or thought I was smiling. "Thank you Susan." I felt her hand brush over my forehead. "Just let the doctors do their job Buck, and don't be so damn stubborn." My body had been train wrecked—I nodded with the strength remaining.

Her silhouette graced the door. Dangling her fingers lightly—maybe it was the medication making me loopy. I thought I saw a flash of fury explode behind her. Blinking my eyes, it was gone. The orange jumpsuit shoved on a roller by uniformed officers. Surrendering my head onto the sheet, it had to be a dream.

Chapter 60

— Lieutenant Remi LeBlanc —

JERKED FROM MY CHAIR BY an unholy noise, my ass ended up on the edge of the seat. Wide-eyed, the dim office offered no source for the sound. Only the light creeping beneath the hallway remained—all else fell silent. Willing my pulse to slow down, I pressed my ear toward the open bay area. Faint, an intermittent faint buzzing skipped through the air. I pressed my palms against the old chair—curious where the sound went.

"Agent Blue, progress?" He looked stunned to see me. I kept a distance from the welded metal contraption.

"Remi, good to see you. Thought you'd gone already my brother." He held up a gloved-fisted salute, but was careful with the cutting tool. Usually unaffected, I didn't have the stomach to look at what they'd done to killer number three. It'd been about three days and he hadn't broken—or died. Tough bastard.

"Not yet. Got business to finish, made a promise." Canting my shoulders away from the cage. I heard his moans, but not his confessions.

"Boss man, you know how we feel about ya. Never abandon, but if ya gotta go, we understand. Always be brothers. No matter this shit or not." A snarled Creole smirk beamed as he lifted the welding shield. "No matter what."

"Let's focus on finishing this for Ruiz. What's this one got to give?" Pushing the crook of my elbow over my mouth, the stench of exposed flesh washed over me as the industrial ventilation fan kicked on. Gagging, I wretched forward—then mused at my weak stomach.

"Losing your nerve for getting truths boss man?" Sweat dripped from the hair matted across his ink-ornamented forearm. It brushed down dropping the shield as he sparked up the torch's hot blue flame. Killer number three moaned. I glanced at his nude, almost skinless body stretched prone across the metal frame.

Damn, reminds me of the torture my dad endured. How much more can this one take?

"Gig pole. Don't forget to ask." His sinister laugh bellowed from beneath the robust plastic facemask. Agent Blue nodded his head yes.

Easing my truck along the space reserved for ambulances, I jumped the hedges to slide through the staff only entrance. Marci Perque pressed her hand against my chest as I rounded the corner.

"Excuse me Mr. Remi, but where you think you going?"

"Marci, here to see Buck. Room number?" I let her hand press deeper into my chest. She was always a flirt, but harmless. Her naughty grin, flattened as the lines in her oval face etched deeper than I'd last known.

"Buck's way down the hall, last door on the left past the nurses' station. He's in and out of it boy. Don't go disturbing him you hear?" Snarled lips surrendered to a sassy smile. Wrapping both arms, she squeezed her bosom against me. "He loves you Remi." Her wet eyes lost within a sweet shaded complexion.

Bustling with purpose, curious glances cast as I coasted through sterile spaces. Eyes down, I nodded to a few of the hospital staff I'd come to know. Most were single, but never interested me. They knew RJ was gone—two even thought it was the right time to console me. Bad move.

Her smooth, freckled arms folded loosely over each other. An encouraged smile. Her eyes cut back to her peers—obviously an effort to impress the others, or draw courage from them.

"Hey Remi. How ya doing suga, you here to see that man?" Her flirtatious tone was like nails down a chalkboard.

"What man Toni?" Slipping in front of me as I moved aside. Cupping her mouth with her thin, painted fingertips, her ponytail dangled as she tiptoed up toward my ear. My knees buckled with her words.

Walking away, my wobbling legs and spiraling mind grappled with the brilliant whiteness of the hallway illumination. Hiding within my hairline, wetness soon charged down my neck and into both ears. The deputy posted outside Buck's door grabbed my elbow, "I'm sorry sir, no one past this point." Fear rent across his unwrinkled face, his partner stepped across the open threshold. Concern on the older deputy's face and hand on his Taser.

"I'm here to see Sheriff Walker." Still gut wrenched by nurse Toni's news. I understood the deputy didn't know me—underground was my job.

"Remi, so glad you're here." St. Pierre gasped, swinging her head around the corner. She patted her hand against the deputy's arm. His grip on the stun gun eased. "Darn place is a madhouse." St. Pierre scanned the hall and led me in the room with an unusually hard grip across my bicep.

Quietly, I slid the chair next to his bed. The metrical hum of machinery filled Buck's room. Genevieve sat dutifully next to him. Coolness mercifully came from the rumpled sheet against my forehead. I hunched close to him as I processed his condition.

Memories flooded my spirit. I watched my dad agonize until taking his own life. There was no fancy hospital caring for him. Grinding my teeth until I heard them popping in my head, I thought of how I also watched Emory Ballard suffer till his death. I couldn't lose Buck—I couldn't sit here and watch him die.

Her hand patted my neck. Worry struggled with peace. Fear battled fury. Genevieve said nothing. She allowed me to process. Gently, I cupped my hand over the IV tubes to hold his fist. His shallow pulse steadily batted against the heart rate monitor's blip. My breathing settled into a synced rhythm with his, and I finally accepted the comfort of his presence.

"Gen, what happened?"

She leaned closer. Her spiraled hair brushed across my right fore-arm, "We don't know yet. Chief Roberts is refusing access to media and outside agencies."

"So... Big Johnny just up and died?" Prying my eyes open, her image was blurred by wetness clinging across my lashes.

"Guess so. According to Tom Roberts." Her spark of sarcasm wasn't directed at me, though I felt her disgust.

"Gen, you're next in command, so watch your six. Don't underes-timate these people—you saw what they're capable of doing." Clutching the buzzing cellphone, I let the glow from its screen reflect against the bed frame.

"Everything okay Remi?"

"Just what I've been waiting for. Gotta a promise to keep."

"Keep for who?" She reached across the chair.

"For our Sheriff." I dropped her fingers onto the mattress, and patted the boss' leg. "I need you back Buck."

Chapter 61
— *Lieutenant Remi LeBlanc* —

CHIEF ROBERTS WOULD BE WRAPPED up with covering up Johnny Chiasson's jailhouse murder. Number three had finally surrendered his information and his life. Shaking my head as I ribboned my way through the hospital's parking maze. How that idiot survived Agent Blue's interrogation was beyond me. I'm just glad I never ran across that hardy bastard on the street—this parish is better off that he's dead.

Squeezing the steering wheel until white-knuckled, I roared home and prepared to honor my word to Buck. Confiding months ago, I was still shocked by his lack of attention to sanitizing a scene. Leaving that gig pole at Bell Cove was a giant screw up. His initial admission signaled that I shouldn't bring it up unless he did. He knew it would destroy him if that thing were found. It had been.

Dragging a whopping bag of chow for the hounds—they'd not been out of the kennel in the last two days. Sitting in the yard as the night crept across the south, I scratched their bellies as thick tongues scraped across my neck and face. These two had been with me a long time—never judging, just present.

I jumped in the shower—first one since swimming Turtle Bayou. If Agent Blue's boy surrendered honest information, it should be a quick in and out job. Chief Roberts had a series of sheds and outbuildings on his property. Nothing guarded, only a few stray dogs. Like I said—in and out.

Night lumbered flat and heavy over Bayou Parish. Opening and squeezing my fist, I tried working out the soreness from my fight in the lake. Must'a jammed it on a stump or something. Now wasn't the time to worry about that or the sinus infection. Between the black waters and burning sugar cane, my lungs were catching hell.

Sinking in the soft soil's underbelly, I made my way through a grove of pecan trees and rice fields converted to crawfish ponds. Sunrise was my only obstacle, so I took my time sneaking onto Roberts' property. Hunched at the clearing, I watched as the mutts clattered back and forth near an old shed. Sniffing the dirt and each other's asses. The property leading back to his house was scattered with tractor parts, aluminum boats and vehicle odds and ends. Not at all orderly like his work persona—I wondered if I was at the correct location.

Catching my breath, I remained out of sight and switched off the night vision goggles. Too many spotlights and string lamps creating blind streaks. I wasn't sure whether the Chief was even home—figured the dogs would've moved toward the house if so.

Time to move.

Opening the cellophane baggies filled with dog chow, I launched them toward the trio. Curious, but ignorant—furry ears perked into the saturated air. The smallest dog caught wind and tail wagged it toward me. The followers followed. Easiness settled over me watching the dogs enjoy the snacks—odd attitude for an operation, but my mind drifted peacefully. I needed the moment of calm.

They'd taken to the chow. Movement would be clear to the shed. Pressing against my sore right wrist to push off the soil, I winced. Back onto both knees I shook my hand out. My mouth perch to sound out, but I clamped quiet.

Crack.

My body crooked stiff at the sound except for the frigid sliver of fear snaking its hate-filled influence along my spine. Back against the canopy of brush and shadows, my heart raged within the cavity trying to contain it. I was shocked Chief Roberts didn't hear the thumping.

"Get over here." He barked out to his pets while fumbling with the chained padlock across the weathered wooden doors.

Son of a bitch, I never heard him coming.

Dim overhead lighting rocked back and forth as it escaped the shed's interior. The feisty mutt tried following him inside. The sharp yelp caused my body to constrict. I saw the small dog's frame fly airborne from the interior. "Stay the fuck out of here. You know this is daddy's special place." Cruelly sinister, Roberts' voice pierced the evil of night's darkness.

Belly pressed against the earth, I slithered among the uncut grass. Careful to mesh within the shadow, I buried my face behind a log as two of the dogs retraced the snack trail. Rolling onto my side, I grabbed the last baggie and silently launched it as far from me as possible.

Grunting reverberated within the shed. Yellowish light broke across darkness in jerking, uneven motions. The small animal shook as he lay prostrate on the cement foundation—poor pup cowered at the opening.

Muscles aching, I slipped further along the tree line. Saturated by the moist bog, my clothes meshed with marshland. Small brush tugged at my garments while I angled a view between the structure and the slightly opened door.

Primal sounds pulsed as his body heaved—Roberts' right arm violently beat out a hedonistic rhythm. Straining, my eyes narrowed to see what was in his left hand—couldn't see. Except the dog's whimpers, there were no other external sounds. Arching his nude torso, sweating head thrashed backward. His neck stretched as the blood-flushed color of his body's heat rising seared across his jawline and into thick, huffing cheeks. Spastically, his body lurched up and forward as sound again spewed from his throat.

His shoulders rolled forward as the momentum slowed—he leaned against what looked like a workbench. Air expelled heavily from his mouth as his rubbery neck struggled to keep its head from toppling onto the bench.

"Come here boy." I jumped hearing him say that.

Oh Lord don't let there be a child in that shed.

Holding the wet air filling my lungs, I pressed an ear for a small voice or movement. The slice of view was difficult to breach. My fingers tore into the muddy bog while both legs flexed in preparation to attack him.

"Here now." He demanded.

The small dog's body reeled off the ground. Trembling, it moved toward the door—nose to the ground. I saw Roberts' shoeless feet and the puppy hovering between them. The animal looked to be licking semen from the cement floor.

"Good boy. How's daddy taste?" His disgusting taunt ignited a panting of yelps from the little dog.

Bitterness flooded my tongue and cheeks gulped back the bile balancing against my uvula. Pressing my head beside the sod to quiet the thunderous pounding of my pulse, I was reassured my time working in this hell was limited. Light marbled behind my eyelids and anxious tears exploded from beneath them. Spittle leaked between quivering lips till it mixed with the grass and mud. It was hot and tasted like hell—I was fuming to attack this sick bastard.

Creaking rusted hinges, and then the shove of splintered wood against frame sent the small dog sprinting for cover. Roberts shuffled his slippered feet along the edge of the cement foundation. My body meshed with the overgrowth as I fought to suppress a coughing spell. Standing mere feet away from me as he adjusted the elastic waistband on the grey sweat pants, I pressed my face into my bicep to choke back the sounds. His gut dropped below the white wife beater as he tugged the hem to wipe his face. His glazed eyes swept past me. I clinched both fist, but he still seemed disoriented from the ferocious orgasm I'd just witnessed.

Motionless for about twenty minutes, I began to fidget—I had to know what was inside his *special place*. Blinking, I crushed my brow together as my nose wrinkled to survey the area. All clear—even the mutts.

Slinking along the terra firma, my lips fell slightly parted as I struggled to breath through my nose. The thick linked-chain dangled and I caught the shiny padlock before it struck the concrete. Pausing to examine the lock and chain, it was obvious he valued the shed's contents.

I took my time prying the door away from the solid wooden threshold. Deep darkness lay within the walls. Slipping my NVG back over my head, I flipped the power switch. Immediately the items came into focus as the night peeking goggles conquered the blackness. Sweeping my eyes from top to bottom, and then along each wall, I dropped to both knees. Humanity irreparably fractured.

What the fuck?

Chapter 62

— *Sergeant Earl Brooks* —

I'M TOO OLD FOR THIS shit.

Agent Jones' phone call stirred my spirit—I wanted, but also didn't want anything to do with what I knew would involve more violence. I'd seen my share in Vietnam. I didn't duck it, but damn it, this is south Louisiana—not Khe Sanh.

Scratching my ass while I groaned rolling onto my side of the bed, I fumbled for the lamp switch. Her hand lay softly across my shoulder.

"Earl, please don't go. This is too much for you right now."

"I know baby, but they need me. We too close to stop now." Shutting my eyes—I didn't want to get any more involved than I had already.

"I know you love your job Earl, but you're the supervisor. Send that young boy. Todd Stone." Her worry caused that comment to waiver across the mattress.

"Momma, Stone is dead." As I'd done for years, my shoulder rolled from beneath her touch. Duty called.

"Oh, I'm sorry. Poor boy. You be careful Earl Junior." Anticipating her calling me Earl Junior usually brought a smile. That vanished with the despair in her voice.

"I'll be back Momma. I'll put the dog out." Involuntarily, I dressed and meandered through the garage door. My chest ached from late night ice cream and whatever hell these Task Force boys were about to unleash.

Coded telephone conversations with Agent Jones as I crept through the quiet neighborhoods, I headed down the bayou. Soon, I was backing my unmarked police cruiser into a far corner of the pitch-black parking lot.

Prickles of suspicion crawled across my skin. Why was I was called out in the middle of nowhere—this was a whites only biker bar. Hell, even I knew what they'd do to me. Cop or not. Revolver under my thigh, I laid the Remington 870 sawed-off shotgun along the front seat.

A clear view across jacked-up pickup trucks and tricked out motorcycles, and I radioed to Agent Jones that all was clear at the Iron Horse Saloon.

"10-4 Sarge. Target number four, Aaron Malborough is inside." Agent Smith whispered across the encrypted tactical radio channel.

"How will I spot him?"

"He's about four hundred pounds. Riding that last hog on the front row. The one with the ape hanger handle bars." Agent Jones added.

"Sounds simple enough." I laughed uneasily as my left hand riveted to the rubber grips on my trusted pistol.

"10-4 Sarge. Big bastard looks like a monkey fucking a football on that Harley." I didn't recognize that voice, but understood the reference.

The rigidity in my physique eased after the first few hours watching a bare parking lot become sparser. Nodding off once, I jerked my head off the headrest.

Maybe I was getting too old for this shit.

It had steamed beyond hot inside my car. No engine meant no air conditioning. Parked in a mosquito haven also meant no open windows. My right hand caressed the shotgun's polished wood stock—the short barrel remained cool to the touch.

Exhaling in exacerbation, my body sat in a soggy roux of ass and underwear. I knew this was for Ruiz—how dare I complain about being uncomfortable. For Ruiz.

"Eyes up, movement." Ducking below the dashboard, my mouth met the microphone. Damn right, Malborough's fat ass looked just like a monkey fucking a football. It was my first laugh in anguished hours.

"Anyone out there? Target on the move." I lifted my binoculars over the steering wheel to scan for other surveillance units. The night remained still, except for the dim tail light on Malborough's hog.

Punching the steering wheel, I cursed aloud. This wasn't like them boys—I had begun to trust Agent Jones. What were they up to? Mashing the radio button again, I saw the transmit light flash across the liquid crystal screen.

"Agent Jones, Smith. Y'all out there? Target left the parking lot."

Grinding my jaw, I pulled lips back across my dried teeth. Twisting the ignition, the angry eight cylinders sprung to life. Lights out, I sidled to the edge of the oyster shell parking lot. The taillight disappeared into the earliest of morning's fog. Loud pipes now a faint whisper, I gunned it. Smoke and dust hurled from beneath my chassis as I fishtailed onto Highway 51.

Hearing the rumbling screech, I clutched the steering wheel and jerked it to my right. Skidding across grass and debris on the narrow shoulder, I came to rest inches from the basin's brackish waters. Heart thrashing, I saw the vehicle that almost slammed into me swerving back into the northbound lane. Exhaust spewed from its tailpipes.

Shit, I never saw that damn van. I'm way past fatigued.

"Task Force Agents, this is Sergeant Brooks. The target's motorcycle is heading northbound on Highway 51. Be advised there's a dark colored van driving like a bat out of hell heading his way." The radio crackled—still no one replied.

Fuck this—I'm heading to the house.

Tapping the brakes after another a mile or so up the road, my calf muscle cramped from the lack of sleep and abundance of bullshit, "What now?"

The pistol grip molded into my right hand, the barrel was pointed just below the open driver's side window. I approached the blacktop chaos. Screams blended into the chorus of crickets. Squinting arid eyes, I saw Malborough's Harley Davidson scattered across Highway 51.

That same black van sat canted across both lanes, while a truck I recognized as Agent Jones' idled south of the crash. *Must've been one hell of a collision.*

Agent Jones jogged toward my door—I lowered the revolver. "Sorry I didn't answer the radio. Hard to get into position and chat." Sweat and purpose blanketed his hollow glare.

I killed the car's headlamps and watched. Malborough thrashed like a wild bore as Agent Blue emotionlessly duct taped his hands and feet. Nodding his chin, he signaled Agent Smith to help roll their catch into a thick plastic body bag. Usually reserved for corpses, we all knew he'd soon become one—he obviously did too.

Climbing out of the car to help the Agents allowed a chance to stretch my legs. They needed help lifting the flailing plastic satchel. Every bit of four hundred pounds rolled, flexed and bent his way to avoid being transported. Agent Blue waved everyone back as he peeled the heavy metal zipper back a few inches.

Jamming a cattle prod into the opening, I soon heard the snap and popping of five thousand volts of electrical viciousness. Killer number four's big body exploded in pain. His resistance grew intense, so Agent Blue calmly mashed the switch again. Duct taped grunts seeped through the industrial grade plastic bag.

"Lay still." Agent Blue quietly instructed.

The black container crumpled in half as Malborough sat upright. Agent Smith's gloved hand pressed across my chest to stop me from pushing it back down. Agent Jones shoved a large rubber siphon hose through the unzipped section. Five gallons of water were emptied inside the sealed bag. It sloshed like mad as the biker's body wretched inside the shallow pool. Replacing the rubber hose, the cattle prod continued the torture.

"Enough fun, get him in." Agent Jones looked to each as he tossed me a pair of rubber gloves. "Coming?" he squared at me. I nodded yes. We heaved the big bag into the van.

I strapped the shotgun back beneath the front seat of my car, and felt around for my sunglasses. Morning's sun reminded me of its fury. A few chilled nights still had no dominion over the day's torturous temperature intentions. Shielding my eyes from the glare of the rising Creole red ball, the color-streaked sky rolled in over the silhouetted inky marsh and still waters.

Chapter 63

— *Sergeant Earl Brooks* —

I'D SPENT YEARS WORKING FOR the Bayou Parish Sheriff's Office and never once stepped foot into the warehouse. Hell, I didn't even know it existed until all of this shit started. A large industrial fan sucked at the humidity in the bay area, but the rancid stench of torment saturated the air. Knowing what writhed in the van's cargo area, my gut twisted.

"Brooks, I mean Sarge. Could ya grab that corner?" Agent Smith's hulking frame contracted with each pull. Wrapping his sledgehammer fists against the thick plastic bag, he began jerking it inch by inch. At least I had the legs end, so I heaved with what I had left—it wasn't much. Unevenly, the bag spilled onto the cement floor headfirst. Snorting like an animal, Malborough soon whimpered.

"Sorry son lost my grip." My weary eyes struggled to hold contact with the massive Task Force Agent. Hunched back resting against both knees, Agent Smith slid a wooden stool under my ass. "Thanks. I don't even know your first name Smith." Curiously, a weathered hand rubbed below my chin craning my neck to see his face. The greasy shock of ragged hair hid an angular face, "I have none." His hand drew back a collection of tangled mane and his face softened to a half-smile. "I'm nobody sir."

Wheeling a cart of five-gallon water bottles, a sprawling matrix of dark green ink covering Agent Jones' shirtless upper body rippled to life. United States Marine Corps symbols decorated his bowling ball sized shoulders and thick chest. Sliding the button down shirtsleeve over my triceps, only an Army Calvary tattoo made its way back from Asia.

Setting the cart over a metal grating in the center of the room, he bobbed his head. Agents Blue and Smith jerked at the body bag until it rolled onto the drain.

"Let's get this over with. No three day marathon for this pig." Agent Blue looked at each of us—silently nodding in agreement. He pulled on the over-sized metal zipper tongue. A big fat head popped through the small opening. Bleeding and wet, Malborough's eyes sprung open with horror behind them.

"Aaron, I will ask you only one question. I will ask it only three times. You will refuse the first, lie the second and consider the consequences of answering on the third time I ask. Let me be clear. You will die. How fast you die is up to how you answer the question. Understand?" Pressing my fist against both lips, I expelled the air bubbling in my intestines. Unsure if I was getting sick, my nervousness grew as I watched Agents Smith and Jones turn their eyes away from the center of the room.

"Where's your partner Jess Duplantis?" The calm in Agent Blue's voice sounded like he was reading a bedtime story to children. He peeled the grey tape from Malborough's meth-cracked mouth.

"Fuck you."

"That's one." He nodded to Agent Jones who hoisted a plastic bottle into the small opening. Sergeant Ruiz's killer shook his head with eyes sealed as the five gallons of water rained over him and into the sealed plastic coffin.

"Where's your partner Jess Duplantis?" Agent Blue ran his gloved hand across Malborough's eyes to wipe the water residue from them.

"I don't know no Jessie Duplantis. Let me out, you gonna drown me. I confess, I killed that bitch. Bring my ass to jail right now." He thrashed inside the bag. Hands taped tight behind him, his breathing became more labored as he panicked.

"Is that your answer?"

"You deaf? I told you." Malborough look saddened as Agent Jones reached for the next large bottle to empty inside the bag.

"He gonna give the man a chance to think it through?" I tapped Agent Smith on the knees to whisper. Leaning in, he easily towered over me. Pursing his lips together, he shook his head no. Then he pressed his index finger across his mouth—I got the message.

"Where's your partner Jess Duplantis?"

"Take my ass to jail. Big Johnny already dead, ain't nothing to worry about there."

"Aaron Malborough, is that your final answer?" Calm, Agent Blue looked easily into the doomed man's eyes.

"Fuck'n ayy."

"Thank you sir." Agent Blue pressed his beleaguered body from the metal step stool. Flicking his finger at Agent Jones, he walked into the office section of the warehouse.

"Dat's it?" Malborough laughed though confusion etched its way deep across his face.

Agent Smith pressed his hand into my shoulder as he stood to join Agent Jones. The echoed rip of duct tape cracked between Agent Smith's fists.

"No need for you to say anymore." He swathed the three-foot stretch of reinforced adhesive around Malborough's mouth and head. The biker shook his skull violently in rebellion. Agent Jones emptied bottles of water into the plastic body bag until it spilled over the small-unzipped hole.

Malborough's muffled grunts flitted away into the metal grating that covered the drain. His body bounced and squirmed against the floor. I stood back and looked away—my own lungs felt constricted as I imagined what he was going through inside that water grave. Then he was still.

Chapter 64

— *Deputy Chief Genevieve St. Pierre* —

IT WAS TIME TO STOP resenting Susan Lambert. She'd done nothing to me, nor took anything from me. She had Buck's attention, but in a personal tone—I was being petty. Leaning back against the overnight sleeper, I let her rustle Buck together for discharge.

"Stealing my patients again Doctor Lambert?" Cloaked in a starched white coat, the tall Hispanic filled the threshold to the dimly lit private room.

"Oh hello Doctor Perez. I'm just helping an old friend escape." Susan chortled uneasily. I figured she teetered on an ethical edge whether or not she and Buck had engaged in a physical relationship. Perez's look reflected no concern, but Susan's did—strictly by the book.

"What's the damage Doc?" Buck sat up, groaning in exhale. His colorless hand clawed into Susan's forearm for balance. I leaned over the small bed to steady him with a hand on his back.

"Buck, you escaped the big one this time. Not a heart attack, but stable angina. Its chest pain brought on by activity or stress. I'm sure you've got plenty of both." I watched Susan's hand squeeze Buck's arm. Her head dropped in relief—red eyes glistening.

"When can I get out of here?" His voice already sounding stronger.

"This morning if you'd like. I'm sure the hospital needs the bed space for paying customers." Doctor Perez's hardy laugh helped ease the natural tension. "I don't think you need beta-blockers right now, but let's look at you early next week." He glanced at each of us, nodded to Susan and disappeared into the hall.

Patting Susan on the shoulder, her slender frame surrendered to my touch. Immediately, I regretted being a bitch to her over these last months. Buck needed someone outside of the Sheriff's Office—she was becoming that someone.

"Susan, I trust you'll get him home? I've a swarm of chaos to tame at the office. Seems they found another of Sergeant Ruiz's killers. Crashed his motorcycle and landed in a ditch along Highway 51. Drowned." The sting of passing along the deception mattered less these days—revenge for RJ now mattered most.

"Drowned? Let the Task Force know, I'm sure they be happy to hear." Buck's voice waivered between shocked and informed.

"Buck, I'm sure they already know." My eyes misted hugging this man who'd been so strong, but now struggled to sit upright. The opened back hospital gown made him look older—weak. Susan's hand on my arm sent chills along the skin. I blinked away the tears and smiled at her. "I'll get him home Gen."

Hurrying through the Sheriff's Office complex, I managed to reach my office without seeing anyone. Running my free hand along the wall, I swiped at the light switch. "Please. Leave it off." My heart startled, "Remi?"

"Gen, we gotta talk." His long wiry frame stretched over the length of the old couch. The crook of his elbow bent across his eyes, only his mouth moved.

"Remi, how'd you get in here?" Sliding my feet to slice the darkness once the door fell shut—I dropped everything onto my desk. "Were you the one who found number four?" My weight surrendered into the leather chair.

"No." I saw his chest flexing as he heaved with whatever the burden that drove him into hiding out here. "But I'm sure they did. Drowned by chance?"

Leaning across the desk onto my elbows, "Yes, he did." I watched his reaction. Only his scarred leather motorcycle boots rocked in motion.

"Saw the body bag in the warehouse earlier."

"Body bag?" Running my hands through tangled curls, I swept them behind both ears.

"And jugs of water." He never moved. The arm stuck over his face, and body seeming to ease at the positive confirmation of number four's passing.

My computer's screen added a hint of light to the darkened office. I tried to adjust myself behind my desk, but the lights out effect had me baffled.

"Remi, is that why you're hiding out here? In the middle of the Sheriff's Office building?"

"Gen, we need Buck in on this."

"Out of the question. He's just getting home from the hospital Remi. You want to kill him?" Slamming my open palm against the desk, I leaned to pop on the lamp. He growled.

"It's big, too big to discuss here. Either he's in, or I handle it myself—my way." Rocking his torso until he loomed over the sofa, his mouth quivered. His hands shook—my stomach twisted. I picked up the phone.

Chapter 65
— *Sheriff James Walker* —

RUBBING THE PURPLED SKIN WHERE the IV breached, I pulled myself up before moving to the couch. Sure they'll understand. Susan looked displeased with company coming, but her medical training had to tell her my chest pain wasn't going to kill me—not yet. Offering another cup of tea, her hand lingered over mine. I was lost in the natural silver shine of her cropped hair as it swung along her sharp jaw line. I smiled with a careful nod.

"In here Remi." His distinctive one knock and then enter reflected the way he handled everything—full speed.

"Boss man, good to see you getting around. Sorry we gotta do it like this, but you'll understand soon." Remi bit his bottom lip as I held onto his hand longer than usual. I saw the pool of emotion stirring beneath his fragile surface.

I pulled him down until his ear sat next to my lips, "Son, I'm going to be okay. Stop worrying, you didn't cause this." Remi's head nodded slowly but his gaunt eyes cast away.

Susan returned with Genevieve, Brooks and Graza. Nervously, she flitted about the living room hurrying to accommodate each with chairs or pillows. My heart beamed watching her. She'd never been inside my house before, yet she moved with sincerity to make sure everyone else felt at home.

Greeting the others, my eyes glued to Remi. He folded and unfolded his arms while fidgeting in an otherwise comfortable chair.

Swiping a palm across his forehead repeatedly, accumulated moisture glinted above his lips. I motioned to Susan and asked her to kick up the A/C.

"Thank you all for coming out to the house. When I took over this job, I thought we'd gather here for personal and family times, but the BBQs will have to wait." Attempting to laugh sent a razor sharp pain through my ribs. "Remi, let me turn this over to you." I leaned back against the armrest and pillows Susan stuffed behind my shoulder.

Remi sat silent. His shaggy long hair draped over his face as his head hung low between his knees. I watched his back rise and fall with each exaggerated struggle for air. Pressing his palms against his knees, he sat upright. Clearing his throat and swallowing more often than usual, his lips parted. Silent.

"Go on son, its okay." I gave him an awkward thumb up.

"Last night I went for a walk to feed some dogs. I saw Chief Roberts walking in the same area. It happened to be right next to his property. He went into a locked shed, so I stopped walking. He did some nasty shit to a puppy, so I sat in the dark waiting for him to finish. I wanted to make sure the dog was okay, so I went into the shed after he left." Remi guzzled half a bottle of water, and then arched his back. "Couldn't hit the lights, so I used my dog walking goggles." His hands mimicked switching on NVG.

I scanned the group. Bodies forward capturing every word. Always the investigator, Detective Graza sat with a pen and notepad.

"His shed is full of trophies." Remi buried his lips against his left hand. Angst stricken, his torso vaulted forward.

"Sports trophies?" Susan asked. Then awkwardly recoiled in regret.

Her question sidetracked me, though I instantly grasped what Remi intended. My heart began to fail as I fought forming the words to ask him one question. Trembling lips over grubby teeth, I couldn't shove sounds beyond a simple grunt. My hand fumbled across the end table for the bottle of nitroglycerine.

"He kept pieces of the children's clothing." Remi's eyes half closed as his head cranked across the room to face me. A single nod yes.

Thank God Wyatt Cash was closer to closure.

"Team, we need to decide right now how to handle this." Revenge replaced my concern over body aches. Leaning forward from the couch, Gen helped me balance on the edge.

"Buck, Councilman Chiasson goes before the State's grand jury this afternoon. If he flips on Roberts, and he goes missing or dead—fingers point back to you. Back to us." Genevieve calmly rationalized. Pulling back a finger for each point she argued, the others sat connected shaking their heads. "Why not get a search warrant, recover the evidence and expose him for the murdering devil that he is? Otherwise his death becomes a mystery and you rob every child's family of closure." Genevieve continued.

Finally, my gaunt face fell into my hands. "Closure."

"Boss man, going this way might wrap up Chiasson too." Graza said.

"Don't forget Johnny Jones. I'm itching to put his slime ball ass away." Remi growled from the middle of the living room.

"That mean you sticking around Remi?" Hands scrubbing his dehydrated yellowed eyes, Sergeant Brooks asked the obvious question. No one moved. Remi's body froze, hands juddered into pants pockets—he shook his head, no.

"Well, let's put this case to rest first." I refocused the team. "Graza, what's your feel about the State Violent Crimes Task Force? Bring them in now or after?"

"Sheriff, my mind says now, but my gut says after we have Roberts' ass in custody. There's been a string of vics over the last ten years—wasn't important to them then, why's it now?" He slammed his notepad closed, and shoved the pen in his shirt pocket, "Fuck them glory hounds."

"Gen, I know what you think. Earl?" I leaned close to this trusted gentleman.

"Sheriff, I'm too damn old and tired to play politics. Let's clean up our own house." The tattered detective righted his posture and walked next to the couch. "We do this your way—for your boy." Brooks' leathered knuckles brushed against my t-shirt. I felt the surge of energy radiate from his hand.

It was time to take Police Chief Tom Roberts' murdering ass down.

Chapter 66

— Detective Jose Graza —

SERGEANT BROOKS LOOKED LIKE HELL, so I let him snooze. We had a long, boring ass drive ahead anyway. The southern most part of the parish—The Point. There was nothing much there beyond salt domes and offshore supply companies. Deputy Chief St. Pierre was typing the search warrant affidavit for Roberts' property, so Sheriff Walker sent us to recon leads that might help strengthen it. Remi's account of his being out for a walk might have entertained us, but a magistrate would hold us all in contempt. The stakes were too high.

"Hey Deputy Chief. I'm whispering so I don't wake up sleeping beauty."

"Graza, what's your ETA?" Sensing tension in her questions—I understood why.

"We're about half hour out. Not sure who or exactly what our goal is, but we'll give it a shot." I tried shaking loose more mission information.

"One of the victim's family members just skated on drug charges. Word is he shared a cell with Big Johnny. Maybe they talked." She sounded determined.

"What's this guys name anyway?"

"Roy Blanchard."

"Roy Blanchard?" I repeated. Didn't ring a bell.

"Roy Blanchard?" Sergeant Brooks repeated while peeling his face from the plastic interior door panel. Rubbing his eyes, he mouthed to ask whom was I talking to. I flinched—his stale breath was fierce.

"Yes, why?" I eased off the gas pedal heading into heavily commercial areas with stop and go traffic. Sarge became so animated, I was afraid he'd gone insane. He motioned for me to hang up the call.

"Deputy Chief, connection is really bad, let me call you back." I held the cell up to Brooks' face. "See?"

"Jose, cut the shit. Roy Blanchard is dead."

"Well then we heading to a graveyard, because that's who we going to see." I turned my eyes back to the single lane highway heading toward the Gulf of Mexico.

"Remember when Ruiz got shot during that meth lab raid? The two girls found in there were brokered by Blanchard." My crooked look must have told him I wasn't following. "Blanchard set up the deal to swap the girls for crank to the parents. The girls were used to help cook meth and for sex." Brooks was emphatic.

"So how did Blanchard end up dead? Or undead?" The grogginess of fatigue fogged my mind.

"That's the mystery. He was being held by the Task Force and flipped on Big Johnny. SWAT runs a raid on his place, and that's when Buck almost killed Johnny in a pursuit. Jail was waiting to book Blanchard on child molestation charges, but all of a sudden he no longer existed." Brooks flipped through his notepad while refreshing his memory.

"Think he escaped?" Twisting my brow, I knew it was a stupid question.

"No, I think the Task Force released him in hopes of luring a bigger fish. Obviously it worked. It's our job to reel that fish in." Brooks wrote and then circled the words, Roy = snitch. My mind raced to connect the dots before we arrived. Unsure what we were reeling in, but I wasn't getting caught off guard again.

The old shed was an oyster shack and bait shop. Unbuckling the safety belt, my hands shuffled the steering wheel through the narrow gate. Brooks crumpled the paper directions and readied himself for the unexpected.

I saw the guy standing by the pirogue's hull. Hearing the revolver zip out of Brooks' leather holster, my eyes squinted and glanced back and forth across the blighted property. The guy looked unarmed—Brooks wasn't screwing around. He never did.

"The idiot in the Cajun Reeboks must be him." Brooks quipped with disdain.

Except for the do-it-yourself prison tattoos covering his body, cut off denim shorts and white rubber shrimp boots were all he wore. He slowly drew from a cigarette as his eyes zeroed in on us. His head swiveled.

"Watch him Sarge, he's gonna run." Hand gripping the shifter to throw the car into park if he even flinched. Running down dirt bags was my specialty. He drew off that cigarette again—slowly. His knees look to be shaking, what was up with Blanchard?

"Son, you looking to talk to us?" Brooks asked from behind his door, I swung toward the left to cut off one possible escape route. The haggard looking guy said nothing. His hands shaking. He couldn't match the cigarette to his lips anymore.

"You looking for us?" Brooks raised his voice. I sensed his patience wearing thin. Keeping an eye on the nervous wreck of a man, I continued scouring the area for anyone else. I still hadn't shaken off what Stone did, and I sure the hell wasn't getting myself in another ambush.

"Detective, I don't want to die. I surrender." The cigarette fell from his twitching fingers. "Save me from the Asian Triad. I beg ya."

Cutting eyes to Sarge, my shoulders shrugged at his plea. I saw Sarge raise his revolver—I raised mine.

"What'cha talking about son?" he asked.

"I'm Jess Duplantis. I surrender." Stringy muscle fibers quivered, the guy fought to lift his hands above his head. "I did it."

"You did what?" I saw Sarge's face wrinkle. I began to snort through my nose—I hadn't noticed the stench. The discarded fish and seafood being processed was suddenly overwhelming. This guy's actions stunk more.

"I killed that lady cop. I'm Jess Duplantis. I know Task Force killed the others—the Triad is also in the parish. Save me."

"Where's Roy Blanchard?" I asked. This felt like a set up.

"He called y'all to meet, but he's trying to save me. I'm his cousin. Now arrest me." Demanding, though his voice trembled.

"Who knows you're here Jess?" Sarge's voice changed—sinister sounding.

"Not a soul. Just Roy, but he ain't saying a word." His blondish red hair matted to his freckled skull.

Sarge nodded for me to cuff him. His weapon trained on Duplantis' head, it was time to get out of this scenario before things changed for the worst.

"413 to Headquarters." Pulling the radio microphone to my mouth once onto the Highway 308, Sarge looked hard behind him. Then leaning across the console, he pushed the mic away.

"What'cha doing boy?"

"Calling in this 10-15 for transport." I watched Duplantis in the rearview mirror. Heavily, his eyes nodded.

"Think this through. We want this one hanging out there? He killed Ruiz. You heard him—no one knows where he is. For all anyone cares, he's already dead. I say we drop him off at the warehouse." My gut wrenched at his suggestion. I hated this killer, but he surrendered.

Doesn't he deserve due process?

"Let me guess, you think he deserves due process, a fair trail, a jury of his peers?" Sarge had taken the microphone from my hand. His reddened eyes pulsed, as a funk from unbrushed teeth filled the air. "Where you gonna find a jury of peers who done hatcheted a female cop to death. We already judged him Graza." His right hand chopped down against his left palm.

"Sarge, you gotta be shitting me. We can't execute him. Even if he is a murderer. We gotta be better than this." Squinting against the sun's glare, I cranked the A/C up and tried to ignore what Sarge was jackhammering into my ethical core. My pulse quickened as he relentlessly chewed on my ear.

"Just stop Sarge. You're asking a lot of me sir."

"We gotta long drive ahead, just think it through son. We promised to do this for Ruiz." His words hurt—I knew he was right.

Chapter 67

— *Sheriff James Walker* —

SUSAN PULLED AGAINST ME. TEARS moistened her eyes as I walked away. It was just the second time we kissed. I had a job to do—she knew it, she just disagreed with it. Pulling the Polo shirt over my head, the sticky spots on my skin from the hospital's electrodes grabbed at the material.

"Buck, I'm not going to beg you. You heard Doctor Perez's orders." She sat on the bed—shoulders usually sharp, now slumped. Her soft hair hung forward as her chin rested close to her chest.

"Susan, I feel fine. No way in this world I'm not going to be there. That son of a bitch stole my life—I'm going to take his." I felt a rise in temperature creeping up my neck and into my cheeks. Shoving the bottle of nitro into my pants pocket, I had to will myself to calm down.

"We don't know for sure he killed Wyatt. Maybe involved, but it might have been Councilman Chiasson for all we know. Let Chiasson's deposition unfold before the State's Attorney General today. Play this one by the rules. Everyone will be watching to see how you handle this." Sliding off the mattress's edge, she collected her keys and phone. A trembling hand pressed against her stomach.

"Let it unfold? You heard Remi. That monster has Wyatt Cash's red rubber boots in his shed. I'm supposed to wait for who to solve this—the Police Chief?" Flecks of light behind my eyelids nipped. The dizziness forced me back onto the bed. Hunched over, my body's weight leaned heavily across both elbows as my chest expanded and emptied. Lifting my head I saw his little picture. Dressed in his Team Bayou Lightening swimsuit, Wyatt Cash's photograph still sat curled cornered against the lamp.

Just where he left it.

"Buck, you're not the only one suffering the lost of a child. How many other children's families continue grieving? You mess this investigation up by making it your crusade for revenge, and they all lose—including you." Snorting through her nose, she spun on her heel to leave.

Easing over to tug the tattered leather straps, I yanked both boots over my feet. Rising slowly, I waited for the weakness to pass. "I'll stay in the truck. Promise." The revolver scraped against my spine—I was ready for closure.

"Buck, your cell's ringing on the table. I'll let myself out." Susan's refined demeanor wouldn't allow her to slam the door, but I knew she wasn't pleased. Mashing my foot down into the old shit kicker, I glanced through the curtain as a trail of dust rose behind her sedan.

"Gen, sorry I missed your call. Where are we with this?" Gritting my teeth, I pressed the cell to my ear. My gut stung with Susan's exit.

"The search warrant's almost ready. Waiting to hear from Brooks. If Roy Blanchard rats it'll help finish the probable cause for the affidavit."

Walking away from the window, I drove a fist against my thigh, "Damn, hope letting that child molester walk was the right thing to do. He'd better come straight with info."

"Buck, it was the best call at the time. Roy can always be found." Genevieve was right. I just hated leaving loose threads hanging.

"Okay. Call me once warrant is signed. We'll meet at the warehouse before heading to Roberts' place. Quick and quiet Gen." Finding myself in the threshold once again with cement legs, I couldn't enter his room. Sternum feeling like it had been cracked—the giant gulp of air only increased the pressure, "Later Gen."

"Graza, Buck here. Update?" Scanning Wyatt Cash's room I was anxious—needed word from the detectives.

"Uhmm, Sheriff. Got a dilemma. Blanchard was a no show."

"What? That piece of shit. I knew he'd turn on us." Kicking the kitchen chair, it flew across the braided rug and smashed into the dishwasher.

"Not really sir. He traded up." Graza's voice cracked and I heard him swallowing hard but remaining silent.

"Is that Brooks in the background? What's he bitching about?" I sensed hesitation, "No time for bullshit, fill me in."

"Jessie Duplantis turned himself in. Blanchard convinced him to do it." Graza blurted out. I heard Brooks gasp in the background.

"What?" I picked the chair off the floor.

"Blanchard was in jail with Big Johnny. Seems Chiasson liked to brag while getting oral sex. He told Blanchard about his brother's fetish of getting his rocks off hearing about how Tom Roberts tortured and raped those children."

My gut knotted as bile shot up my throat—I heaved into the stainless steal sink.

"Sheriff, I'm sorry. I'm so sorry."

"No need son," Wiping a napkin across my lips, "I gotta check it at the door. Job to do. Please, go on." Rinsing my mouth and face, the running water echoed through the call.

"Blanchard made a monitored call from your jail. It got snatched. Next thing, Big Johnny was transferred to the city jail by Chief Roberts. His brother came in to visit several times, but always left after heated arguments. Seems Big Johnny was placed in isolation a few days. I'm sure Doc Lambert will detect the torture in the autopsy."

"You mean Roberts has an insider working at my jail?" Leaning my face toward the ceiling fan, I let the cool air bathe over my neck and shoulders. Sensing I was reaching information overload, what would be my saving grace?

"More like Johnny Jones. He's running the muscle behind WIP. One of his boys. We'll flush him out soon." Graza promised.

"These fuckers are like cockroaches. They need to be stomped out for good." My thumb and forefingers traced my chin. *How deep does the corruption go?*

"Well, Duplantis was telling us the Asian Triad is here to deal with WIP. Seems Tommy Chang was a high-ranking member in his chapter. Maria Sanchez was his old lady. WIP fucked with the wrong one. Also another reason Duplantis surrendered." I could hear Duplantis' voice in the background demanding an isolation cell.

"Fill in the Deputy Chief so she can finish the search warrant affidavit. And Graza."

"Yes Sheriff?"

"You made the right decision by bringing Duplantis into custody." Not completely excited about it, but I knew it was best.

"Thank you sir."

Chapter 68

— *Sheriff James Walker* —

ONCE AGAIN THE RATTLING CLANKING-CLANK jerked and jolted until the corrugated metal door cleared the sally port's entrance. Killing my headlights, I piloted the truck next to the row of other cruisers. Their faces flat of emotion, the faintest haunt of relief shone as I approached the group.

"Remi, looks like your relationship with old Judge Boudreaux paid off." I gripped his palm as solid as I could muster. Strained smile rutted my face.

"That, and another fifth of whiskey. Told you he'd sign anything placed in front of his empty glass." Remi looked better—first smirk I'd seen in weeks. I knew he wasn't coming back though.

"Whatever it takes son." I swung around, "Brooks, I trust you got Mister Duplantis tucked away nice and safe at the jail?"

"Yes sir brought him over to Jean Lafitte Parish just like you ordered. Sheriff Breaux said to leave him as long as needed."

"Not sure I can trust Gaston too long, but it's what we got to deal with. Now, let's get started on this plan." I pulled a stool against the workbench. My skin crawled with a conflicted energy among the group. Their eyes narrowed with focus—but their fingers wrenched or tapped the tabletop.

"Sheriff, can I just throw this out there for the good of the order?" St. Pierre rolled her shoulders.

"Sure Gen, shoot." I was relieved she broke the ice.

"We're all committed to this. To you, but I for one, am as nervous as a fat cat at an alligator farm." Tension in her face erased any age and made her look neutral—almost grey. The others silently bobbed their heads.

"If it helps, I am too. I'm taking strength in knowing it's the right thing to do. Not for my own revenge, but what's right for this community. The families who've lost hope deserve our best. Isn't this why we do the job?" A hand landed firmly on my forearm—Graza's eyes were glistening as his head shook in agreement.

Finally, my pulse eased and I sat back in the seat. It was time to do this and do it right.

St. Pierre lifted a finger as she walked away from the table. Her face reddened as her mouth fell open. I saw her eyes bunch against the bottom corners while nostrils flared—fury raged across her face.

"Jess Duplantis is on his way to the emergency room in Jean Lafitte Parish." She slammed her cell onto the workbench while collapsing against the solid wooden block. "Sheriff Breaux said he was accidentally placed in a general population block. Gang raped, and barely alive. We gotta move out now." She demanded while tightening the Velcro straps to her ballistic vest.

"Why so?" Blood rushed into my brain as I rocketed out of my seat. My fingers clamped into Graza's shoulder.

"Trustee said they kept asking if he ratted out to the police." Her hands nervously rattled while pocketing the phone. "He wasn't close enough to hear whether Duplantis said anything." Remi stared straight into my eyes as his chin popped upward. He was right—it was time to move.

"Guys, don't let this distract you. Stick to the ops plan. All we're doing is serving a search warrant signed by a judge. Keep it simple." I shook everyone's hand as we moved to our cruisers. Agent Jones mashed the button setting off the noisy chains jerking the door.

"Buck, remember—you promised to stay in your truck. Deputy Chief will handle Roberts on scene. Right?" Remi called out over the hood of his vehicle while strapping the bulletproof vest against his torso. I nodded yes.

Dust and gravel vomited walls of debris as the caravan flew down country roads and over the pitted asphalt. My fists strangled the steering wheel. Mind racing over how Jess Duplantis was fingered as an informant so fast. It'd become a race to the finish for Tom Roberts. If anyone knew about this search warrant—he would.

Crossing the Bayou Rond Pom Pon Bridge, I saw smoke in the distance. Rolling up my window, the sugar cane burning in the fields after harvesting always caused my chest to tighten. Not today—couldn't afford the stress on it.

Brake lights exploded. I backed off the fleet of cruisers as they lipped tight left turns onto the freshly paved stretch of street leading to Roberts' home. Remi radioed to the team to get ready to move into positions once we cleared the last three patches of standing cane stalks. They were about ten feet high and made seeing anything impossible.

"Shit, everybody move. Now." Remi screamed orders over the encrypted radio channel.

My heart raced as I nudged Graza's bumper trying to hurry him around the last section of harvest. *What the hell is happening up there?*

"I'll take the target shed in the back. Don't park. Drive over his shit. Hurry." My gut knotted at the panic in Remi's instructions. I struck Graza's vehicle from behind, "Go. Get outta the way." I yelled.

Graza looked back through his rearview mirror and throwing his hands up in the air, his cruiser lurched forward into a ditch. His rear tires almost off the ground, he spun them like devil trying to back out. He had the driveway blocked.

"Forget it, just go." I radioed to him.

I shoved the vehicle just around the corner to see the scorched bunches of light. My mouth dropped open and an ungodly noise drummed from it. The chaos looked like hell on earth. Satan himself, Tom Roberts was flying along his property on a four-wheeler with a torch—setting his property ablaze.

My deputies were in cars and on foot sprinting through the smoke and flame. Clutching my chest, I fought to jerk the door handle open. Smoke was creeping inside the cabin. I turned off the A/C.

Roberts had out distanced my staff and headed toward a crossroads leading into the forty arpent fields and swamp. I knew where he was heading—I'd cut him off.

Banging the truck into reverse, I spun around a three-point turn and steered toward an old board road used for land-based natural gas drilling. Hearing Remi yell over the radio that it was all going up in flames, my eyes watered. Vision blurred, I grit my teeth as my neck stiffened to focus on the narrowing path.

I saw him behind me off to the left. He was looking back at them. Approaching a canal, I saw the front of his four-wheeler dig into the dirt as he down shifted for the watery crossing. Gunning the big v-eight engine, I smashed the accelerator into the floorboard.

Both machines came to sudden, violent stops.

"It's over Roberts. You're under arrest." Climbing out the driver's side door, I slipped into the thigh-deep water. Weapon drawn and held unsteady, "It's over."

"About time Buck. Hell, you know how hard it was keeping that secret? I didn't even know it was your boy at first." His four-wheeler idled—I didn't see a weapon. His smile indicated me otherwise.

"I said it's over. Turn off that bike and raise your hands." Shaking my left hand to get the stale water and mud from it, I struggled, but couldn't escape the canal. My eyes dropped for a second to crawl from the debris—his engine revved.

"Don't do it Roberts. I'll shoot you." I was now more than soaked. My throat was drying and felt like it had swollen closed. I gulped for spit or air—neither.

"I ain't going out like this Buck. You know better than that. I'll take my chances with you out here. Always wanted to kick the redneck out of your ass." His left leg swung over the bike's saddle.

"Stay right there or I'll kill you." Trembling, I slapped both hands together to steady the weapon. My shoulders quivered—I felt cold twist its way up my backbone. His step toward me cast a giant shadow. I leaned back against the truck, looking up at him from the canal. My left leg was still sunk in the muck.

"Buck, you're not going to pull that trigger." He came closer. "I got the gig pole from Belle Cove Plantation. You're prints are all over it." He laughed.

Both shoulders pressed against the metal cab, I fought for a puff of air. The muscles in my arms popped and quivered as I slid my index finger inside the trigger guard.

"Stop Tom. I swear. I'll kill you." Fixed vision along the sights, I flexed my forearm sending steady pressure through my hand. I heard the shot erupt from the barrel.

Chapter 69

— Lieutenant Remi LeBlanc —

"HE GONNA MAKE IT DOC?" Crawling across a grey screen, the green blip slowed. The dark room offered shadowed streaks casting eerie glooms of despair. Deputy Chief St. Pierre's watchful glare was concealed as she stared at medical instrumentation. I pulled the shirt tighter across my shoulders as dread crept across them.

"Remi, where the hell y'all find him? He's lucky to be alive." Doctor Perez never pulled punches. Sliding the black plastic eyeglass frames back up the long bridge of his nose, he dropped the metal clipboard onto the foot of the bed.

"We gave him CPR until Brooks got a police unit out from behind Graza's cruiser." St. Pierre stepped out of the shadows to brief the tall physician. "No time wasted waiting for an ambulance." She leered while placing her fingers along the wafer-thin mattress.

"I don't think there'll be permanent brain damage, but tests will tell. Water submersion is tricky. I know you want to get a statement soon. That'll have to wait." Doctor Perez patted Genevieve on the shoulder and turned to shake my hand. "Remi, you need rest boy. You look like death itself." I nodded.

A slender flash bolted through the unguarded door and slipped past Perez's big body frame without effort or contact.

"Buck. Oh my God, what happened this time? I begged him not to go out there." Susan Lambert was hysterical—I'd never seen her like this. I wasn't comfortable with it. I walked Doctor Perez out of the room—they were cohorts after all.

Peeking my head back in, Genevieve motioned for me to help her. My spirit was empty and without empathy for anyone at the moment. My hand held stiff, I tried patting Doctor Lambert on the back, but it didn't help. She wailed over Buck's body.

Wiping the smeared make up from her darkened orbs, "Please tell me what happened to Buck."

"Susan, best we figure, he confronted Tom Roberts in the wooded area just before a shallow canal. Seems like he tried shooting him, but passed out. Already stuck in the canal, he landed between his truck and the bank. His face lay just underwater. Not sure how long, but we came as soon as we heard the gun shot." Genevieve wrapped her arm around the much taller surgeon—compassion knew no height. The doctor leaned with her head against Genevieve.

I heard Lambert whisper, "Where's Tom Roberts?" I eased back, "Doc, we don't know. Saw four-wheeler tracks over crossroads disappearing into the wooded areas. Search and perimeter teams set up."

"He got a huge jump on us Susan. Our focus was Buck." Genevieve squeezed Lambert tighter.

"He's lucky to have y'all Genevieve." Craning her head back, "You too Remi."

"Thanks Doc." Shoving both hands in my soiled pants pockets, I broke eye contact with her.

How do I tell them I'm done?

"What's the plan for capturing Roberts?" Lambert turned back to St. Pierre and she leaned away from her. Genevieve dropped her head.

"I'm more focused on Buck right now. Sergeant Brooks is heading up the search teams." Coughing several times, I noticed Genevieve's throat bobbing as she swallowed. Her eye cut back toward me.

"Remi, you know the swamps better than anyone. How come you're not out there tracking him down?" Doctor Lambert's shoulders straightened until their full measure of height towered over Genevieve.

Her cheeks twitching—fear and hate shook them.

"Doc, Buck will recover. Genevieve will serve as Sheriff until he returns. Me? I'm at a crossroads." I dug my hand deep into my back pocket.

"What does that mean Remi?" Lambert demanded. Her fists balled and wrists shook.

Genevieve's flushed face lacked tension—closing her eyes, her body lurched with anguish.

I pitched my gold badge onto the foot of Buck's hospital bed. Tempted to retrieve it, I resisted—I knew what needed to be done.

It was time for all of us to heal.

The End
Season 1

Squad Room Roll Call

Thank you for reading **Bayou Roux**. If you enjoyed it, please help other readers find this exciting adventure.

Your mission:

1. Please tell your friends about this series.
2. Help me by writing and posting a review.
3. Sign up for my new releases on the Amazon Author's Page.
4. Join me on Facebook at CopsWritingCrime
5. Check out cop life at Bright Blue Line (scottsilverii.com)
6. E-mail with questions or comments at brightblueline@gmail.com.

Check out my other works:

Cop Culture: Why Good Cops Go Bad (non-fiction)

A Darker Shade of Blue (non-fiction)

Bayou Backslide: A Cajun Murder Mystery Series (Special edition)

Blue Love Line: A Cajun Murder Mystery Series (10-CODE Anthology)

Made in the USA
San Bernardino, CA
09 May 2015